Praise for Rick DeMarinis

"Rick DeMarinis, who seems to have warmed his toes by the fires of James Crumley's gonzo genius, is one of that lonesome crowd of writers who love the language but aren't afraid to rough it up to save its life. Still…if civilization is headed for the caves, it's nice to know that De-Marinis will be there, scribbling on the walls."
—Marilyn Stasio
The New York Times Book Review

"DeMarinis has produced a masterpiece in this bittersweet coming of age story."
Publishers Weekly
On *The Year of the Zinc Penny*

"Rick DeMarinis has long been one of my favorite writers; wherever he has cast his gaze, he has taught me something new about the way to see things."
—Robert Olen Butler

"It's one thing to be good, which, Lord knows, Rick DeMarinis certainly is. Funny, however, is not a given. And *The Mortician's Apprentice* is the funniest book I have read in some time."
—Beverly Lowry

"DeMarinis is a contemporary avatar in American short story writing that, by way of Melville, Faulkner, Welty, and Cheever, is essentially religious, and, because rooted in the everyday, comic. His art…is comedy of a very high order."
—Russell Banks
The New York Times Book Review

"You simply can't move your eyes from the page."
—Mark Smirnoff
The New York Times Book Review

"I have always believed that Rick DeMarinis is one of the most talented and versatile writers of my generation…*Mama's Boy* is one of the best novels I've read in years."
—James Lee Burke

Also by Rick DeMarinis

STORIES

Apocalypse Then

Borrowed Hearts: New and Selected

The Coming Triumph of the Free World

The Voice of America

Under the Wheat

NONFICTION

The Art and Craft of the Short Story

NOVELS

The Burning Women of Far Cry

Cinder

A Clod of Wayward Marl

A Lovely Monster:
The Adventures of Claude Rains and Dr. Tellenbeck

The Mortician's Apprentice

Scimitar

Sky Full of Sand
(Introduction by Scott Phillips)

The Year of the Zinc Penny

Mama's Boy

EL PASO TWILIGHT

Rick DeMarinis

ISBN-13: 978-0-9623789-7-3

Manufactured in the United States of America

Published in the United States by

Bangtail Press
P. O. Box 11262
Bozeman, MT 59719
www.bangtailpress.com

Cover photographs:
www.shutterstock.com/Alex Emanuel Koch (Silhouette)
www.shutterstock.com/maradonna 8888 (Woman in Car)

Book Design by Allen M. Jones

EL PASO TWILIGHT

CHAPTER ONE

Luther Penrose begins all his novels with a weather report from the dark side of Disneyland. My favorite: *Chalcedonic clouds, like the stained undergarments of the gods, clung to the carnelian hips of Calexico's enchanted hills.* This is choice stuff; you take it one word at a time to get the full benefit. Exposing yourself to his prose is like falling down a velvet staircase: you're disoriented, stupefied, amused, but not hurt. Today's piece, *Gotterrdammerung Now,* had its own dash of the Magic Kingdom's dark-side atmospherics: *Whispering mists of silvery fog wreathed the Black Forest, strangling the neugeboren sun in its ascending astral crib.*

He always shows me his work in progress. He thinks I know some German. I don't. But I know *neugeboren* means newborn, and, he informed me, *Gotterdammerung* means twilight of the gods. Why the "now" is anyone's guess. ("My subject," he said, "is birth, death, and the unholy free-for-all in-between, which is what great literature is always about.") I'd heard it before, sometimes accompanied by window-rattling, Germanic thunder—in stereo. For no reason I could think of, he wants my untutored opinion.

We were friends by default, thrown together by time and place and the perversity of fate. We'd gone to school together, all twelve grades, and after a few wasted years of wondering what to do with the rest of our lives we joined the army like a pair of fugitives, which we were—fugitives from the dull and ordinary future looming on the flat horizon.

Back in our high school days he was too smart for his own good. In the classroom he always knew the answers and raised his hand too often in a show-off way—which attracted the wrong kind of attention. In grammar school he was a star, admired by teachers and students alike. But in high school his precocity was dangerous. The playing fields now reeked of testosterone. Luther was big but not strong or athletic. He was easy pickings for the bullies who hated smart show-offs who knew the answers before the questions were asked.

I became his protector—again by default—which involved me in a dozen parking lot fights on his behalf. When I won he was jubilant. When I lost he became paranoid and disoriented as if the last bastion between him and catastrophe had been breached.

So we shared a history, such as it was, and that counts for something. I knew even in those early days that his thinking was a little off the tracks. He claimed the army changed him. Of course it did. It changed me. It changed everyone who was there.

I'd read fifty manuscript pages of *Gotterdammerung Now,* every page choked with similes and metaphors indigestible as iron filigree. Luther was a turgid writer and like most turgid writers he believed his work was visionary. "Talent," he once said, "consists of one's ability to penetrate the fog of events and trends in order to discern the hidden truths that impel them. The vehicle for this quest is a superior prose of a certain gravitas." Luther was never deficient in self-importance.

I handed the fifty dog-eared pages back to him. "It's not very sexy for a romance novel, Luther," I said, knowing he was bulletproof against critical opinion.

"It's not a romance novel, J. P. It's an historical bildungs-roman based on little known facts regarding the familial, spiritual, sexual, and political education of Wagner, the central character."

"Honus Wagner? The Flying Dutchman? Pittsburgh shortstop and Hall of Famer?" I pronounced Wagner the way he did: Vaahg-ner. V followed by a throaty hiss and a clamp-jawed r.

"No, smart ass. *Richard* Wagner of *Der Ring des Nibelungen.*"

"Sounds very romantic," I said.

Luther—six-foot-two and two-hundred-ninety pounds—heaved himself out of his recliner. His thirty-pound Manx, Gretchen, leaped from his lap with an operatic yowl.

"You feed that cat too much, Luther," I said.

"So now you're a veterinarian *and* a literary critic?"

"Just pointing out the obvious," I said.

"That's just like you, J. P. You think everything's obvious. You've got a simpleton's grip on reality. There are more things in heaven and earth than dreamt of in your philosophy, my friend."

"Walt Disney?" I said.

"Shakespeare, dolt. You might try reading the masters someday to feed your impoverished intellect. The rewards are gratifying beyond measure."

"I read *you*, Luther."

"Not very well, it seems. Get yourself a beer."

His fridge was loaded with beer and little else. I pulled out a six pack and carried it to the living room where I watched Luther ease a 1958 Met recording of Gotterdammerung out of its jacket with the care of a neurosurgeon removing a brain tumor. He put the disk on his beloved 1963 Marantz turntable and adjusted the weight-balanced tone arm so that the diamond stylus touched the grooved vinyl with the impact of eider down.

Luther was not a fan of modern technology. He wrote his novels on a steel 1926 Underwood Standard, a glossy black typewriter that could serve as an anchor for a forty-foot sloop, and he kept only vinyl LPs in his music library.

"I'll stick with analog sound reproduction, thank you," he once said, dissing the CD. "Digital recording corrupts the integrity of the diatonic scale. Most people don't notice the difference, but my hearing is ultra sensitive. I hear the micro-second intra-digital *omissions,* you see. It's one of my gifts."

He had other gifts. He was ultra sensitive to all the gadgets of microchip technology. Cell phones, palm pilots, iPods and iPhones, digital cameras, computerized navigation systems ("What the hell's wrong with the Rand McNally *Road Atlas*?") made him erupt with Luddite crankiness. These devices were proof the world had been hijacked by satanic forces whose minions were the pinched-face geeks who spoke a technoglot no one but they could understand.

"They want to wire us together under the excuse of anti-terrorism," he said, "so they can have us tethered, under fingertip control. Someday you won't be able move your bowels without the issue being instantly analyzed for Baba Ghannooj and other Osama bin Laden favorites by Homeland Security. The Japanese already have wireless toilets lined with microchips capable of reporting abnormal intestinal activity to a centralized medical authority empowered by law to alter your diet and change your prescriptions. Illegal substance residue in the bowl? You'll hear Interpol knocking on your door before you get your pants up."

Luther's creative paranoid logic tended to spiral out of control. He smoked copious amounts of Paregoric-laced weed to calm and focus his inventive mind. He thought of himself as a pioneer in the medical and artistic applications of marijuana.

The beefy sopranos shrieked, the hearty baritones bellowed. The house shook with detonations of high-fidelity analog thunderclaps. I thought of something Mark Twain once said about Wagner: "Actually his music is much better than it sounds."

LUTHER, SUPINE AGAIN IN his recliner, suspended our conversation. His eyes focused dreamily on the myth-infested past as he hummed along with the music. His thick fingers danced on the leather armrest of his chair to the rhythm of the galloping iron-breasted Valkyries.

At one point he pulled a box of cigars and a tin of

makings out from under the recliner. They were expensive cigars—Arturo Fuentes "Hemingways." He ran one of them under his nose, sniffed, clipped it with a bullet cutter, then dug a cave in it with his penknife. He packed the violated Hemingway with sensimilla—virgin bud with high THC content grown on the high plains of Chihuahua and trucked into the city daily. "The milk run," the cops called it. Token busts every now and then at the border customs station kept everyone happy. Luther called this black zeppelin his "super blunt."

He took a mighty operatic puff, held it, then let the smoke wheeze slowly out. A self-satisfied grin split his face. Ringlets of his curly blond hair clung to his forehead. He looked like a debauched Roman, refreshed after a visit to the vomitorium.

"How dee fucking doo," he said, grinning like a teased ape.

"Wagh agh," he added, choking a bit.

He didn't offer to share, which was fine by me. The last time I smoked mota, over ten years ago, I rolled a car into a deep irrigation ditch and almost drowned.

Luther puffed the souped-up stogie with a rich man's indifference to waste. He had a rich man's indifference to a lot of things.

The music stormed toward its thunderbolt climax. I imagined a herd of rhinos cluster fucking in a tea shop. Thor's or Wotan's hammer fell, the walls of the tea shop collapsed, the crazed rhinos thundered into the surprised streets.

Luther sang along with the howling sopranos in a gravelly voice that could only deliver a single unstable note. It wasn't singing; it was inspired barking.

This went on for a while. I picked up a magazine. "Do Borders Matter?" was the title of one of the articles. The writer wasn't sure they did. Subtitle: "An Arbitrary Line in the Sand." A photograph of brown men in straw hats accompanied the article. The men were in handcuffs, INS agents—la migra— loading them onto a bus. The photo didn't flatter the agents: They looked like big-bellied storm troopers, towering over the small brown men they were arresting.

Luther had called me earlier that day: "My life's a bloody mess, J. P. Help me sort things out, okay buddy?"

"Your life is privileged, Luther," I said.

"I need you to be sympathetic just now, J. P.," he said. "Sarcasm won't do. Please come over."

By the time I'd finished my third beer Luther's mood had soured. The music had lost its hold on him. His sensimilla-fueled trip to the mythic world of Wagner was over. He crushed the blunt in his ashtray, mumbling darkly. Arturo Fuente "Hemingways" run about two hundred dollars a box, but Luther treated them like Mexican cigarettes.

He rose out of his deep chair, trailing litter and grunting with effort. "Let's get the hell out of here, J. P.," he said. He raised the tone arm off the vinyl Valkyries, then slipped the record back in its jacket. "I need to sound you out about a serious matter."

"The novel about Honus Wagner? Lifetime batting average .320? Hit over a hundred career home runs in the dead-ball era?"

"Richard *Vaahg-ner*, goddamnit! And no, not the novel. I asked you to come over because my life is in the toilet."

We drove out to Sergio's in Luther's restored 1941 Packard Clipper, an eggshell-yellow beauty with perfect chrome and wide whitewalls. Luther wouldn't drive a car made after 1970. He also drove a 1950 Hudson Hornet, a 1946 Studebaker Champion, and the first true muscle car, a 1964 DeLorean-designed GTO. They were in perfect working order without the help of microchips. He bought the cars from restorers who charged what you could buy a new Mercedes for.

Sergio's was a taqueria out on Montana Street, just past the drive-in triple-X porno theater. Luther liked Sergio's because it was pure retro—no TV, no annoying fluorescent lighting, and everything was fried in unadulterated lard. Sergio never heard of transfatty acids or cholesterol. Except for a few tired-looking transvestites, the place was empty.

"I'm going to leave her," Luther said. "She's forced my hand."

"Who's forced your hand?"

"Jesus, man! Who do you think? Who do you leave when you say you're going to leave someone?"

"*Carla?* You're going to leave the only woman on the planet who can put up with you?"

"That's what I said, didn't I?"

"Big mistake, ole buddy."

Carla, an instructor of Latin American Studies at our local branch of the University of Texas, was formidable—smart, idealistic, and a passionate pro-bono activist on behalf of Mexican illegals who cross over the Rio Grande and get caught. She was a dissertation defense short of her Ph.D, and on the tenure track in her department. In spite of all this, she was real people. She spoke the language and took the simple pleasures of common folk. Carla was an aristocrat with calluses.

She was not beautiful by most standards, not even pretty. Maybe it was her expression: always serious, always intent, always soldiering for a cause. Her eyes didn't invite; they challenged. She could make moral demands on you without saying a word.

She was memorable. And, oddly enough, desirable. You normally wouldn't give her a second glance. If you did you'd find yourself thinking about her the next day while relieving your pent up libido. I think she had that effect on a lot of men who saw her politically passionate nature as something transferable to the bedroom. She was a saint for putting up with Luther as long as she had. How she hooked up with him in the first place ranks as one of life's bizarre mysteries.

"She's knocking boots with some home-wrecking swine," Luther said. His fleshy unlined face darkened with the injustices that had become his lot. He looked like a petulant child.

Twenty-five years ago in the Saudi desert he'd been kicked out of the army for assaulting a bird colonel. "Sieg heil, Mein Herr!" he'd said to the colonel. He'd raised his arm in an aggressive Nazi salute. He was standing too close to the colonel and his snappy Sieg heil! knocked the man's hat off. The colonel had ordered him to report to the medic's tent and take his anthrax shot and Luther had refused. This bit of foolishness got him an Article-Fifteen court martial plus time in the stockade. When he still refused the required inoculations, he got more jail time and a bad-conduct discharge which was downgraded to a Section Eight. The Section Eight was justified: Luther had become more than a little unstable. They sent him home a medicated zombie. When he checked out of Walter Reed, Section Eight papers in hand, he joined as many anti-war groups as he could find. It was his way of getting back at the army.

He lived on his dead father's estate, in an ancient twelve-room house with gargoyles carved into the portico's pillars. The house was crumbling at the edges from neglect, and the yard had been given back to the weeds. Neighborhood children thought the house was haunted and that a monster lived in it. They weren't all wrong. They ran past Luther's place every day on their way to and from school, thrilling themselves with imagined horrors.

Now and then Luther would make an effort to groom the old place. In jodhpurs, pith helmet, shin-high Wellingtons, and tapping his palm importantly with a riding crop, Luther played *padrón*—a role he enjoyed a little too much—to penniless Mexicans who waded across the river looking for wages. He turned them loose with mowers, hoes, and rakes in the tangled field of Johnson grass and broadleaf weeds that fronted his house, handing out ten-dollar bills at sunset. If Carla was around, she'd give the men food and make Luther pay them twice as much.

"Carla's loyal as they come," I said. "No way is she two-timing you, Luther."

"You don't know what you're talking about, J. P. You don't know the half of it."

Actually, it made sense. In the shape he was in now I couldn't imagine any woman sticking with him for more than a year. Carla, who was ten years younger than Luther, had stuck it out for almost eight. If she had a boyfriend, she was overdue.

"So what did you want to talk about?" I said. "You've already made up your mind."

"This isn't easy, J. P. I don't take divorce lightly. I grew up Catholic, you know. I've got a lot of things to consider before making my move. You can understand that, can't you?"

"I guess."

"You *guess*? Don't trivialize my problems, J. P. I've got a lot on my mind. I'd like you to understand that, if it's remotely possible."

Luther took himself very seriously. He felt he had the right to since he'd finally published a book and was now a legitimate author. In the photo on the back cover Luther looked handsomely distressed. His chin rested in his cupped hand, his shadowed forehead nobly creased, eyes focused past the camera: Here was a man in possession of a dangerous vision capable of subverting the values by which people lived. If you didn't know him, you'd believe you were looking at young Kerouac hardened with Hemingway steel. He assumed this pose now, as he examined my character.

His novel, a six-hundred-page family saga—*I am Pedro Morales*—covered the entire twentieth century, with overlaps into the nineteenth and twenty-first. It began with the Spanish American war and ended with the drug wars of contemporary times. It was published by a small press in Nebraska that went broke shortly afterward. Luther carried the dog-eared paperback around with him and read aloud from it during lulls in whatever conversation he might be having. Fearing this, I kept talking.

"I mean, sure, Luther, I understand completely. But I doubt that Carla is bonking someone. It's not like her."

"I want you to follow her, J. P. Find out who the son of a bitch is. I want you to take pictures. I need hard evidence before I go to my lawyer."

"I don't do that sort of thing, Luther. Besides, you're not exactly an altar boy in the area of fidelity."

He'd had a girlfriend a few years ago up in Las Cruces, a chain-smoking waitress with three kids and no husband.

Luther set himself up as her sugar daddy, giving her money whenever she asked for it, which was often. The money was habit forming. When he broke it off, she had withdrawal symptoms and went ballistic. She wanted him to divorce Carla and marry her. She said she'd sue him for alienation of affections if he didn't. When that didn't work she had her brother, Marco "Crippler" Monzón, a former professional wrestler, threaten him. "Marco knows how to make you a drooling quad in three seconds flat," she said. "Marco gets through with you, you'll be sitting in day-old shit breathing through a tube in your neck and watching your dead dick grow knob cheese." Luther gave her fifteen thousand dollars and a vintage Coupe de Ville to leave him alone.

"It's different with men," Luther said. "I've never taken a romantic interlude seriously. But when a woman strays, it's always serious. Christ, don't you *know* that? You believe that New Age crap that women have the same sexual freedom as *men?*"

"You can find yourself a creepy peeper in the yellow pages to do your dirty work, Luther," I said. "You don't need me."

He sipped his beer, his pale blue eyes fixed on me over the rim of his glass. "I want you to do it because you're my friend," he said. "I don't want some stranger following Carla. I still love her, goddamnit. I don't want some leering son of bitch taking snapshots of her fellating the bastard in a Motel 6. I want you to do it."

"I work insurance gigs, Luther. Not domestic stuff. Anyway, I'm too busy to follow your wife around town."

In fact, I wasn't busy at all. Sundown Fidelity had let me go in favor of a west-coast outfit whose operatives all had law degrees and wore Hart, Schaffner and Marx suits. By exposing phony claims I'd saved Sundown thirty-odd million over the six years I'd worked for them as a salaried investigator, but somehow that wasn't a factor. They fell for the west-coast outfit's pitch: more resources, more flexibility, global database, multiple operatives, etc. And they liked the suits. I didn't have a pitch, just results, and my best dress-up gear was pressed Levi's, ostrich skin boots, and Mexican wedding shirts—loose-fitting guayaberas. I buy them in Juárez a dozen at a time.

"You want me to *beg?*" Luther said. "All right, I'm begging, J. P. I'm on my knees here begging you. Please. I'm going out of my mind. I've got to know."

"I'll get back to you."

"Don't say that. People who say that never get back to me."

"I need to think about it, Luther."

"Think about this: I've got money falling out of my ass! I had to liquidate my El Paso Pipeline stock because I was paying too much in taxes! I can't spend it faster than it *grows,* for Chrissakes! How about I give you five hundred a day and expenses for as long as it takes?"

By local standards Luther was rich. His money was in stocks, bonds, trust funds, property, and annuities, all inherited from his father, Big Bill Penrose. Luther didn't have to work, even if he could have held a job. He spent his days smoking reefer, listening to Wagner, and typing novels on his vintage Underwood. Big Bill Penrose, who'd been a county judge for thirty years, had amassed a fortune. It was common knowledge that he'd sold favors and had never turned down a mordida—a bribe. The judge always had his hand out, and not just for handshakes.

"I won't take your money, Luther. Not for that kind of work, even if I decided to do it. Anyway, like I said, I really don't have the time."

His cherubic lips spread back over his teeth. His fawning smile was more unnerving than his frown. "You've got nothing *but* time, J. P. I happen to know that. I can be a rotten s.o.b, I happen to know that, too. I don't deserve a friend like you."

Or a wife like Carla, I thought.

His expression turned abruptly sad. He expelled two fat crocodile tears from his calculating eyes.

"I'll give it some thought, Luther," I said.

"That's the least you could do. You *owe* me, buddy."

CHAPTER TWO

O we? I hadn't seen him in weeks. What did I owe him? If anything, he owed me a lifetime of favors. I needed money. What I'd stashed away was slowing evaporating. But I'd never borrowed from Luther. Maybe he thought our friendship, such as it was, came with markers.

Allegiance. I guess that's what he meant. You owe allegiance to your friends. That's the definition of friendship.

Wives, on the other hand, require more than allegiance. My wife, Kat, decided she could not stay in partnership with a man of zero ambition.

"I've got no future with you," she said, "because you've got no future in mind for yourself." She said this without judgement or hostility. She loved me but could not squander a lifetime with me. It was a simple evaluation of our two years under the same roof. "Damnit, there's no *fire* in you, J. P.," she said. "You don't *want* anything. You live in the present tense.

No past to speak of, no future. Nowhere to go. No reason to change."

It was a body blow, but she was right. I had no ambitions and wanted no part of anyone's rat race. I saw what it did to my father, dead at forty-four of a worn-out atrioventricular valve. A successful man by some lights—a man with three late-model cars, a summer cabin in the mountains of southern New Mexico, a hacienda-style house in El Paso's Upper Valley, and the humped shoulders of a man who'd been holding back the weight of a fiscal tsunami for twenty-two years. Twenty-two years hustling insurance policies to people who couldn't afford them. Always coming home late and washing down a few bites of supper with a tumbler of bourbon because he was too tired and edgy to eat and unwind properly. This is the image I carry with me: a sad gray face sagging with early old age. He died at the kitchen table of an unemployed smelterman named Gabriel Ruiz, trying to sell Ruiz and his wife a term life policy with a double indemnity rider attached, a policy they'd pay for out of their food budget. He fell over dead, face first into an open portfolio just as Mr. and Mrs. Ruiz were beginning to warm up to him.

My parents, Jim and Velma Morgan, were decent, hard-working West Texans who wanted a better life for their children. They named my older sister "Aïda"—not because they loved opera but because, like many working class Americans, they pined for the exotic. They believed a daughter named Aïda would escape an ordinary life of household drudgery and the paralyzing dullness that went with it.

I was introduced into the world as J. P. Not John Pierpont, as in the railroad tycoon, just the rootless initials, J. P. My father believed those famous initials alone had power, that they were magnets that would attract wealth. He was disappointed when I went to college on the GI Bill and majored in English and History instead of Business Administration and Accounting. ("What do you do with an English degree? *Read?* What good is history to someone who has no future? It's okay for women to do these things"—a reference to Velma, who taught high school English for thirty years—"but not for men who need to get *ahead*.")

When she was nineteen Aïda married a San Antonio fireman who beat her whenever guilt over his extra-marital affairs turned into booze-fueled self-righteousness. Aïda has six kids and looks ten years older than her forty. The fireman left her for a nineteen-year-old beautician. He started his life over again with another teenager hoping, I suppose, for better results the second time around.

The man without a name, J. P., became an insurance investigator after a stint as an El Paso cop. He was often behind with his rent and credit card payments. But he was satisfied with the status quo. It was the only thing he could count on.

I missed Kat for a long while, missed her badly, but did not blame her for jumping ship. Now remarried to someone who has a future, she sends me birthday cards, Christmas cards, and now and then calls to see if I'm still safely on course to nowhere. I still love her, or the memory of her. But memories are unreliable—warped mirrors we look into to justify what we've become. In any case, I've never had a relationship with another woman that measured up to memories of Kat.

My apartment building is in the historic Sunset Heights district of El Paso. My south-looking windows open to the dry plains west of Juárez, Mexico, where Pancho Villa set up his muzzle-loading McGinty cannons to bombard the barracks and fortifications of the Mexican army. A hundred years ago the occupants of this building could sit on their verandas and watch an actual war in real time. The building is nicked here and there with stray machine gun fire from both sides.

El Paso is isolated from mainstream America by hundreds of miles of desert on all sides. The isolation isn't just a matter of distance. Established in the 1500s, this city has always marched to its own drummer. It's a piece of America that held to its own less frenetic pace. Think of it as American civilization in retrograde. The town looks modern enough—freeways, the usual glass and steel buildings, the usual shopping malls, the usual briefcase-carrying men in thousand-dollar suits giving the impression of vitality and purpose—but deep within its poetic heart it nurtures a secret desire to apply the brakes to the machinery of enterprise. It's a poor town—the unemployment rate a perpetual 10 percent, twice the national average—but the ambitionless feel comfortable here. My father went against the grain, and it killed him.

Kat was from Chicago and couldn't understand the El Paso zeitgeist. It's not something to understand, it's something to experience. I had no explanation other than to say, "It's my town, it's how we are, I can't be anything else."

"This town is crazy," Kat once said. "On the surface it's mellow and easy going, but that's a thin veneer. It's nothing more than articulated chaos."

I had think about that. "That describes most of the world, doesn't it?" I answered.

Who you are is where you're from and what happened to you there. The city, the desert, the river, the tawny Franklin mountains that divide the town into two halves—these things define you, starting from the cradle, ending in the grave. You carry out your life to the strains of mariachi guitars carried on the breeze. If I said I loved the place, I'd be misstating the facts. I am the place: Articulated chaos. Me.

Not that the town doesn't have citizens on the make, legal and otherwise. We have plenty of crime. Except for the occasional gangbanger firefight, very little of it is violent. A stray bullet from a barrio might land in your garden or bounce off your car. Once, in an east side Luby's parking lot, a small hail of bullets fell harmlessly out of the sky a few yards in front of Kat and I—a volley shot from a barrio some distance away. Gang war spillover. But the professional crooks are generally laid back and not entirely convinced they are the bad guys.

My last fraud case, the guy confessed—after I pointed out some telling inconsistencies in his story—that the accident was scripted, a rear-ender with the usual whiplash injuries. He couldn't explain satisfactorily the presence of neck-braces in the car full of claimants or the fact that the cops had been called ten minutes *before* the collision. "These clairvoyant people travel with neck-braces?" I said to him. Even so, he thought there was still a reasonable chance Sundown Fidelity would pay out damages to the "victims."

"Yeah, okay, it started out as a set-up," he admitted. "But the driver of car number two went totally mental, you know? The daredevil got a little too much into the gig. He had a hot date waiting for him and so he got impatient. He called the cops ahead of time, then jumped on the gas. The people in car number one *were* actually fucked up some. See, it *was* an accident. No one planned it the way it came down. If there's no plan, and people really get hurt, then it's an accident by definition, right? You got a problem with that?"

SOME SAY IT'S THE water. The Hueco bolson is rich with lithium salts. The bolson, a pristine aquifer of unreplenishable, unpolluted ice-age water, hidden deep under the desert, is the source of the city's drinking water. It's precious water, tens of thousands of years old. I hate to see people wasting it on lawns. I have been known to vandalize Rainbirds.

Thanks to this lithium-rich bolson, we are a naturally tranquilized population. Polar behavior, at least the openly aggressive kind, is rare and usually exhibited by people passing through on their way to the brighter lights of Dallas to the east or Phoenix to the west. Other forms of madness aren't affected by the water. Luther's for example.

I was thinking about all this one late morning about a week after my visit with Luther, when my phone rang. I waited for the answering machine to kick in.

"Come on, J. P.," a woman said. "Pick up the damn phone, we've got to talk."

The voice was familiar but I couldn't put a face on it. I only knew it was someone I didn't want to talk to. I didn't pick up the phone. I went downtown to the Hollywood Café on South

El Paso Street, bottom floor of the old St. Charles Hotel, a place you can get a gordita and a beer for under three dollars.

My sweet retrograde city.

CHAPTER THREE

The Hollywood Café was so poorly lit you couldn't see the roaches crawling around your shoes but you knew they were there by the occasional crunch when you shifted your feet. The Hollywood wasn't exactly a dirty place, it was just old. Any old building in El Paso is owned by roaches. And the roaches of El Paso are as big as field mice. As long as the cooks kept them out of the gorditas, empanadas, and menudo, I was fine with them. If you're not fine with super-sized roaches, find another city.

I was working on my second Corona when my cell phone began to massage my thigh. I pulled it out, flipped it open.

"I'm having lunch," I said.

"You're lucky," a woman said. "Some of my clients are being fed mush through a rubber tube."

It was the same woman who called me at home. This time I recognized the voice and the woman who owned it. Pilar

Mellado, an agent for Adult Protective Services, a state agency with Gestapo powers.

"What's up, Pilar?" I said.

"I think you know."

"You been checking up on Velma," I said.

"I have, J. P. Bottom line? You can't stall any longer. You've got to put her into a home. I'm recommending El Descanso. They're competent and reasonable."

"An agent of the state shouldn't be recommending nursing homes, Pilar. You could be accused of taking kickbacks. The appearance of wrongdoing can be as damaging as the wrong-doing itself."

"You're the kind of guy that works hard to prove his ignorance, J. P. It doesn't become you."

"She won't go."

"She's talking to the Virgin again."

"What virgin would that be?"

"The one that comes and goes. The one in her pantry. The one in her shower. You name it. Oh wait, there's a new one in the backyard. Our Lady's face outlined on the lawn by fairy rings. Your mom's got some of her more gullible neighbors worked up. They've been seen kneeling in front of the toad-stools, praying out loud. The old girl's losing it, J. P. But you know that already, don't you?"

"Sounds like her neighbors are losing it."

"They don't count. They don't qualify for our services, age wise."

El Paso is known for its sightings of la virgen. She appears in the burn-patterns on tortillas, in woodwork, in the patina of old leather, in water-stained plaster walls. She once appeared in the mole-pattern on a bank teller's back: connect the dots and voilá, the Holy Mother. If the likeness persists long enough the faithful from all over the city and beyond come to petition it for forgiveness, restored health, salvation, or money. Some-times the owner of the object that bears the miraculous pres-ence charges a fee to the supplicants at his door. When Our Lady appeared on a grilled cheese sandwich, it sold on eBay for twenty-eight thousand dollars. The Virgin is a definite blue chip asset.

"I'll talk to Velma tomorrow," I said.

"Today is yesterday's tomorrow. Look, J. P., don't put this off. It's for her own good. It's for *your* own good, too. If you don't take action, we will. You'll be bumped out of the loop."

It was the usual threat. "Bumped out of the loop" meant they'd remove Velma from her Upper Valley house over my objections, or hers. They'd padlock the place and eventually auction it off to pay the nursing home expenses. Whatever money she'd saved would be confiscated by the Public Fiduciary. The Fiduciary would then assume guardianship as well as conservatorship. I would be isolated from the process, out of the loop, without say-so or leverage.

"I'll take care of it, Pilar," I said. I tried to keep the anger out of my voice. Pilar Mellado was just doing her job.

I'd said pretty much the same thing of myself after dismantling an idiotic insurance scam dreamed up by some chump who thought he'd solved all his financial problems the easy way. Just doing my job, sir.

Like the moron who stole his own twelve-year-old Grand Prix then parked it, covered with a tarp, behind his cousin's house a few doors down the street, hoping to collect about nineteen-hundred dollars in theft insurance. I found the car the day after he made his claim. My job, sir.

A guy too dumb to be scared stepped in front of a downtown bus. An accomplice on the bus stashed a half-pint of Cuervo and a half-smoked joint under the driver's seat when the driver got out to check on the "victim." They figured they had the driver and the city nailed for half a million, minimum. The city's insurance was carried by Sundown Fidelity at the time, so I was called in to have a look. It was a slam dunk. The driver tested negative for drugs and alcohol by the cops, and I rounded up three witnesses who saw the accomplice plant the tequila and roach. I visited the busted-up scammer in his hospital room.

"I get nothing?" he said through the pie hole in his head cast.

"Just a bill for a broken headlight on the bus," I said, plus some jail time after you heal up."

"Fuckhead," he said, the expletive funneled through plaster.

"That's my job description, sir."

People live in varying states of self-delusion. I don't exclude myself.

AFTER MY FATHER DIED, Velma began to get strange. At first it looked like zest. She was energized. She cleaned the house until it looked unlived in. She bought new furniture, had the Salvation Army pick up the old stuff. She read obscure poetry out loud in the backyard. When my dad's life insurance money began to run out she took a job with the local school district as a crossing guard, the same school district where she'd spent her life as a respected teacher. She also moonlighted at a bakery where she made the breakfast pastries that she'd have to deliver at five in the morning to Upper Valley grocery stores and cafés. She learned how to drive one of my dad's almost unused sedans for this purpose. One night the shift boss caught her drinking vanilla straight out of the bottles it came in. Stoned on vanilla, she ran her car through the front windows of a 7-11 store. This cost her the crossing guard job as well as the bakery job.

A few years later she began talking to Dad. I heard her scold him once. "If you only had listened to Doctor Arroyo, honey," she said. "He warned us. He told you a hundred times to slow down and take care of yourself." I heard her saying this to the wallpaper across the room while seated at her new dinette set. After scolding Dad, she read him poems. The sort of poems she'd read to her high school students to bump them out of their slumber.

"Who you talking to, Mom?" I said.

"Your father," she blurted. Then she realized what she was saying. She became coquettish. "I mean *no*," she crooned, "not your *father*. I was just thinking about him. Thinking out loud."

I caught her doing it again a month later. I didn't ask her about it that time. A lot of old people talk to the walls, I told myself. It doesn't mean anything.

Then she started seeing the Virgins. She was an avid reader of books dealing with the occult. She read books that argued for the existence of angels. She read books on events unexplained by science. She read science books, too. She read a non-mathematical book on the latest thing in theoretical physics, "string theory," and claimed to understand it. She said string theory explains how beings from other dimensions not only exist but can visit us if the harmonic vibrations of the strings are just right. The Virgin was one of these visitors. UFOs?—they also were trans-dimensional travelers. Bigfoot?—a creature from dimension number five. Hitler? Idi Amin? Saddam? Jeffrey Dahmer?—monsters from the dimension commonly known as Hell. "The true world is divided eleven ways," she said. "Every one of them different but every bit as real as the one we live in. There are eleven versions of yourself, J. P. Your father is still alive in four other dimensions, dead and buried in seven, unmourned in one. That's why I can talk to him. And you know what? Just because you're from dimension five, six, or eleven, you're not a whit smarter or wiser than you are in dimension one or three. It's always just the same old you, warts and all. The one thing you can't escape is you."

"Please don't tell this to the Adult Protective Services people, mom," I said. "They're probably not up to speed on string theory."

Her tired old face stiffened. She was only seventy-four, but she looked eight-four. "I'll fight them," she said. "I'll not give up my home."

She drank several water glasses full of iced muscatel every afternoon, claiming it was good for her nerves. She always poured one for me. I always emptied it into the sink first chance I got.

"You can't fight city hall," I said. "They come by checking on you, you'd better not talk about virgins in the woodwork. That kind of talk makes them eager."

She began to fidget. She knew I was right but she wasn't about to lie to anyone on the subject of visitors from other dimensions, backed by string theory. Lying when you knew the truth was the greatest sin she could imagine.

"You're not religious, Mom," I said. "Or scientific, for that matter. You were a high school English teacher."

"You don't know me at all," she said. "I've always been religious, I just don't believe in church-going. I've always been as interested in science as I've been in literature. I'm not stupid and I don't like being treated as if I were."

And so it went. She'd found her truth. Whether or not it originated in neurological damage or trans-dimensional visitations was probably beside the point. Truth is truth, whatever bus it arrives on. Mere logic can't dislodge it.

When I got back to my apartment, Luther had left a message on my machine. He was choking back sobs. I called him back.

"She's gone, J. P.," he said. "She didn't come home last night from work. I found a note taped to the front door this morning. A nervous scrawl. Her handwriting is usually perfect. I called the cops. I wanted her listed as a missing person. They goddamned near laughed at me. Then they asked me if we'd had an argument. Said it like our arguments were common knowledge. They practically accused me of running her off, the sons of bitches."

"Did you?" I said.

"Jesus, not you, too." His misery came through the phone. My ear felt damp.

"What did the note say?"

"Not a hell of a lot. 'Luther, I need some time for this. Do *not* worry about me. Don't forget to feed Gretchen and to clean her litter box. I'll be back when I get back.' Why is she doing this to me, J. P.? What the hell does she mean, 'I need some time for this'? For *what*?"

"I'll come over tomorrow."

"Tomorrow! It's always *tomorrow* with you, J. P. The original mañana man."

"You might be reading too much into the situation, Luther."

"Fine. Thanks so much for your support." He slammed the phone down. It rang again a minute later. I got into the shower before the answering machine picked up.

I made myself a generous bloody Maria, watched a little TV news—the greater world was still on the Midnight Express to hell—and went to bed.

THE DREAM VISITS ME occasionally: I'm on the upslope sands of a wind-rippled wadi. Fifty meters ahead on the other side of a long berm someone's waiting for me. I can hear my accelerating heart even though I'm asleep. It's one of those please-kill-me berms that are supposed to hide their type sixty-two Chinese-built light tanks except the turrets stick up like carny ducks, vulnerable to 40 mm RPGs. Sergeant Apostoli says, his voice rasped by Kuwait grit, They're probably all dead, Morgan, but be ready to eat sand. Apostoli, forty-nine, survived Khe Sanh and now he's in Kuwait. Through a screen of blowing sand I begin to see the shepherd coming up the other side of the berm, a smoking turret behind him. He's carrying the usual AK 47. Sometimes in this dream it's not an AK but a shepherd's crook. Sometimes he's in camo, sometimes in shepherd's garb. But where are the sheep, or goats, or whatever these sadass people have? He points his crook at me, moving closer, smiling in a friendly way. Good people, these Iraqis. I tell him in my two-week Arabic to drop the crook. Please drop your fucking weapon, sadi kie (my friend). Get on your knees, hands behind your head! Where are your fucking sheep, sadi kie? But a forty-knot shamal is howling and my eyes even under the goggles are stinging. He keeps coming up toward me out of the please-kill-me berm, smiling, not understanding, wanting to surrender but not clear on just how to do it. He looks friendly as Jesus in an Easter play. Jesus with his finger inside the trigger guard of an AK. An armored personnel carrier is burning behind him, draped

*with the recent dead. If you're surrendering, drop your piece! I
say in English, but he keeps moving, sideways against the wind,
smiling, and there's no time to figure it out. You see any fucking
sheep? I say to Sergeant Apostoli. He's your fucking sheep, Apostoli says. Take the simple shit down! Allah Akbah! the shepherd
yells and my mouth goes dry as the blowing sand, and I thumb
the selector to auto. He figures out what I mean a second too
late. He drops the AK but I've already put a three-round burst
into his chest. He takes a hard flop and muscle seizures make
him bounce down the steep slope of the berm. His eyes are not
yet dreamy with death but alive with the fear of it. I put another
burst into his still pumping heart and he's finally dead, dead as
Jesus. I stand over him, studying his eyes. You dumb shit, sadi
kie, I say, but I'm shaking. Boos teezee, sharmuta, I say, a mangled insult, meaningless to him now.*

I don't wake up in a heart-pounding sweat anymore, just
a little bemused, wondering why the dream sticks. It's been
decades since Kuwait, decades since I lit up the Iraqi conscript
who surrendered a heartbeat too late.

CHAPTER FOUR

Luther lives in Kern Place, an old, upscale neighborhood nestled in the western foothills of the Franklin mountains. A number of the houses in Kern were old Spanish-style manses: red tiled roofs, inner courtyards surrounded by stone walls with broken glass embedded on top to discourage intruders, the windows and doors covered with wrought iron bars. The iron bars are antiques, turned by metal smiths in the early years of the twentieth century. They were nice to look at but they weren't just ornamental. Kern is a prime target for the ladrónes—thieves—who wade the Rio Grande looking for items that will get a good price in the fencing operations that thrive in the back streets of Juárez. Computers used to be first to go but now it was flat-screen, hi-def television sets. But anything electronic, from blue ray DVD players to smart phones, are popular items among the Rio-wading burglars.

Luther had company, a tall wiry man with quick narrow eyes and a wolfish look. He was wearing a three-piece pinstriped banker's suit and Gucci wingtips. The suit and shoes were at odds with the jade studs in his earlobes and the soul-patch tuft under his lower lip. His silvery hair was wired in dreadlocks, completing the contrast. He was white but everything about him said: *I'm as hip as any brother you can name. Don't think you can play my game.*

He stood up when I came in. I knew what he was before he uncrossed his legs: Luther hired a creepy peeper after all. We shook hands. His hand was damp and he held mine a beat too long. He bared his teeth. I'd seen that thousand dollar smile walking toward me in a dozen used car lots. I didn't recognize him at first, but I recognized the style.

"Ham Scales," he said.

"Excuse me?" I said, thinking I'd misheard.

"Ham for Hamilton, but I can't have people calling me *Hamilton*. Too formal, too many syllables. Hard to warm up to someone you've got to call Hamilton. You'd feel the need to curtsey or bow." He winked at me, handed me his card:

HAMILTON SCALES & ASSOCIATES
DISCRETE INVESTIGATIONS

"You working for Luther?" I said.

"We're addressing the issue," Scales said. "And you are…?"

"J. P. Morgan."

"I've heard of you," he said.

"Very funny."

"No, I mean I know your rep. You're a local hero, dawg. You did some quality work for the Sundown people. You want to join my crew, give me a call. We're always looking for good skip-tracing muscle, and you look pretty buff. Does that sort of thing appeal to you?"

"Excuse me all to hell," Luther said. "But I think we were talking about *my* problem here."

"I don't think it's a problem, Luther," I said.

Luther scoffed. "My brilliant friend doesn't think I have a problem."

Luther was drunk and wallowing in self-pity. Seven or eight empty beer cans were scattered next to his recliner. Which meant he was off his meds.

Again I wondered what Carla ever saw in him. But then he wasn't always like this. He'd changed over the years. Ten years ago he had movie-star looks and could convince people who didn't know any better that he was the genuine article, a hot young writer about to stand the literary world on its stuffy head. Carla was impressed, believing he was a serious person with serious talent, if a bit eccentric. A few years later his demons came on strong and he let himself go. Went from a lean one-eighty to a sloppy two-ninety. He was inconsistent with his meds, too consistent with his booze and grifa.

Scales turned to me. "You don't think Carla Penrose has something going with Hector Martinez?" he said.

I looked at Luther. "Who is Hector Martinez?" I said.

"Our team boiled it down to two or three possibles," Scales said. "A couple of older grad students—and this Hector guy, also a grad student. He seems to be the most likely, even though he's a little young for her. We estimate his age to be about twenty-three."

"You're confusing him, Ham," Luther said. "He needs it spelled out. Show him the pictures."

Scales pulled an envelope out of his jacket pocket. He handed it to me.

"I think you'll find I have grounds for annulment, if not divorce," Luther said piously. "The church will usually grant annulments in this type of case."

I looked at the pictures: Carla handing a manila folder to a man wearing a straw ranchero hat and sunglasses. Carla at a lunch counter, sitting next to a kid in his late teens—not a likely candidate. Carla laughing wonderfully, like she hasn't laughed in years, a shadowy figure next to her with longish hair, a man possibly, but it could have been a tall woman wearing a blazer and slacks. In this photo Carla looks happy, a sight that explained Luther's beer-fueled pout.

"This is Hector Martinez?" I said, pointing to the shadowy figure.

"The one and the same," Scales said. "Carla Penrose is his, ah, graduate *advisor*."

"I'll kill the son of a bitch," Luther said through his teeth.

"There's nothing here," I said. "These pictures are supposed to be incriminating? Carla's a popular professor. She interacts with all sorts of people all day long. Her students are crazy about her. These pictures mean nothing."

"There's more," Scales said. He took a mini-recorder out of his pocket. "My team tapped her office phone." He studied the recorder, found the play button. "This is Carla Penrose talking to a male individual, most likely Martinez."

A tinny voice speaking in guarded whispers, said: "I need to see you right away." It sounded like Carla, but the quality was poor.

"I understand, Carlita," a man said. "I know what I need to do. I want you to know that I'm grateful for what you've already done for me. The gringo pig and his agents do not worry me."

There was a long pause, then the woman, Carlita, said, "We have to be careful. If they find us, expect the worst."

"Ai, Carlita. Their threats mean nothing. Not here. Not in Mexico. En ninguna parte—nowhere."

"Don't be reckless, Hector," the woman said. "Your courage is admirable, but acting recklessly would be a mistake."

Scales put the mini recorder back in his pocket. "If that's not enough for you, J. P., then think about this: Carla Penrose and an Hispanic male, possibly Hector Martinez, flew to Las Vegas this morning. We believe the note she left on the door was a stall. My man saw them board Delta flight 3901."

Luther moaned. "Goddamnit," he said. "I gave that woman the best years of my life. And this is my reward? Some home-wrecking son of a bitch calling her *Carlita*? What's this *Carlita* crap? Her name's Carla, not fucking Car-*lee*-ta!"

"It's a term of endearment," Scales said.

"I know what it is, for Christ's sakes. And me—I'm supposed to be the gringo pig in their little dialog?"

Scales put his hand on Luther's shoulder. "I understand what you're going through, Mr. Penrose," he said. "But when all the cards are face-up on the table, you'll be able to put your life back on course."

"I loved her," Luther sobbed. "I *still* love her. I've never loved anyone but her."

"That's a quality attitude, Mr. Penrose," Scales said. "It shows your basic decency. You deserve better than to be disrespected this way."

"I also have the capacity to forgive," Luther said. He looked at Scales expectantly. A saintly smile distorted his face. The man was shameless.

"It takes a big man to forgive," Scales said.

Luther, playing the wounded but still resolute martyr, sipped his beer. "I can forgive, but not forget," he said. "This kind of wound doesn't heal overnight. It's not exactly a paper cut."

"No, it runs deeper than that," Scales said. "It cuts to the heart. I've seen the whole spectrum of human behavior, Mr. Penrose. When I say I feel your pain it's not just polite conversation."

"I was in Desert Storm, 1991, and came out unscathed," Luther said with quiet dignity. He studied the palms of his hands. "Now look at me. I'm bleeding. I'm nailed to the cross."

"We'll do our best to start the healing process, Mr. Penrose," Scales said. "You deserve swift closure in this case."

"I need some air," I said. I went into the kitchen and opened the solarium doors.

A small green lizard looked up at me from the flagstone tiles. There seemed to be a question in his flat black reptilian eyes.

"Don't ask," I said.

CHAPTER FIVE

"He's pond scum, Luther," I said. After Scales left I remembered some things about his "crew" and their reputation.

"Really?" Luther said. "His outfit's been in business twenty years. They've solved cases the police couldn't close. But a track record like that doesn't impress you, the greatest investigator since Sherlock fucking Holmes. To someone as god-like as yourself he's *pond* scum. Pardon me if I pass a little global warming methane in honor of your professional opinion."

He raised a cheek and spent a trumpeting fart.

"That guy eats out of dumpsters, Luther. He goes after cold cases with an eye to after-the-fact litigation. They dig up an injured party—years later sometimes—and scare up enough evidence to make him into a plaintiff seeking damages from some secondary source. Like the woman who received anonymous death threats, then a year later collected compensatory damages for emotional stress from Southwest Bell because the threats came over *their* lines. They were "facilitators." The lawyers Scales and company work with are personal injury specialists. The shameless humps find a money connection, no matter how unlikely, and go after it with punitive recompense suits. The way courts are handing down damage claims these days, they almost never lose. Scales came to Sundown a couple of years back looking to secure fidelity bonds for his motley crew of ex-felon skip-tracers. They were turned down flat, on principle. Luther, this guy is a lamprey in Gucci shoes. Get rid of him."

"Nice speech, J. P. but I don't think you know what you're talking about. All I know is they get results. Besides, weren't you the genius who told me to try the Yellow Pages? Now you've got your shorts all bunched up because I followed your advice."

"How much are you paying that creep."

"I think that's between Mr. Scales and me."

"I hope to hell you haven't signed anything."

"Again, that's none of your business."

"You'll lose her for good doing this, Luther."

"I've already lost her."

He looked up at me, his eyes damp, his lower lip trembling. "I treated her like shit, J. P.," he said. "I admit it. But that doesn't mean I don't love her."

"What *does* it mean, Luther?"

"Nothing, damnit! It's just the way I am. I can be an asshole at times. She knows that. She knew it years ago. She bought the whole package."

"I don't think she knew what was in the package. You should count your blessings she stuck it out as long as she did."

"Go fuck yourself, J. P."

"He'll bleed you until you wise up or he hits dry bone," I said. "That's how he works." But Luther wasn't listening.

SCALES WAS WAITING FOR me outside. He stroked the soul-patch bristles under his lip thoughtfully. "Yo, dawg," he said.

"Let's be straight about something here. The gig is *mine*. Are we clear on that? It's small change, but we've already got the wife dead to rights, practically in flagrante delicto. It may take us a few weeks to get footage of Martinez feeding the lady his chorizo, but have no fear, J.P, we'll get it done. Love, like the old song goes, always finds a way."

"What's your take?" I said. "Six bills and no cap on expenses?"

"You're really an amusing man, J. P. You should have your own radio talk show. 'Morgan in the Morning—Advice for the Intellectually Disadvantaged.' Has a ring to it, don't you think?"

"He offered me five hundred a day, flat," I said, just to see his reaction.

Scales scoffed before he could stop himself. The condescending scoff told me what I wanted to know: he'd probably nicked Luther for at least double that.

"You work on the cheap these days, J. P.," Scales said. "You having a hard time getting gigs since Sundown canned your ass?"

"Maybe I'll just do Luther a favor and locate Carla myself, gratis."

Scales made himself look sturdy under his pin stripes. "Looky here, cowboy. If this is going to be a turf thing, you lose. I've got the man's retainer. That qualifies as a legal contract. This is a small-change deal for us, but we like to think no job is too small or insignificant. Our aim is to aid and comfort the citizens, for a profit. So go find your own nickel and dime gigs."

I stepped close to him, within uppercut range. We were about the same height but I was two weight classes above him and my face had a history of old brawls. "This may be a hard concept for you to grasp Scales, but the man, such as he is, is my friend. If I want to do him a favor, I will."

He stepped back out of reach and pointed a stern finger at me. "You fuck with me, Morgan, I'll have your license. I've got friends who shit in marble toilets. Are you so marginal you don't *know* that?"

"I don't need a license to do Luther a favor."

"Do yourself a favor and butt the fuck out. What are you going to do when they pull your ticket, dawg? Bus tables at Luby's?"

"Thanks for your concern, *dawg*, but I think I'll get by."

We left it at that. Scales drove off in a lipstick red Porsche. I had parked one of my dad's relics, an oxidized 1971 Chevy Monte Carlo, behind it. I went back inside.

"He's got his hands in your pockets, Luther," I said.

Luther was still in his recliner sipping a fresh beer. *The Flying Dutchman* was on the stereo, rattling the china in the sideboard. The big Manx howled at something under the sofa. It was all very operatic.

"What do you care?" Luther said. "I needed help, and you, uh, *hesitated*. Jesus, it's great to be blessed with friends you can count on." He gave me a wounded look, then turned pensive. "The last time I had real friends was in the army. Combat does that. You bond. They say combat strips away your humanity. That's bullshit. It *exposes* your humanity."

"You weren't in combat, Luther. You spent the war typing battle damage reports in Riyadh."

"Everyone who was there was in combat," he said. "One of those Russian Scuds landed two hundred meters from my hotel! And don't forget, Riyadh was crawling with possible suicide bombers."

"You were TDY in a *hotel?*"

"I was on temporary duty the day I enlisted. I was only in Riyadh five weeks. And you know what? I didn't take a shit the entire time I was there! I didn't leave a single turd in the Saudi desert! When they put me in Walter Reed I had an impacted bowel, along with Gulf War syndrome and a neurological disorder due to a chemical imbalance—thanks to incompetent army docs who shot me up with all kinds of so-called anti-toxins. They had to use a Roto-Rooter to clean out my bowels. It was as painful as any goddamn gunshot wound, J. P. But did I

get the Purple Heart I deserved? Fuck *no!* They sent me home
with a package of Ex-Lax and a Section Eight."

Luther, whose loyalties tended to be flexible, was on temporary duty the day he was born. I couldn't help laughing a little.

He stared at me, then through me. "You think it's *funny?*"
he said. "You *laugh* when you see amputees and quads? Human suffering is your idea of knee-slapping humor?"

He'd practiced and perfected the baleful thousand-yard
stare. It was humbling to civilians. He intimidated waiters and
store clerks with it. The stare said: *I've seen more than you've
seen in your worst nightmares.* He'd conveniently forgotten
that I was with the 24th Infantry and had been shot at from
fairly close range by troops in Saddam's Hammurabi Division.
In Luther's version of reality he was the only significant actor.

"I'll find Carla," I said. "I won't charge you a nickel."

He ignored me. His manuscript was in his lap. He held up a
page and studied it, his Ben Franklin reading glasses down on
his nose. I started to leave.

"Wait a minute, J. P. Listen to this:

> Richard flushed a bright lobster-red, nearly swal-
> lowing his caviar spoon. Meyerbeer, his host,
> didn't understand the significance and import of
> Lohengrin at all! Richard, nauseated, gagged. He
> went out into a black misery of spiteful rain and
> strode toward the odiferous sewer that was the
> river Seine as the Parisian night fell heavily with
> an oddly ominous and joyless gaiety. "There is no
> opera like Lohengrin!" he told a nameless dere-
> lict who held out his filthy hand for alms. Rich-
> ard suddenly *hated* Paris! He struck the derelict's
> filthy hand with his walking stick. "Schwein!" he
> said, moving on. He looked forward to residing
> in Meudon! The Parisian Prefect of Police had
> no power to arrest him for his debts in Meud-
> on! Meudon, where he vowed to take the only
> revenge available to absolute genius: He would

stun the world with a new music taken directly from the haunted realms of the great Teutonic gods themselves! Soon Cosima—daughter of the moody Hungarian genius, Franz Liszt—would be in his arms again. Cosima! Beautiful wife of von Bulow, a decent chap who did not object to the affair! Cosima! Cosima! In his mind's eye he saw the tender gates of her sex trembling like the moist petals of a rose opening to his Valhalla-forged manhood as if to the very sun itself! "There is no opera like Lohengrin, Cosima!" And why should von Bulow object? Giving your wife to a possessor of absolute genius would be an honor for any man! What is more precious and rewarding than the devotion of such absolute friends? What is more pleasing to the palates of the eternal gods?

"What do you think of *that*, my friend? Melodramatic? Too much *Sturm und Drang* for your bourgeois soul?"

"Vintage Penrose," I said. "Top of your form, Luther."

Luther nodded in agreement, pleased with himself. Luther, the hero of his own delusions.

CHAPTER SIX

The following morning I walked into a replica of Bhutan. The university was less than a mile from my apartment building yet every time I came here I felt ten-thousand miles away and a thousand years back in time. It's the buildings. They make no sense. No university anywhere in the country has buildings remotely like this. This is what Shangri-la must have looked like.

The wife of its first president was responsible for the time/space effect. She was thumbing through a *National Geographic* and saw photos of the *dzongs*, the fortress-monasteries of Bhutan, transplanted from Tibet. This was over a hundred years ago. There was no campus yet, no buildings. She pointed out the terrain of Bhutan to her husband. Pointed out that it was similar to the terrain of far West Texas. The architectural style of the great Buddhist monasteries would be perfect for the new school—the West Texas School of Mines and Metallurgy. She convinced her husband of this.

It made no sense. Colleges needed to look like colleges, not Buddhist monasteries. The buildings should have vertical walls with climbing ivy, classic arches, grassy quadrangles, solemn bell towers that chimed the half-hour and the hour. They shouldn't have shallow, red-tiled roofs. They shouldn't rise up from ground level like trapezoidal monoliths, and the walls shouldn't be studded with exotic bricked-in mandalas significant only to Buddhists. If anyone in a position of authority made this argument, the president's wife defeated it. As the years went by the campus grew, but all the new buildings conformed to the original mandate. They all looked like Tibetan *dzongs.* The school dropped its mining and metallurgy tag in the 1960s and became the University of Texas at El Paso. I called it Bhutan. Bhutan on the Rio Grande.

I liked to stroll through the campus on Sundays, when the students were gone. The feeling of being transported through space and time was greatest when I had the place to myself. The wind funneling through the channels between buildings was pitched low, like the *oms* of Tibetan monks. Sometimes I'd bring my lunch and find a place to eat it in the small mulberry-shaded park in front of Old Main Hall, the oldest of the *dzong*-like buildings. I'd settle in there, sitting cross-legged on the grass, and think my best lotus thoughts as time slowed to a crawl and sometimes stopped.

I wasn't thinking my best lotus thoughts today. The campus was crowded and because it was Friday there was a rock band exercising itself in the plaza of the Student Union. I asked a distracted man in seersucker and bow tie—my guess: an economics professor—where I could find Latin American Studies. He pointed the way. The over-amped band drowned out his voice. He said something that sounded like War Hell. Close enough. I found *Worrell* Hall, on the south end of the campus.

"Where can I find Carla Penrose's office?" I asked the departmental secretary, a narrow, tightly-strung woman in her fifties. She was one of those perpetually exhausted office workers who could look aggravated in a coffin.

"She's taken sick leave today," she said, not looking up from her paperwork.

"Tell me anyway," I said.

She looked at me briefly. "Why should I do that?"

"I want to slide a note under her door."

"Give it to me," she said. "I'll put in her mail box."

"It's personal. Kind of a billet-doux. We're old friends. I'd rather just slide it under her door."

Her lips tightened to a sharp red line. Kissing them would be like kissing a cheese slicer. "No one will read it, sir," she said. "We respect privacy, even that of our non-tenured faculty."

I guessed she was letting me know she had a sense of humor, but she didn't smile.

"Skip it," I said.

I walked down the hall adjacent to the departmental office, checking the nameplates on office doors. I checked all the nameplates on the first and second floors. I found C. PENROSE, on the last door of the third floor hallway. Whoever assigned her this office must have wanted to exile her. Troublemakers in some institutions are given remote work places before being fired. The bosses, possibly out of guilt for what they are about to do, don't want to face the soon to be jettisoned. I wondered if Carla had made enemies in high places. I decided she had; she was the type—a born boat rocker.

The door was locked. I checked the other offices. Most of them were dark. I listened at the door of two offices that had lights showing in the transoms. No sound. Probably a couple of profs reading papers. I went back to Carla's office. I had my pick kit with me. The lock was old, probably going back forty or fifty years. Even so it took me about a minute and a half to get the pins moving with my homemade snake pick. Too long, but this was a relatively safe place to work the nefarious trade. I went in, closed the door behind me.

Carla lived well in exile. The office was a statement: exile has its plus side. It was attractively decorated. It had the feminine touch—Persian-style rugs, chintz curtains on the window, a floor lamp with a tiffany shade, a small fridge festooned with decals and magnets. Prints of the Impressionist masters on the walls. The walls painted a non-standard teal green. There was a plush divan with plump satin pillows and a leather armchair with matching ottoman. The divan was wine red and long enough to lie down on. Her scent was still on the pillows. It was more a hideaway crib than an office, ideal for romantic trysts.

The view from her window provided contrast: Across the Rio Grande was one of the poorest sections of Juárez, the Cedepista area. The Cedepistas claimed to be communists, and gringos were not welcome there. You took your chances walking or driving through that neighborhood. Even the Juárez judiciales were careful patrolling the dirt streets and miserable shanties of the Cedepistas.

The first thing I did was screw the cap off Carla's phone and remove Scales's bug. Then I checked the overhead light fixtures and A/C ducts for mini-cams. If Scales's crew had planted one I couldn't find it. I turned on her computer and guessed at her password. I got it on the third try: Rosepen. I called up a dozen files that had to do with course descriptions, proposals for new courses, and memos, none of which had anything to do with Hector Martinez.

After that I went through her desk. She kept it messy and wouldn't notice my pawing through it. The top drawers were filled with the kinds of things teachers hoard: gum erasers and white-out, a dozen pencils and as many pens, push pins and thumb tacks, staplers and sticky notes, rubber bands and rolls of Scotch tape, rolls of postage stamps, stacks of pre-stamped departmental envelopes, labels of all kinds, bottles of aspirin and Tylenol and an empty Percoset vial.

The bottom left drawer was a file. It was packed tight with student papers. In the back of the file there was the literature of protest and change. There were papers with titles such as "Open la Frontera Now!" "Stop Persecuting the Working People of Mexico" "This Land Was *Their* Land." A paper titled, "The Aims and Methods of the HBB," seemed to address the problems created by a civilian vigilante group bent on the violent interdiction of illegals.

There were some enlarged photos of Carla and several

Mexican women wading across the Rio Grande, and other photos of them using bolt cutters to open a large hole in the chain-link fence that separated the two countries. Another photo showed the women crawling through the hole. The next photo in the series showed INS agents handcuffing the women. Carla raised her cuffed hands high for her accomplice, the photographer. She was smiling brilliantly, without fear. The photo, subtitled "Conscience and Disobedience—the Border Today," made the pages of *Newsweek*.

I remembered the incident. It happened last winter: It was a guerilla theater event, styled after the Vietnam war protests of thirty-plus years ago. Carla spent a night in INS custody then was fined heavily for her part in the demonstration. I remember Luther raising hell with city officials, throwing his weight around, identifying himself importantly as Big Bill Penrose's son. No one took him seriously. Big Bill was an embarrassing memory for most people in town. If he had weight, he took it with him to the grave.

None of this explained Carla's absence.

I left after making sure the door would stay locked after my tampering. Down the hallway a man stepped out of an office. He was bald, dressed in a saffron robe and sandals. He wore round, dark-rimmed glasses. A Buddhist monk.

He was the real deal. When the monks of Bhutan learned of this campus decades ago, they were fascinated, sure that it had some sort of metaphysical significance. They visited the campus, and the university president at the time offered the monks free office space. Shortly after that the school opened a Himalayan cultural center on campus.

The monks were like ambassadors from another planet, but they weren't just exotic decoration. They came to West Texas as if they'd discovered a lost district of their own country. They offered classes in the Eightfold Path and meditation sessions for those who needed to re-orient their lives. Now and then they made sand mandalas designed to bring good fortune to the university. In a crafted ceremony a monk would take the sand from one of these mandalas and sprinkle it into the

Rio Grande, blessing and purifying the polluted water. It was probably going to happen one day, but no one as yet had sued the university for violating the constitutional dictum separating church and state.

The monk saw me and smiled. "So, how is your day going so far?" he said, as if he was really interested.

"Haven't stubbed my toe yet," I said.

He laughed good-naturedly. "Well, it is still early, is it not?"

CHAPTER SEVEN

I was almost home when Luther's Packard pulled up beside me. He cranked down the window. "Get in," he said.

"What brings you to the low-rent part of town, Luther?"

"I've been looking all over hell for you," he said. "She took money out of our joint checking account before she left. Scales told me she paid cash for her tickets."

"Carla?"

"No, Queen Elizabeth the second. Who the hell do you think?"

"Has she been in touch?"

"No." I got in the car. Luther looked as if he hadn't slept and was running on coffee and amphetamines. He seemed to be vibrating—uncontrolled spasms shivered through his body. He was unshaven and his clothes were speckled with food. He also stank of beer and fried meat. Carla wasn't a great cook, but all Luther could do to feed himself was to fry club steaks in a skillet full of hot grease.

"I want you to go to Las Vegas, J. P.," he said. "I want you to find her and then reason with her. She's always liked you. Maybe you can talk her into coming home. Explain how contrite I am. She'll listen to you."

"What about Scales and company?" I said. "They've probably set up bugs and spy-cams inside her hotel room by now. Isn't that what you wanted? Hard evidence for the divorce?"

"I don't want to lose her, J. P.," he said miserably. "I *need* her. I want you to tell her that I forgive everything. Remind her I'm Catholic and an expert in atonement. She's had her little fling, but I am her goddamned husband! That counts for something, doesn't it? The fact that I'm able to humble myself and forgive her should bring her to her senses, don't you think?"

I thought, Maybe this whole Hector Martinez thing was about Carla coming to her senses, but didn't say it.

Luther parked in front of my apartment building. He took out his wallet. He gave me all his cash. "There's about two thousand here. I'll send more if you need it. Do what it takes, J. P. Kidnap her if you have to. If you talk her into coming home, I'll give you a five grand bonus."

"You ought to get the Scales people off the case first."

"I'll do it. First thing tomorrow."

"Did they find out what hotel she's in?"

"The Riviera. Room 821." He looked at me, a glimmer of hope in his eyes. "They have separate rooms. Martinez is in 823."

Separate but adjoining, I thought. "I want to know something first, Luther," I said.

He looked at me, started to frown, then looked away. *"What?"* he said.

"I want to know exactly what you did to make her run off."

"I'm not a wife-beater, if that's what you're getting at."

"Something happened between you two, Luther."

He slumped glumly into the thick mohair seat of the Packard. "Maybe there was something," he said, barely audible. "I knew about this Martinez prick before Scales identified him. I mean I knew she was seeing someone on a regular basis. I didn't know his name. I saw her with him in the Paradise Café. Heads close together, intimate over piña coladas. This was a couple of months ago. I raised holy hell but she insisted the guy was a graduate student and they were just talking about border

issues. Goddamn but I'm sick of border issues! J. P., I *wanted*
to believe her. But it was all bullshit. It might have started out
innocently, but it looks like they took their little border-issue
meetings to the next level."

"That's all?"

"Isn't that enough? Jesus H. Christ, what more do you want?
You want me to tell you that she quit sleeping with me?"

"Did she?"

"Go to hell."

"I want you to understand something, Luther," I said.

"What?"

"I won't kidnap her."

He looked at me, eyes full of misery. But the misery faded
into worry, then fear. His lower lip trembled. "There's something else," he said.

"Saved the best for last, did you?"

He ignored the taunt. "You know I'm paranoid, and even a
tad schizoid at times, right? And the bi-polar thing…"

"I've seen you spar with your demons once or twice, Luther."

"Maybe I'm being paranoid now. I don't know. But there's a
pair of supersize thugs parked in front of my house. I saw them
when I left. They're driving a rental. I don't know who they are,
but I'm afraid to go home."

"Probably just lost tourists, wondering how to get to the
Alamo."

"They didn't look like tourists—more like old-school Klan
goons. I could almost smell the grits and fatback."

"There's no Klan chapter here," I said. "Not since the 1920s."

The Klan might have come to El Paso looking for trouble
after UTEP won the NCAA basketball championship with an
all-black team back in the early sixties which pissed off a lot of
white roundball fans down south. But it didn't happen.

"They just sat there," Luther said. "Just looking straight
ahead like they had a lot of time to kill."

"If they're still there when you go home, call me. I'll check
them out."

That seemed to calm him down a bit. He stopped vibrating, but there was a sick waxiness to his skin. He really believed he'd contracted Gulf War Illness—nightsweats, fatigue, joint pain—and that he'd brought the sickness home. It looked like he was having a relapse. His forehead was beaded with sweat and he looked paler than ever.

I said, "Carla may be having an affair with Hector Martinez, Luther, but I think there's something else going on. I think she's in some kind of trouble. That's why I'm willing to do this. I don't want to see her get jammed up with the law."

"It's her goddamned lefty politics. She's pissed off people on both sides of the river. The Mexican feds, the coyotes, the INS—and there's no stopping her."

He started banging the steering wheel with his fists. His eyes lost focus. He wagged his head as if trying to stem and organize the chaos in his brain.

"Luther," I said. "Go home and take your meds. I'll get some answers for you."

CHAPTER EIGHT

Luther called me when he got home. The car parked in front of his house was gone but his paranoia wasn't. "Sit tight, Luther," I said. "Take a Prozac, light up a blunt. I'll check in with you tomorrow."

"Everything's so easy for you," he said, sarcastically.

"Some of us are just blessed," I said.

The next morning I went to Las Vegas, a two-hour flight. I rented a car at McCarran and headed for the Strip. The superficial dream-like beauty of Vegas made you feel like the star player in a bigger than life drama. The place was orchestrated, intentionally or unintentionally, to produce that effect. It made you believe in new starts and happy endings. You didn't feel like the sucker you were about to become.

I took a room on the tenth floor of the Riviera. My window looked out on Las Vegas Boulevard, a long avenue packed cheek to jowl with the palatial architecture of other times and places. Some of it was from no specific time or any known place, denying both history and style. It could overpower your sense of reality if you let it, and most people let it—that's why they were here. *What happens here, stays here*—was the town's new motto. It gave the go-ahead to hopeful hedonists from Milwaukee and Wichita and Saskatoon. Even daylight seemed amped up, too dazzling to be natural.

I don't think the Virgin Mary has ever been sighted here. Not her kind of town. Yet it was full of believers. The sidewalks on both sides of the street were jammed with pilgrims in shorts and sandals looking to fill the casinos' collection plates with their retirement money. The hope of the true believer: If the gods of Vegas receive enough tribute they might bless the pilgrim with a lucky draw, a lucky roll, or a lucky spin. There is no salvation here other than luck.

I didn't spend much time looking out the window. I went down to the eighth floor, listened at the door of 821. The TV was on, and above the canned laughter I heard a woman, Carla I supposed, and a man, Hector Martinez no doubt, talking. I couldn't understand them, but they were talking fast, with intensity. I felt the tension in that room through the door.

I went down to the casino and found a slot machine opposite the elevator doors. You can't get out of a Las Vegas hotel without walking through the machinery. There was no easy escape from the slots, the blackjack and craps tables, the roulette wheels. A quarter-mile zigzagging promenade takes you past hundreds of games before delivering you to an exit. A design feature subtle as a gun in your ribs.

I wore a blue, long-billed UTEP cap, shades, and a twenty-four hour stubble—enough of a disguise to go unnoticed where you were unexpected.

I sat in front of a poker machine with a cup full of quarters, refilling the cup every hour or so. Next to me a heavily made-up dowager with a dead cigarette hanging from her lower lip worked the Jokers Wild option on her machine. She had a noticeable hump from years of leaning over the electric bandits. Her movements were mechanical and tireless—years of hope petrified into habit. There was no pleasure in the ritual for her. She reminded me of an El Paso grandma, an abuela grim in solid black, sitting in the front pew of the San

Patricio cathedral on Mesa Street, mumbling her way in Spanish through the Stations of the Cross.

My stakeout ended around three in the afternoon. Carla and Hector Martinez stepped out of the elevator and headed toward the front doors of the casino. I gave my half-full cup of quarters, about fifteen dollar's worth, to the old slots junkie next to me. She looked at me, her watery eyes dim with suspicion. Then she smiled, her dentures reflecting a rainbow of color from the festive lights of the casino. "This is going to double your luck," she said. "Jesus is on your side now, hon. You wait and see." I didn't think that doubling my luck was a necessarily good thing, but I thanked her anyway.

I got through the doors of the casino just in time to see Carla and Hector get into a cab. A fat guy in a fifty-dollar Walmart suit got into the cab behind Carla's. He reminded me of Bluto from the Popeye comics. Big and nasty and not at all shy about it, his sloped forehead suggesting a shortage of frontal lobes, the part of the brain responsible for civilized conduct.

I had a Chevy rental in valet parking, but there was no time to retrieve it. I got into the cab behind Bluto's. I told the driver to follow the first cab. All three cabs headed down Las Vegas Boulevard, then took an on-ramp to 515 south, the interstate bypass. We were all headed, at high speed, toward Henderson or Boulder City or beyond. The cab behind Carla's cab dropped back into traffic. I figured the fat guy in the cab behind Carla and Hector was one of Scales's hirelings who didn't want them to realize they were being followed. For the same reason, I told my driver to let some traffic fill the gap between us and the fat guy's cab.

The geography began to change after we left the city. Tracts of upscale houses grew on either side of the interstate like a fabulous terra-cotta fungus. I could almost hear the collective hum of air conditioners and swamp coolers. The streets of these developments were empty. It was as if the houses had been evacuated before an expected disaster. And then we were past the housing tracts and into the part of Las Vegas that was here before the casinos came. On the outskirts of Henderson, still on the Boulder City highway, we came to a stretch of haphazard construction: corrugated steel sheds, warehouses, a café shaped like a 1940 Airstream trailer, a storage lot full of wide diameter culverts, and the inevitable skanky trailer court, filled with forty-year-old single-wides that were rusty at the skirts. Carla's cab took an exit ramp and drove into the trailer court, "Shamrock Meadows," a descriptive so wrong that it must have been the developer's idea of hilarity.

Bluto's cab also went into Shamrock Meadows. I asked my driver to let me out at the café. He was a mild looking guy with a crepey neck and small, nervous hands. He reminded me of my father.

"How you going to get back?" he said. "No cab's going to come all the way out here from town."

"I guess I'll worry about that later."

"We're pretty close to Boulder City," he said. "You could probably walk there in a couple of hours."

"I'll keep that in mind," I said. "Maybe I could bribe a Boulder City cabby to come get me."

"And take you where? They're sure as hell not going to run you all the way back to Vegas."

"For no amount of money?"

He looked at me closely. "I didn't take you for rich," he said. "I took you for one of those guys who leaves the house deed on the craps table."

"I'm not one of those guys," I said.

"Well, hell. If I can keep my meter running, *I'll* wait all day for you."

I gave him a twenty. "Get yourself a sandwich," I said. "I should be back in a half hour or so."

CHAPTER NINE

An empty cab pulled out of the main street of Shamrock Meadows. It was a dirt street and the cab raised a tan fog of hardpan dust. A pair of dusty tots sat on the edge of the street running Tonka trucks in and out of a puddle they'd made. They had a pail of water to replenish the puddle. One of them looked up at me as I passed by. "Want to play?" he said. "Come on mister, *play.*"

"Not today, buddy," I said.

"You can use my truck," the other one said. "I'll be the water man."

"You kids quit bothering the gentleman," a woman's voice said. The voice came from the screened slit-window of a single-wide trailer.

"Don't mind them, mister," she said to me. "They just miss Jared. *I* don't miss the butt-head but he was always decent to the kids."

The screen door opened and she came out to the small steel-mesh porch. She was as hard and lean as the desert that surrounded her trailer. She held a cigarette in one hand, a beer

can in the other. She flipped her cigarette into the kids' mud
puddle and jutted her hip. Her translucent housedress was
printed with blue forget-me-nots. Her legs in silhouette were
good, all the way up. She wore flip-flops on her dusty feet. Red
toenails.

I'd seen her before in a hundred different trailer courts. She
had the look down pat. The car parked next to her trailer also
fit the mold—a late sixties Chevelle with a cracked windshield,
flat tire, and flaking landau roof. If I looked inside I would
have seen cracked vinyl upholstery and a split dashboard. I almost smiled. Her quick eyes studied me as if I was a possibility
she shouldn't overlook.

"You huntin' for Jared?" she said, her eyes narrowing. "You
look like a repo man. They wantin' to take back his Quad
Cab? The butt-brain put two thousand down on a fully loaded
chili-pepper red half-ton Ram Quad Cab *knowin'* he'd never
make the six hundred a month payments. The two thousand
was his work-comp money. It was all the money we had after
he got busted up on the job. You got a better example of shit-
for-brains stupid than that?"

"No ma'am," I said. "Jared takes the prize."

Actually I had a few dozen better examples of shit-for-
brains stupid. She probably did too. She laughed cynically. I
laughed cynically. We agreed that Jared was butt-brain of the
year and she was better off without him.

"He's decent to the kids, but I come in a poor second behind
his truck," she said.

"The man's a fool," I said.

"Repo man can see that chili-pepper Quad Cab a mile off
like a blister on the Pope's nose. I don't know why I put up with
the dumb sumbitch long as I did. The only thing he can hold
onto is his dick. Even then he spots the bathroom carpet."

"The world is full of Jareds," I said.

"Tell me somethin' I don't know," she said. She looked at me
as if I might be an exception.

I touched the bill of my cap and started to move off.

"Hey, sir? You want a cup of coffee?" she said. "I'm just

about to put a fresh pot on. You take leaded or unleaded? Maybe you'd like a cold beer?"

"No thanks, ma'am. I've got some business down the street."

"The repo man," she said. "I'd a known you anywheres. Goddamn but all you muscle boys look alike. They give you a repo man makeover when you took the job?"

I could have asked a similar question of her but held back. She had trailer park genes. And Jared would always fall in love with big red trucks he couldn't pay for. I guess everyone's stamped out by one cookie cutter or another. She went back inside. I ambled down the street of overdue payments and unrealized dreams, feeling like a repo man on a mission. Which, in a way, I was.

Bluto's cab was parked in front of a nice double-wide. There was even a lawn out front with pink flamingos on it. Bluto was sitting low in the back of the cab, talking on his cell phone. Asking for further instructions, no doubt. I stopped and tapped on his window. He lowered it.

"*What,*" he said.

His mournful hyperthyroid eyes looked me over. He looked like an enormous mutant frog stuffed into a bad suit. "You working for Luther?" I said.

"Who's Luther?"

"Luther's the guy paying your wages."

"Fuck if he is. Ham Scales pays my wages." He waved Ham's business card at me.

"You got Ham on the line right now?"

"Who the fuck wants to know?" He bared two rows of small mossy teeth. If frogs had teeth, this is what they'd look like.

"J. P. Morgan, a friend of the Penroses."

He rolled his window up and said something into his cell phone. He rolled the window back down. "Mr. Scales says you shouldn't be here. He says if you try to contact the cooze, he'll get a restraining order and have city hall pull your ticket."

"Tell Mr. Scales to watch his language. You might also tell him to pound sand up his ass."

He grinned and repeated my message into the phone. He probably didn't get many chances to tell his boss to pound sand up his ass.

He folded the cell and put it away. "Mr. Scales advises you to get yourself a life," he said. The window scrolled back up.

I went to the front door of the double-wide and knocked. A sign on the door said *No Solicitations*. A frail man in his late fifties answered. He was wearing a salmon-pink leisure suit with big lapels, white shoes with gold buckles, and smoke-tinted aviator's glasses. His hair was dyed tarslop black, which only made him look doomed. His sideburns were bushy and would have come down to his jawline if he'd had one. His nose was violet with a fine tapestry of shattered capillaries and his prolapsed stomach looked like it was carrying a forty pound tumor. He looked like Elvis might have looked if he'd lived ten more years and stuck to meth and bourbon. "What is it?" he said, annoyed. "I'm not buying anything."

"I'm not selling anything, sir. I'd just like a word with Mrs. Penrose."

Doomed Elvis looked over his shoulder. "Do you know this man?" he said.

Carla came to the door. "Good God, what are you doing here, J. P.?"

"Looking for you."

"Luther sent you."

"He did. He's worried sick."

"Luther worries about Luther," she said.

She was wearing tan slacks and a pink sleeveless blouse. Her short brown hair had amber sun-streaks in it. She had a beaky nose, freckled at the bridge. Her eyes were her best feature—sea-gray eyes that changed with the weather. Sometimes they were an oceanic gray so deep you thought you might drown in them if you didn't break contact. Right now they were steely with anger and possibly fear.

She looked past me through the open door. "Who's your friend in the cab?"

"That's Bluto. He's not my friend. Luther sent him, too.

That's how worried he is, using redundant trackers."

"I don't want either one of you here. Please go, and tell the man out there to go, too. I can't believe Luther did this."

"Luther thinks you're having an affair with Hector Martinez," I said. "He thinks he wants a divorce. The guy in the cab has been taking pictures of you and Hector, for evidence."

"Oh for Chrissakes," she said.

"I'm here to ask you to drop Martinez and come home to Luther. He doesn't really want a divorce. He wants you."

"He doesn't know what he wants. Luther just *wants*."

"He seemed genuine, Carla."

"Genuine my ass. Goddamnit, you're ruining everything! All of you!"

She turned away from the door and looked at Hector Martinez who was seated across the room in a sofa, listening to us. He was a tall, good-looking kid. An Indio, with a broad Mayan nose, prominent cheekbones, strong supraorbital ridges. He looked uneasy, if not downright scared. Doomed Elvis was saying something to him, but Hector's attention was on Carla and me. He stood up and stepped close Carla. If they were lovers he would have touched her—a hand on her shoulder or elbow, even a blatant arm around her waist. He didn't make any of these possessive gestures. He looked like a nervous kid who had never possessed anything.

"What's going on?" he said. "Does this mean we have to cancel the surgery?"

"Be quiet, Hector," Carla said. To me she said, "I want you and the photographer in the cab to get the hell out of here, *now*."

I handed her my cell. "Tell it to Luther," I said. "He's paying the bills."

She punched in the numbers. She didn't give him a chance to talk. "Call off the dogs, Luther," she said. "I'll be home in a couple of days. I'll explain everything then. This is not what you think." The conversation was short but she apparently managed to placate Luther.

"Now go," she said to me. "I can't tell you how delicate our situation is. You and the guy out there are fucking things up for me and Hector."

"For you and Hector," I said.

"Goddamnit, get your brain out of the gutter. This is a life and death deal, J. P., and you being here just makes things worse."

"What surgery was the kid talking about?" I said.

"Get fucking *out*," she said.

CHAPTER TEN

Bluto was busy on his cell phone, getting instructions from his boss. I dialed up Luther again. "I don't think the relationship is necessarily sexual," I said. "There's something else going on."

Luther took his time answering. I figured he was toking on a blunt. "That's not what Ham Scales thinks," he said, wheezing. "He wants to continue surveillance."

"Of course he does. He wants to keep the meter running. Take my word for it, Luther, Carla and Hector Martinez look too rattled to be having fun and games in Vegas."

"You don't know that. Besides, if it's not an affair now it could develop into one later."

"That's what Scales says?"

Luther paused, took in a choppy breath wet with emotion. "Ham suggested the possibility. He said the situation is in flux and anything might happen. He said it might just take one little incident to make them fall in bed. Like a friendly kiss suddenly becoming an open-mouth face-eater. No, I'm going to keep Ham on the job."

"He's got a lurid imagination, Luther. You'd better tell him to be more discreet. If Carla sees Bluto every time she turns around she may get permanently pissed."

"Who the fuck's Bluto?"

I turned my cell off.

I walked back to the café. The cabby was inside, staring into a cup of coffee. He picked up his check, paid it with the twenty I'd given him, and we headed back to the Riviera.

I had a few hours to kill before my flight back to El Paso. I showered, changed clothes, and went down to the casino where I found an empty blackjack table. I lost fifty then won a hundred by splitting a pair of aces and hitting them with a ten and an eight. Idiot's luck.

I went into the restaurant and ordered a roast beef sandwich to go. I carried the sandwich and a beer out to the swimming pool area. Next to my table a tapped-out player in Bermuda shorts and polo shirt rooted around in a trash can for empty martini cups. He was after the untouched olives. He ate them hungrily, without shame. Sometimes he got lucky and found unchewed pineapple chunks in a piña colada cup. I figured him for a roulette freak, the most efficient way to put the mortgage payment down the toilet.

"A little short?" I said.

"I find myself financially embarrassed at the moment," he said. "My stock holdings tanked last month. You know how it is."

"The house loves the wheel," I said.

He looked at me, unsure of my intentions. Malice and scorn were not among them. He seemed to recognize this. "I won't go near the wheel," he said. "The wheel was made for masochists."

I nodded agreeably. The whole place was made for masochists, but I felt no need to point this out.

"Yesterday I was up five large at the craps table," he said. "I made it all on pass-line bets. Then she turned on me, the fickle bitch."

I didn't ask what he meant. Lady luck, the fickle bitch, killed his streak. I gave him half my sandwich and ten bucks. He thanked me and headed back into the casino where the Lady waited patiently for his return. Humiliation wasn't a problem for him. He was beyond such middle-class responses to life.

I got to McCarran an hour before my flight. I played the slots outside the boarding gates, lost my casino winnings, cursed the fickle bitch, and boarded the Boeing 737 hoping that luck played no part in the air-worthiness of aging commercial jets.

CHAPTER ELEVEN

A nasty wind shear turned the plane into a paper kite just as it was about to touch down. It landed on its left wheels, yawed a bit, bounced, became airborne again. When the right wheels slammed into the runway a second later the plane shook like a wet hen. The Bloody Maria I'd been nursing jumped off the pull-down tray and into the magazine pouch on the back of the forward seat. The tray was supposed to be up and locked, but I sneaked it down after the flight attendant finished her walk-by check.

"Shit," I said.

The elderly woman next to me went white, then splotchy red. "My God!" she said, "what *was* that?" Her chestnut wig had slipped down on her forehead. A twenty-year-old's hair on a seventy-year-old head. Distracting, but not fetching.

"El Paso," I said. "We get a lot of curious wind."

"They should fix it," she said.

Fix the wind? My Bloody Maria? Her hair? I didn't pursue it. We filed out, all of us a bit wobbly in the knees.

"Nice landing," I said to the pilot as I deplaned.

"Got you down, didn't I?" he said, a bit defensive.

I recalled an old pilot's proverb: Any landing you can walk away from is a good landing. "Hell, Captain," I said. "I wasn't complaining."

I found my car in long-term parking, paid the ransom, and headed toward town on I-10. It was dusk, and the lights of Juárez bloomed toxic orange across the river. A geometry of blue lights within the orange marked the foreign owned factories, the maquilas, that dump pollutants into the river and into the canopy of air Juárez and El Paso share. If you could separate the orange and blue lights from the poverty and poison under them, they made a lovely display.

The gusting wind came from the west. By the time my old Monte Carlo rumbled up the hills of Sunset Heights it was gale force. A pumice of desert sand made my teeth gritty.

A dozen roaches were napping in my kitchen after having gorged themselves stupid on microscopic toast crumbs and other bas-cuisine fallout. They'd had the house to themselves for a while and were feeling secure. I stomped the floor and told them to go back into their holes, and after a moment or two of panicky indecision, they did.

Panicking roaches remind of panicking humans. They lose their heads, run into each other, make suicidal leaps off countertops and other high places, try to hide behind chair legs with their brittle asses sticking out waiting to be squashed. Ridiculous creatures really, but they'll inherit the earth after we're long gone. One of God's minor jokes. The planet will be theirs, but they won't know what to do with it. You gotta love the little buggers.

I put a frozen veal cutlet dinner in the microwave then fixed myself a Bloody Maria, replacing the one I'd lost to wind shear. Three parts tequila, one part V8 spiked with Tabasco, a little lime juice.

I still had most of the money Luther had given me. I'd give it back to him, but not tonight. Tomorrow I'd try to convince him he was an idiot and did not need detectives tracking his wife around the country. I didn't know why she'd brought Hector Martinez to a trailer court south of Las Vegas, or who Doomed Elvis was, but her purposes didn't seem carnal. Carla was a political activist. If Luther needed something to worry about he could turn his paranoid imagination loose on the consequences of whatever noble cause she was involved with. She'd crossed swords with the INS before and had made enemies on the other side of the border as well. The state police of Chihuahua had arrested her for leading a protest march against the living conditions in Cereso, the infamous Juárez prison. She'd marched with Jane Fonda and Sally Field along with thousands of others in an Amnesty International sponsored protest of the unsolved serial killings of hundreds of young Juárez women over the last decade. There were a lot of reasons a husband could worry about a wife like Carla, but wantonness had to be way down on the list.

I had two more Bloody Marias after my dinner, listened to some vintage jazz on the public radio station, went to bed early. An old bad dream tracked me down, the one where Kat is packing her bags and I'm drunk in the bedroom, convinced that she is only trying to make a point. "I know you're not leaving," I said. I held up the newspaper as proof. "It says right here in the headlines that they've cancelled all flights to Chicago until the war's over." She kept packing anyway. "There's always an alternative way to go," she said. I watched her walk away until she was a speck on the horizon. At that point in the dream the newspaper headline changed. It became: ALL FLIGHTS CANCELLED BUT THERE'S ALWAYS AN ALTERNATIVE. In bold, black print the truth seemed inescapable: There is no lock-step certitude about anything. I always wake up from this dream nostalgic for certitude and calling her name, *Katherine, Katherine,* as if those lost syllables could retrieve a world without alternatives and secure it once and for all.

I woke up, not thinking about Kat but about the Iraqi

conscript. Feeling bad about losing Kat dragged up Kuwait, 1991, someplace I didn't want to revisit just now. *He should have dropped the goddamn AK.* But the justification didn't put the bad feelings away. The trouble was his eyes. The politicians who invent and justify these wars never have to look into the eyes of the people they kill by proxy.

I CALLED LUTHER THE NEXT morning. "You've got nothing to worry about," I said. "Unless my instincts are out to lunch, Carla and Hector Martinez are having a political affair, not a sexual one."

He didn't respond, but I could hear him breathing. "You all right, Luther?"

"No," he said, his voice shaky. "I'm *not* all right. They left an hour ago. The ones that were here before."

"Who?"

"Their car was parked out front. I already told you about them, goddamnit."

"The Klan goons?"

"They aren't Klan. They're some kind of bounty hunters. Crackers in overalls and hob-nailed boots. They beat the crap out of me."

"They give you a reason?"

"What the fuck do you *think?*" He dropped the phone, picked it up, spoke into the wrong end, turned it around. "They wanted to know where Carla was. I said I didn't know. I asked them what the hell do bounty hunters want with my wife? This just pissed them off. I took their best shots, J. P. I didn't break…"

"Okay," I said. "I believe you."

"…until they poured gasoline on my head. Said they'd give me one more chance before they lit the match. I gave it up. I had to. I told them she was in Vegas, at the Riviera." His voice cracked. He choked back a sob. "I'm a goddamn coward, J. P. I'm a sniveling coward. I don't deserve her."

"You're not a coward," I said. "You held out as long as you could. Everyone's got a limit. Did you warn Carla?"

"I called her, but she'd already checked out."

"I'm coming over."

"I ran tap-water over my hair," he said, "but I can still smell the gas."

"Don't light a joint, Luther."

CHAPTER TWELVE

Luther hadn't washed the blood off his face. He kept the marks of his beating available for viewing. I viewed them and was dutifully impressed. Someone had given him a thorough ass-kicking. His bruised and swollen nose was big as a turnip. Crusts of blood rimmed his nostrils. His lips were cut and puffed up twice their normal size. His right eye was swollen shut. He stank of gasoline and sour sweat.

I drove him to the emergency room at Providence Hospital. Luther mangled the insurance forms and then an overworked nurse led us to an examination room. We had to wait another hour before a doctor came in. He was young, upbeat, probably a first-year intern.

"Hey, what happened to *you*, guy?" he said.

"What the fuck does it look like?" Luther said—always ready to bite a helping hand.

The doctor lost his good cheer. He frowned at his clipboard. "Says here you were accosted by intruders."

"*Accosted?*" Luther said. "That's a pretty word, doc. *Accosted* is when someone grabs your dick in the steam room. They kicked the living shit out of me and poured gas on my head, is what they did."

The doctor sniffed Luther's head. "Have the police been informed?"

Luther looked at me, a familiar aslant look, and I knew the next thing he said would be fiction. "They certainly have," he said. "But it was dark. Clouds obscured the moon. No way could I identify them. And let's face it, the cops have better things to do than start a manhunt for a couple of cracker thugs from out of town."

The doc, all business now, cleaned Luther up. He stitched a laceration over his eye, gave him some Darvocet, told him to keep an ice-pack on his nose and wash his hair with a kitchen detergent, then went on to his next patient.

Out in the parking garage I said, "Why did you lie to the kid?"

"I don't want the cops involved. They damn near laughed at me the first time I called them. What could they do, anyway?"

"Well for starters they could track down the hooligans, pummel them with nightsticks and blackjacks then put them in a jail cell. Does that work for you, Luther?"

"They'd just bring more trouble my way. I don't need that just now. Maybe you've noticed I'm trying to write a somewhat serious novel? I don't want to complicate my life any more than it is. I need peace and quiet, J. P., not more aggravation. The muse demands it."

This was Luther playing the Literary Genius card. I always found it amusing when he did that. He put himself on the same shelf with Hemingway, Faulkner, Joyce, and whoever. He'd had a pack of glamorous photographs taken of himself for publicity purposes, if and when he needed publicity: face diagonally bisected by shadow, the brows knitted, the troubled and troubling eyes suggesting literary stardom was not just a gift but also a cross one had to shoulder.

I drove to the Hollywood café. I ordered a brandy for

Luther, a beer for me. He didn't want lunch. I ordered a plate of gorditas.

"You should have had three coronaries by now, the way you stuff yourself with that deep-fried crap," Luther said.

"I work out," I said. "I don't sit around all day smoking grifa and staring at a typewriter."

His mouth twisted into a righteous snarl. "You think *writing* doesn't burn calories?" he said. "The brain, in case you aren't aware of it, uses 90 percent of the body's available glucose. After a day's work, I can barely get out of my chair."

"Wouldn't be because you're a hundred pounds overweight, would it?"

"You're an ignorant Philistine," he said. "You have no idea what price my chosen life exacts."

The waitress came by with my plate of gorditas and our drinks. She gave Luther a long look, then shrugged. Maybe a man with a battered face who smelled of gasoline wasn't all that unusual in the Hollywood. Luther assumed a studied pose for her benefit: attractive melancholy. It might have worked on an eighteen-year-old English major with stars in her eyes, but the waitress, a stout forty-year-old Mexican woman, just shook her head: She'd seen her quota of culos, gringos and otherwise.

I ordered another round of drinks. Outside the wind rampaged, the street foggy with sand. Cars crept along, their lights on. A siren wailed in the near distance.

"By the way," I said. "You told the doc that the goons were from out-of-town. How did you know that?"

"They said so, more or less. Called me a West Texas pussy, like they had a thing against West Texans."

He went into a blue sulk. I shouldn't have been hassling him, but it kept his mind off the beating and the possibility that it might happen again if the "bounty hunters" were unsuccessful in their search for Carla. But there was something else going on. He was being evasive; he wouldn't look at me.

"What's bothering you, Luther?" I said.

"You have to *ask?*"

"You want to tell me what you're not telling me?"

"Jesus, we're talking in riddles now? All I want you to do is tell me what Carla's been up to. I want to know why she won't come home."

I took my wallet out, gave him his money minus my expenses.

He shoved it away. "Keep it," he said. "I may need you again."

"For what? I told you I didn't think she was having an affair. That's what you wanted to know, isn't it? This is one of her noble crusades, Luther. It looks like she's on some kind of rescue mission. Don't be surprised if la migra shows up at your door with arrest warrants."

"What about the crackers? Why did *they* show up at my door?"

"I don't know. Maybe there's a price on the head of Hector Martinez."

"Goddamnit, why does she get involved with these people? What good does it do? Mexico will always be Mexico, the people screwed and the government corrupt. She can't save them all."

"She's an idealist, Luther. If she didn't put her ideals into action she'd just be another big-talking academic hypocrite. Another Marxist with tenure and fat retirement plan. You know she could never accept that. She's too ballsy for her own good."

Luther moaned. "Why couldn't I have married a waitress?"

"You almost did," I said, reminding him of the Las Cruces woman and her brother, Marco "the Crippler" Monzón.

"That woman was trying to hijack me, J. P."

"Marriage comes in all shapes and colors, Luther, very few of them ideal or even rational."

"What the hell do *you* know about it?" he said.

Not much, I had to admit.

CHAPTER HIRTEEN

I stopped at Sunset Heights on the way to Kern. I left Luther in the car and went into my apartment. I own four guns: an old .357 Smith & Wesson Combat Magnum, a .25 caliber Belgian-made Baby Browning that can hide in your palm, a 1911 U.S. Army Colt .45 I bought from a fellow Desert Storm vet who'd taken it from a Republican Guard Colonel, and a Mossberg semi-automatic 12-gauge shotgun with an illegal fourteen-inch barrel. I picked up the Mossberg and a box of double-oughts, a box of wadcutters for the .357, a box of hollow points for the .25, a box of ACP .45s, 230 grain, and carried them out to the car.

"What are we going to do, go duck hunting?" Luther said.

"Hooligans call on you again, Luther, you distribute their brains around your foyer. Just make sure they're all the way across your threshold. In Texas it's legal to use lethal force to defend your home. The Mossberg is a semi-automatic and it's got a non-regulation barrel, but you won't mind paying the fine if it comes to that. You don't have to be a good shot with this piece, just keep pulling the trigger. You have five rounds to do the job. You can reload if you have to."

"I happen to be an excellent shot," he said. "I won a Marksman medal in basic training."

"Fine. You'll save ammo that way."

None of this made him happy. He moaned, a lung-deep throb of despair. "Shit, J. P. No way is this helping my state of mind. Now that Carla's abandoned me, writing is all I've got. It's everything to me. All this is disrupting the process. I don't *want* your goddamn scatter gun."

"You'd rather face those bad boys without serious backup? You think maybe ignoring the problem will make it go away? And for the record, I don't think Carla's abandoned you. Her work is as important to her as yours is to you. Or don't you think so? Maybe you think your wife's work is trivial next to the work of the great literary master."

He tried his thousand-yard stare on me but his focus fell short. "If she hasn't abandoned me, then where the hell *is* she?" He started to tremble. He crossed his arms on his chest to hold down the shakes. "Please don't mock me," he said humbly. "I'm just asking you to understand my situation, J. P. It's a matter of *balance*, goddamnit. I'm losing it."

I put my hand on his shoulder. I felt his deep instability, an internal wobble, like a gyroscope about to lose its momentum and topple. I had a twinge of guilt. I shouldn't have been riding him, considering the shape he was in.

"It'll blow over, Luther," I said. "You've just got to hang tough for now. I'll try to get to the bottom of Carla's 'Hector Martinez Project.' In the meantime, keep a low profile—and keep the shotgun handy."

I drove Luther up Mesa and into the palm-lined streets of Kern Place. I saw him safely into the house. Carla still wasn't home.

The house smelled of gasoline and fried meat. I opened a few windows. The wind was still up, but a little sand wasn't going to hurt anything. Luther went into the bathroom and came out with a vial of pills. He popped three or four of the blue tablets without bothering to get a glass of water to wash them down. He went into the kitchen and came back with a six pack of Pacifico, which he set down next to his recliner.

"Not a good idea to mix your chemicals, Luther," I said.

He ignored me and went to his stereo cabinet and put on a symphony by Alexander Scriabin. Arrhythmic music bloomed into the house like an invisible flower—slowly, in blossoming measures, spooky and strange. Luther settled into his big chair, pulled his makings out from under it, over-filled a Zig-Zag, spilling weed. He regarded his handiwork for a few moments but did not light up. He set the joint down on the arm of his chair.

"You like to make fun of me," he said, opening a can of beer. "But this Russian lunatic, Scriabin, actually believed his music was so transcendentally beautiful that the human race would be *changed* by it. Jesus, J. P., have you ever heard of anyone with an ego that fucking huge? He thought the sounds he made would create a new race of super humans dedicated to peace and beauty!"

Luther laughed so hard his chair fell back into the fully reclined position. He managed to spill only a few drops of beer. "A new race!" he said, choking a bit on phlegm. "The rotten-to-the-core human race transformed by a tinkling piano! And you call *me* nuts!"

I left him that way—laughing like a B-movie maniac, a can of Pacifico in one hand, a fat unlit joint in the other, and a fully loaded twelve gauge semi-automatic shotgun leaning against the wall next to his chair. Probably not among the smartest things I've done. I drove back to my place, trying to exclude the worst-case possibilities from my mind.

When I got home I packed my gym bag and headed for Gold's on Paragon Street, off North Mesa. I needed a good sweat.

I found my treadmill, set it on the "rolling hill option," and started working. I knew the woman on the Stairmaster next to me. I was glad she was there.

"Hey, J. P. Morgan," she said. "You're late."

Dani Thrailkill, around thirty-five, a 911 dispatcher. Recently, I believed, separated. We'd chatted about our marriages, the unknown sloughs of despond that come with domestic life, the moments of happiness, the long gray interludes between.

I knew her husband, Raymond Thrailkill, a city cop. The year I left the force he came in as a rookie. A ballsy, ambitious kid who had street sense and a solid grip on border Spanish. I figured he'd go far, and I was right. He was now a detective lieutenant, and still in his mid-thirties.

"Late's better than not at all," I said, lamely.

Dani and I had met once or twice when I was a cop, but we hadn't seen each other since I quit the job seven years ago—until we met again at Gold's, a few weeks back. We'd been working out next to each other, by accident at first, then later we began to look deliberately for unoccupied side-by-side machines. Our parallel workouts had been going on long enough to stimulate impulses I thought I'd learned to put on a leash. I liked her, but she'd only been separated from Raymond for a couple of months. She told me this while she climbed the endless stairs and I trudged up the "rolling hill." She still had to be sifting through the emotional debris field, looking for shards of meaning. Which was a good reason for me to exercise some self-control.

Judging from the sheen of sweat on her tanned skin, she'd been working the machine for at least half an hour. She was breathing hard and loud.

I dialed in "Fitness Race" and the machine started to speed up just as hers slowed to the "Cool Down" mode.

"We've got to stop meeting like this, J. P." she joked. She stepped off her machine.

"You got a better place," I said, also joking.

"I do," she said.

No joke now in her tone. No joke now in her serious brown eyes.

"Skip the rest of your workout," she said.

CHAPTER FOURTEEN

"Why aren't you working today?" I said.

"I took some sick leave," she said.

"You're not sick."

"I'm sick of the job. Sick of cops. Sick of the human comedy. I'm going to quit. I've got a new job, over in Tempe—the Phoenix suburb. Working campus security at Arizona State."

"Another job with cops."

"Campus cops. Big difference, J. P. College perps are flashers, date rapers, pill poppers, paintball players, and other mickey mouse fuck-ups."

Perps. You only hear that on TV these days. When they're saying it on the tube, they've quit saying it in the precincts. I took her for a tube junky. NYPD Blue. Law and Order. Next thing, she'd say *skell,* or *moke.* But I wasn't complaining.

The next thing she said took me by surprise: "Don't take this wrong, J. P., but are you clean?"

"Am I *what?*"

"Clean. No STDs?—herpes? Clap? God forbid—HIV?"

"I'm clean."

"Scouts honor?"

"Scouts honor," I said.

"And Scouts don't lie, do they?"

"Only about masturbation."

"Then let's quit the niceties."

"Let's do that."

Her bed was king-sized—red satin sheets, pillows big as duffel bags. All of it would soon be in Phoenix, entertaining someone else. But I wasn't complaining.

Dani had a finely tuned athletic body, compact, strong, eager, and she liked it physical. I pinned her arms. She bucked and twisted under me like a rank saddle bronc. Her legs, locked at the ankles, scissored my waist hard enough to hurt. She raised her head, her teeth bared for an opportune bite. Sex for her was an impersonal athletic competition, seasoned with blood. Even so I whispered a shopworn pledge, "This could be the start of something really fine, Dani." A rag of hope choked me up. My voice quivered.

"Shut up and drive," she said.

I wished I'd spent more time in Gold's. Her gymnastic requirements winded me. She got on top for round two, giving me a break. Her fingers dug into my ribcage as she leveraged her thrusts. Her strong throat glistened. A breathy moan hummed between her perfect teeth.

We showered. We washed each other under the warm spray.

This aroused us again and we went back into the ring for round three. I was tired and started to flag. She had a remedy. She picked up a tube of lubricating gel from her night table, squeezed some out, then reached under me and did something only my urologist had done.

"Whoa," I said.

"*Jesus,*" I said.

"Never had your prostate milked?"

"Is that what this is?"

"You've got a lot to learn, J. P."

"I'm willing. What's the next lesson?"

She showed me. I made sounds I'd never made before.

She pushed me off. "We're done for now."

"For now?"

"For now."

WE SAT AT HER DINETTE table and had tea and scones. I was spent but at peace with the universe, my brain swimming in endorphins. She seemed happy too. My day had started out poorly. It looked like it was going to end on a high note.

I caught her studying me over the rim of her cup.

"You grit your teeth a lot when you fuck," she said. "Especially when you're bringing it home."

"I didn't notice."

"I could hear them grinding."

"Is that a flaw?"

"Do you grind them generally? I mean other than during sex?"

"I don't think about it much."

"You could lose your teeth by the time you're fifty, grinding them like that. Do you floss?"

"God no."

She looked at me as if I'd lied about not having a social disease. I changed the subject.

"I'm going to miss you, Dani," I said.

"You could move to Phoenix. It's a great town."

I thought: *No it isn't.* But why spoil the moment. I shrugged. "El Paso is home. The only one I've ever known."

"This polluted shithole has a *hold* on you?"

"It's embarrassing, I know. But yeah, it does."

She sipped her tea, studying me over the rim of her cup. "You could grind your teeth in Phoenix," she said.

Joking again. Which was good. It meant we could leave this episode behind us and still be friends, floss or no floss.

I kissed her. She kissed back. A friendship kiss—cool, impersonal, dry.

"Catch you at Gold's," I said.

"Not for long, J. P."

On that note we parted.

CHAPTER FIFTEEN

I called Luther the next morning. "She hasn't come back," he said.

"You haven't killed anyone, have you?"

"The shotgun scares the bejesus out of me," he said. "It's an evil entity, J. P. A gun like that is a condensation of a million years of wrath. It's got a mind of its own. Every time I look at it, it *tells* me to put the barrel in my mouth and pull the trigger. Put all your pain out the back door. I'm beginning to obsess on it. I tried not to pay attention to it but my eyes always drift back to the goddamned thing. So I locked it in a closet. Let it talk its evil bullshit to the dust bunnies."

Luther was starting to hallucinate. Not a good sign.

"Won't do you much good in a closet if those bounty hunting bozos knock your door down," I said.

"Why would they do that? I told them what they wanted to know. It's not my fault I don't know where my wife is. She's probably in Juárez, or farther south, swapping bodily fluids with Hector Martinez and his politically oppressed relatives."

I was tired of telling him how wrong he was. He believed what he wanted to believe. I didn't argue with him. It would be a lot simpler if he was right. I thought of my afternoon affair with Dani Thrailkill. I thought of her ex, Raymond—a decent cop who probably still had strong feelings for Dani. We made an insignificant triangle among the greater geometries of the universe. But Carla was involved with something more complicated than an extended roll in the hay with an illicit lover. Something more dangerous.

Strains of *Das Rheingold* rumbled in the background. Gretchen, the cat, howled.

"Have you fed Gretchen?" I said.

"What?"

"Your cat. Gretchen. Have you been taking care of her? You know—water, food, litter box maintenance."

"Sure," he said.

"You don't sound so sure, Luther. You're not really hearing voices are you?"

"Just yours and your shotgun's. Get the thing out of my house, J. P. I can hear it whispering to me now even though I've got Wagner turned up full bore."

"You got anything stronger than Elavil, Luther?"

"I'm not taking any goddamned Thorazine, if that's what you mean. I've had it with that poison. It distorts my face. I can't control my tongue. I can't get a hard-on with that shit running around in my brain. I'll probably never get laid again, but it's nice to think I could if an opportunity came up."

"What about Haldol? You've got some of that, don't you?"

"Haldol's worse. Look, J. P., it isn't so terrible being crazy. Scriabin was crazy. Neitzche was crazy. I think more than a few of the presidents of the U.S. were crazy or doped or drunk. Half the geniuses of the nineteenth century if they were around today would be packed off to the madhouse and shot up with tranquilizers. Isaac Newton was a certified nut case. Jesus, what's so wonderful about sanity in a world that implants microchips into babies so they can be tracked all the way to their graves? You got an answer to that, J. P.?"

"Feed the cat, Luther. I'll drop by later."

"Listen, J. P. I'm thinking of starting an art colony, right here at home—you know, writers, poets, painters. Nothing big, just a little informal get-together of people who think alike. I'm tired of rattling around in this big house alone while Carla's off saving the fucking world. I think it would be good for me to have some kind of meaningful social life, a venue where I could sound out my literary ideas."

"It's all about you, Luther," I said.

"That's what I'd expect from you, J. P. Real support."

"Sorry Luther. I think it's a good idea, your art colony."

"Maybe you could join in. You might meet some interesting Bohemian types. You might even find a woman who'd be glad to haul your ashes any way you want them hauled, no strings attached. What do you say?"

"Bohemians? Not my kind of people, Luther. I wouldn't have much to say to them."

"Shit, J. P., you don't have *any* people. You're going to end up a weird stranger in the world, waxing your dolphin in porno flicks and scaring normal citizens half to death."

"Luther…"

"I'm serious. You're crazier in your own way than I am in mine."

"Good bye, Luther."

I hung up.

CHAPTER SIXTEEN

The minute you feel the need to deny you're crazy is when you cross the line to crazy. I don't think I'm crazier than the next person, but then I don't know anything about the next person, except that there's an even chance he's crossed the line to crazy.

I've seen enough unmoored behavior by otherwise respectable citizens to make me think that most people are mentally adrift in one way or another. It's a premise you need to base your daily expectations on. You'll hardly ever go wrong.

On the other hand you need to believe that people are at least partly rational part of the time and that the world has rules based on reason and the lines from A to B are reliable if not perfectly straight.

Otherwise things fall apart. There is no center. A thin band of intermittent rationality keeps things together. This is a statement of faith. A piss poor one, but it's all I've got.

Take the Matador, for example. He works Mesa Street,

across from the Coronado shopping center, selling newspapers.

I'd spent the morning with my crazy mother and was heading downtown to have lunch at the Hollywood when the little guy with his a bag of newspapers darted off the traffic island into my lane. I swerved, almost ramming a green Suburban. I didn't have to swerve; I knew the Matador's routine, but he caught me napping at the wheel, thinking about Velma's latest visitations.

The newspaper man, holding out an unfolded paper as his muleta, danced away from my front wheels, turning a veronica that would have drawn olés from the crowd at the Plaza de Toros in Juárez. The Matador of Mesa Street. At home in a world of his own.

The light turned red and I came to a full stop. I rolled down my window and bought a paper. "Para usted, señor—cincuenta centavos, nomás," he said. For you, only fifty cents. His little joke: fifty cents *was* the price of the morning paper. I gave him a dollar; he kept the change.

The Matador was about sixty, maybe seventy, and looked like he had ring experience. His gray hair was tied back in the classic pigtail and he was as light on his feet as a ballet master. Most people enjoyed his act; others honked their horns, annoyed. When the light turned green he became the Matador again, up on his toes, shaking an opened newspaper at the grilles of the oncoming cars, egging them on, turning professional quality veronicas as each car passed, pretending that under the muleta he had a steel sword, an estoque, ready to bury in the gleaming hoods and into the guts of the engines.

Was he crazy? Yes. No. Maybe. Crazy people often invent their lives, but most do it clumsily and without regard for consistency or style or self-interest. The Matador, an artist, invented himself with grace and humor.

Crazy or not, the Matador enjoyed his life. If he satisfied the world's qualifications for crazy, then there's not much hope for the world.

In another city in another time, a certifiably rational man was ordered to give his pet chimpanzee to a private zoo after the animal bit a finger off the man's friend. The man retained visiting rights and brought the wayward chimp a cake every year on its birthday. The chimp had been like the man's child.

Two large chimps, a male and a female, were caged next to the birthday boy. They observed this happy reunion. They didn't like what they saw.

Like us, chimps are jealous, territorial, sensitive to slight, combative. Something like this probably went through their simian minds: *What's this son of a bitch doing, bringing goodies to the unranked newcomer? We're the boss chimps here. Why is this man not giving us respect?*

At this point they were probably only grousing. But then the certifiably rational man made a fatal mistake. He looked the already annoyed male alpha chimp squarely in the eye. The chimp understood this as pure challenge. The thin band of intermittent chimp rationality snapped.

The clever female chimp picked up the detached handle of a toy broom and nudged the linchpin out of its hasp and opened the cage door. Both went after the man, amok with rage. "Where's *our* goddamned cake?" they seemed to say through hand signs and eye movement. "How come birthday boy here gets cake and we don't?"

Howling vengeance, they knocked the man down, plucked out his eye, bit off his fingers, lips, and nose, then opened his pants and tore off his genitals. The man tried to reason with them between screams, but they were having none of it. *This is our turf,* they reasoned back. *You show disrespect on our turf, this is what you get. If you had brought us a cake this wouldn't have happened. Even a goddamned banana would have sufficed.*

Chimps are our closest relatives, differing from us by one percent of the genetic code that makes us who we are. Intelligent and good humored—that's how most people see them—but these renegade chimps decided to blind, disfigure, and de-sex a fellow primate over a *cake*. It's never the object itself, it's the gesture. The insulted chimps went psycho. Our personal demons are eons-old genetic mutations. We keep them in a locked box. When they break out, we go "temporarily insane."

LUTHER HAS A THEORY I can buy into: Thousands of years ago on the European continent and on the steppes of Asia, certain men were bred solely for the art of war. They were strong, intelligent, quick, and fearless. The breeders of these warriors recruited virile young males rich with the impulse to dominate, destroy, bash skulls, and pillage. (The notion of civil behavior had not yet been invented.) These killer studs were matched with strong women with similar character traits. The marriages must have been living hells, but the offspring had to be impressive. A few generations of this kind of selective breeding and you produce people who have enough rage in their marrow to tear down the gates of hell itself and buttfuck the devil. Civil behavior is not their long suit.

Luther contends that remnants of these breeds are still among us but society no longer has use for them. We don't need them running around with clubs bashing in the brains of selected enemies. Some go into the military, if there's a war worth fighting. But the military is a mechanized bureaucracy and such men have no patience for it. They don't like to take orders from anyone they can't respect as equals. So how do they fit in? They don't. A few go into sports like boxing and football but even those forms of combat are too restricted by rules to satisfy them. Most are caged in prisons. Some take the dangerous jobs ordinary men see as suicidal occupations. The ordinary citizen, if he has the necessary paranoid intelligence of modern man, knows them when he sees them. If he has any sense at all, he'll not meet their steady gaze.

One of these specimens was having a beer and a taco at the Hollywood Café when I got there. When he saw me he turned sideways on his stool to face me. He was big, six-four two-fifty, sinews thick as hawsers.

"Man said you'd be in about now," he said.

I didn't care for his grin. He had hard-time tattoos on his thick arms. His head was shaved. His jaw was heavy, had a primitive jut, and his teeth were big glistening squares the color of oxidized tin. The pale blue eyes under the bone of his brow-ridge were too merry to be sane. He looked like he could stare you into the emergency room.

"What man was that?" I said.

"Let me buy you a beer," he said, patting the stool next to him.

"I'm supposed to know who you are?" I said.

"Hell no. But I know who you are, Mr. Morgan, and that's good enough."

I sat down, curious.

"Huddy Darko," he said. "Out of Winslow, Arizona."

He crushed my hand in his and showed more teeth. His grin reached back to his earlobes. He was wearing a muscle shirt. His tattooed biceps hung like stained hams. Sculpted pectorals covered his chest like armor plate. He had large "HBB" tats in gothic letters on each shoulder. I recalled seeing those same gothic letters on a document in Carla Penrose's desk.

"What's the HBB?" I said.

His smile faded a bit. "What?"

"On your shoulder. HBB."

"We're not here to talk about my skin art, Mr. Morgan."

"What are we here to talk about?"

"The Cisco Kid and his lady friend. The beaner needs his head ventilated some."

"What's that got to do with me?"

The waitress came by. I ordered huevos rancheros with a side of menudo.

"Jesus," Huddy Darko said. "How can you eat that menudo shit? You know what they put in it?"

"This is my home town, Huddy. I was weaned on menudo."

He swilled his beer, his long throat working like a sump pump.

"You're the one who beat the stink out of Luther," I said. "You and a friend."

"Which Luther might that be?" he said.

"Thumped him but didn't bust him up, which was thoughtful of you. But then you poured gasoline on his head and would have lit it if Luther hadn't caved."

"Sounds like a world of fun, but it wasn't my gig."

"You're the bounty hunter, right?"

"*Bounty* hunter? Bounty for what? I don't do chickenshit work for nickels and dimes, Mr. Morgan."

My menudo came. It wasn't up to par, which is par for menudo. The café has a sign out front: "Menudo—Good Enough to Eat." Mexican humor at its finest.

"How about me and you spend the afternoon together?" Huddy Darko said. "Maybe you'll tell me more about this Luther, and the big bad bounty hunters."

"Afraid my dance card is full, Huddy."

"Let me put it this way: I insist. You finish up that bowl of tripe, then I want to take in the sights of Juárez. I'm new around here, so you can show me points of interest. I was told you know the place inside out. Maybe we go to the red light district and catch the afternoon donkey show. Maybe put gringo wood to the señoritas. You down with that, Mr. Morgan? What do you say?"

"Sorry, Huddy. You're just going to have to get laid by your lonesome, which is what you're probably used to anyway. No way am I going into Mexico with you. Judiciales take one look at you we both might wind up in Cereso."

His forehead creased. "I don't speak beaner, Mr. Morgan, so I don't know what you're talking about. But here's the thing— you don't actually get to choose. We're taking you across the river, bud." He pulled up his shirt enough to uncover the black grips of a stainless steel automatic. The "we" bothered me. I looked around the café. Another shaved-head was staring at me from a dark booth. He was eating a cheeseburger with the slow rotating jaws of a meditative ape eating sweet plantain. He looked mean enough, but unlike Huddy he didn't fill out his muscle shirt and his hard-guy look seemed cultivated. I imagined him practicing in front of a full-length mirror. He was practicing now.

"Cornbelt Nazis?" I said. "White Brotherhood? Holocaust Deniers? Church of the Aryan ass-kicking Jesus? You boys parolees just out of Huntsville?"

"We're not cons or cranks," Huddy said. "We're commandos."

He was dead serious. I knew better than to laugh. There was a zero tolerance gleam in his wired eyes.

"That's a new one," I said.

"Get used to it. We're out to save this raggedy ass country whether it wants to be saved or not. We're heroes, Mr. Morgan. You're going to throw confetti on our parade someday."

CHAPTER SEVENTEEN

Huddy Darko drove a Hummer. It was painted in army camouflage patterns, olive and black, knobby tires for off road work. I sat up front. Huddy's partner, Spode Weems, sat in the back seat, directly behind me. Spode was a Huddy-in-Progress, except for his eyes. They looked pit-bull crazy when they stopped moving long enough for you to fix on them. Right now, he was pressing the snub end of a big bore revolver into the back of my neck.

"Be careful with that thing, Spode," I said.

He jabbed my neck with the barrel hard enough to give me a starburst headache. "You don't tell me diddly squat, Mr. Morgan," he said. "I'm careful as I need to be."

"Be nice, Spode," Huddy said. "Mr. Morgan is here to help us find their crib."

The traffic was light going in. The Mexican border guards gave Huddy and his friend a long curious look, then waved us on. I assumed Spode Weems had kept his pistol out of sight when we crossed over. Taking firearms into Mexico is a big no-no.

"We want to find Avenida Duranzo," Huddy said. His accent was deliberately bad, forcing the Spanish words into English cadences. "We'll do some business there on the ah-vun-ee-duh. If it goes down all right we'll take you home. No harm, no foul. We're not career criminals, Mr. Morgan."

"You snatched me because you needed a tour guide?"

"Don't feel bad, J. P.—you don't mind if I call you J. P.?—we'll need your local expertise to get us where we're going. Not a big deal, it just makes the job a little easier for us."

"Keep going straight," I said. "Turn right on Diez y Seis de Septiembre."

It was hot and bright. Sunlight in Juárez is not the same as the sunlight in El Paso, even though the two cities are only separated by fifty yards of beige water. The Juárez sun is cruel—brutally hot in the summer, stingy with its heat in the winter. In winter the air is choked with the things people burn to keep warm. The summer air has a septic aroma rising from a sewage system that was overtaxed fifty years ago. In all seasons the brick factories burn old tires in their kilns, fogging the air with black smoke.

"Sure is one butt ugly town," Huddy said. "But ain't they all? The beaners got a lock on butt ugly when it comes to these border towns."

"Who put you onto me?" I said.

Spode Weems's gun jabbed the base of my skull again. I could feel the barrel moving erratically in my stiff neck hair. Spode was getting too big an adrenaline rush for this to be a casual visit. I hoped his finger was on the trigger guard, not the trigger.

"No harm in me telling you," Huddy said. "I mean I personally got nothing to hide. The more open things are the better I feel. It was a slick-as-snot PI dude, Hamilton Scales. I think you know him. The oily bastard said you knew both sides of the border like shit knows stink."

The streets were crowded. Many El Pasoans come across to buy their weekend supply of tequila or their month's supply of generic medications. One of the perks of living cheek to jowl with Ciudad Juárez is that a number of pharmacological products are available without prescription. Manufactured in the USA but sold at Mexican prices. Medical work is cheap, too. Until her recent slippage into dementia, my mother had all her dental work done here for a fraction of what it would have cost in the states.

We were getting some critical stares from the transitos, the traffic cops who work the streets. An underpaid, under-respected bunch looking to put the bite on the green turista. One of them flagged us down. The Hummer must have looked like a military reconnaissance vehicle to him. Huddy, not knowing the local customs, pulled over to the curb and stopped. A transito blows his whistle and flags you down, you pretend you don't see him. You turn the radio up and hit the throttle. Huddy didn't know that. He pulled over to the curb and set the handbrake. He rolled down his window, the veins in his neck swelling.

"Pasaporte, señor?" the transito said.

"Passport?" Huddy said. "I don't have to show you any stinking passport, muchacho. We just come over to see the donkey do the girl, get the five dollar blowjob, and stock up on tequila. We're here to boost the Mexican economy. We're goodwill ambassadors, Captain."

Huddy smiled broadly at his own wit.

The transito didn't seem to appreciate the wealth of humor in Huddy's performance. He leaned into the truck. He took a long evaluating look at each of us, trying to figure out what he was dealing with and what it might be worth to him. "Are you soldados, señor?" he said. "Are you soldiers from Fort Bliss?"

"No sir we are not *soldiers*," Huddy said, mimicking the transito's lilting English. "We are civilians, *looking* for bliss."

The transito didn't get it, or if he did, he didn't smile.

This had the makings of a minor international incident. Something had to be done before Huddy's stand-up act landed us in jail. I reached past him and gave the transito a ten. He studied the ten. He'd taken some shit. Ten wasn't going to do it. I gave him another ten.

"Gracias, señor," he said to me. He touched the bill of his cap, gave Huddy a long warning look, then moved off.

"If you're going to let them flag you down Huddy, you'd better show some respect," I said. "You can't treat these traffic cops like dirt."

"I treat dirt like dirt," Huddy said. "But thanks for the tip. Why'd you fork over the bribe, anyway? You didn't have to."

"You ever spend a night in the Juárez jailhouse?" I said. "You were about to talk your way into it."

I directed him past the customs house at the Avenida Juárez intersection, then west until we hit some badly paved streets— Corredor, Aranda, Zapata. The houses here were small, some with stucco siding, some sided with scrap wood taken from packing crates. The address he gave me on Duranzo was nailed to a post in the tiny fenced courtyard of a house so small it could pass for a children's playhouse in El Paso. The tarpaper roof was patched with flattened coffee cans and the walls had chunks of stucco missing as if the house had been sprayed with machine gun fire. It was a fairly decent house by West Juárez standards.

Huddy parked the Hummer, set the brake. We all got out. Huddy and Spode tucked their guns under their belts.

"I can smell lard in the skillet," Huddy said. "The beaner and the woman are in there."

"The beaner packing?" Spode said.

"He killed one man we know of, Spode, so we got to assume he is."

"I want to put him down real bad, Huddy," Spode said.

"We'll do just that,' Huddy said. "J. P., since you know the lingo, I'll let you do the talking. Once we get in, you need to step out of the way."

"Who will I be talking to?"

"Don't game us," Huddy said. "It isn't the smart thing for you to do just now."

Both Huddy and Spode had their guns out now, gesturing me toward the front door of the small house. Spode looked like his head was about to spontaneously combust with excitement.

Huddy hit the door with his fist. "Knock knock, sweethearts," he said. "The big bad wolf is here."

CHAPTER EIGHTEEN

No one was in the house. The door was locked but flimsy. Huddy kicked it open and led the way in, gun raised. It was a shotgun house—front room, kitchen, bedroom, all in a line, walls peeling, and a bathroom the size of a broom closet off the bedroom. Cement floor painted orange. A cobalt blue table in the kitchen was set with two plates. There were some scraps of food left on the plates—refried beans, rice, and bits of tortilla. The kitchen stove was an ovenless, two-burner electric circa 1950. A cast-iron skillet crusty with beans sat on the stove. On the counter a tiny TV was wedged between a breadbox and a sack of cornmeal. The TV's rabbit ears were wrapped in aluminum foil to aid reception.

The only furniture in the bedroom was a small bed and a dresser that was painted the same blue as the kitchen table. There was a framed photo of a young Mexican couple in wedding regalia taken on the steps of the four-hundred-year-old Juárez cathedral. A colorful ceramic Madonna stood next to the photo. The Madonna had twin multicolored fish swimming out of her belly, a jungle bird flying out of her forehead, a green snake coiled around her feet. The snake had the ears of a lynx and the large predatory eyes of a barn owl. Indian art is dense with symbols a gringo won't get unless his brain is functioning on a banned psychotropic substance—in which case his take on it might scare him sober. It was impressive in the bewildering, unpredictable way primitive religious art always is.

"Look at that shit," Spode said. "It's sacrilegious." He smashed the Madonna with the butt of his gun.

"Bad luck, Spode," I said.

"A white man makes his own luck, asshole," he said.

Huddy approached the bed, nudged it with his knee. A painting of Christ on black velvet—his familiar thorn-wrapped heart exposed—hung over the headboard.

Spode yanked the blanket off. The sheet under the blanket was stained. "I believe these be pecker tracks," he said. He pointed at the stains. "See there? The Cisco Kid's been banging Juanita seasick. Hot damn, that's where she dropped her oyster, and fairly recent at that."

"We appear to be about one hour behind Bonnie and Clyde, Huddy said. "Where do you suppose they're headed? South? Back north?"

"Those tracks could belong to anybody," I said. I pointed to the wedding photo. "Could belong to the happy couple."

Huddy ignored me. "Where would a pair like that go next?" he said. "I mean from a shithole like this? Another shithole? I guess a pair of desperados like them could go from shithole to shithole until they found the main sewage lagoon."

I shrugged, but he didn't expect an answer. We went back into the kitchen. There were some bullfight posters on the walls. "Maybe they went to the Plaza de Toros, Huddy," I said.

"What?"

"The bullfights."

"That's what you *think*?" he said.

"No, I'm making it up to confuse you."

I almost slipped the punch. I saw it coming but he had quick hands for a big man. It caught the back of my jaw, just under the ear. It surprised me because he still seemed friendly and mildly amused by the situation. I went down to one knee, got up, grabbed the still warm cast iron skillet off the stove and flung it. It missed Huddy but glanced off Spode's forehead just as he was coming at me with his gun raised. Spode sat down, his jumpy eyes momentarily at peace. Huddy stepped in front of Spode and tagged me again. He had an overhand right George Foreman could claim. I couldn't move out of its way. The punch had the weight of a railroad tie. I blacked out for a second, then found myself looking at the ceiling from the perspective of the kitchen floor.

"I guess it's not your fault they're not here, J. P.," Huddy said. "I'm beginning to wonder if the particular folks in question were here at all. It has the feel of a set-up, and that pisses me off. I don't like playing village idiot to the slickers, J. P. I had to take it out on someone and your name came up."

Spode was sitting at the table touching the lump on his forehead tenderly. "Maybe they'll come back, Huddy," he said.

"Nope. They booked out in a hurry. Didn't even finish their lunch. Someone gave them a heads-up, told them we were coming."

"Or they were late for good seats on the shady side of the Plaza de Toros," I said.

"This is all a big joke to you, J. P.?" Huddy said, instantly irate. His tendency to go from relative calm to full-bore rage was something to behold. "I'd appreciate you not taking this thing lightly, J. P. One of our people, a fine young man—a friend of mine, in fact—is dead because of the beaner who isn't here."

"Mrs. Penrose likes bullfights," I said. "You'd expect a bleeding-heart political lefty to hate the slaughter, but she's a real aficionado."

"People running for their lives don't go to the bullfights," Huddy said.

"The Plaza is a good place to hide," I said. "Ten, twenty-thousand show up for the corrida."

Huddy thought this over. "I hate bullfights," he said. "I rode bulls up in Winslow when I was a kid. I like bulls. They're noble creatures. You think I'm going to sit there and yell olé while a pepper-snapper in tights tortures a noble animal to death? Never happen, J. P."

He kicked the painted table, knocking it over. The dishes shattered on the floor. "Let's get out of here," he said. "Everything is pissing me off just now, and the smell of sex and food makes me so god damned lonely I want to tear things apart."

Just then, and unfortunately for them, the couple who lived in this house came home. The man—a boy really—said, "Qué es esto?" The girl, even younger, a bag of groceries in her arms, screamed, "Ladrónes! Son Ladrónes!"

They were small kids, in their teens or early twenties, wide-eyed at the unexpected presence of three large gringo thieves in their house. The boy, thin as a stick and wearing the khaki uniform of a five-dollar-a-day maquila worker, said, "Vete a la chingada!"

Spode looked at Huddy. "I don't think I care for his tone of voice," he said. "What'd he say, Morgan?"

"He said he wants us to get the fuck out of his house," I said. "Perfectly reasonable request."

"The righteous beaner thinks we're trespassing, is that it?" Spode said. "His little tarpaper shithole is sacred ground? Is that the general idea?"

"He isn't our beaner, Spode," Huddy said, holding a photograph next to the boy's face. "Our beaner's got a bigger nose and more gristle on his bones. This is a goddamned snipe hunt. We been gamed big time."

"Vete biches!" the boy said.

"I think this little stud just called me a bitch," Spode said. "He thinks we're fairies!"

"Fuck to the mouth of your whore mother, gabacho!" the boy said, moving close to Spode, fists up. His tiny fearlessness was almost comical next to Spode. Banty rooster taking on a big dog. To his wife he said, "Llame a la policía, Lourdes."

"The little wetback speaks een-glace, Huddy," Spode said.

"He's a Mexican citizen, Spode," Huddy said. "He's not a wetback until he crosses the river."

"Pre-wetback, then," Spode said. "Spawned right here in Armpit City."

"Your mother sucks the donkey," the boy said.

"He keeps saying dirty things about my mother," Spode said.

Spode hit the side of the boy's head with his gun butt. The boy crumpled to the floor. The girl screamed obscenities at Spode. Spode grabbed her and tore her thin dress open from neck to waist. He took a step back, admiring discovered country. The girl's small brown breasts were poor as Mexico but Spode looked as if he'd found El Dorado. The girl covered herself with her thin arms.

"Didn't you change my sheets in Denver?" Spode said to her.

She looked bewildered. "No comprendo, señor," she said.

Her thin body began to shake.

"Vacuumed my room in Tucson? Changed the towels? You were the girl, weren't you *Lourdes*? You polished my knob in Nogales, right? That was you, *Lourdes*, wasn't it? Or maybe it was your sister. You got a lot of sisters, don't you? Like fifty zillion?"

"Lo siento," she said, shaking violently now. "Lo siento, señor."

"Leave her be, Spode," Huddy said.

"I'm having some of this, Huddy," Spode said. "I'll even *pay* the scrawny bitch. They all got eyes for the dollar down here, don't they? I mean, everything's for sale, right?" He took a five-dollar bill out of his wallet. "She's probably not worth five, but I feel generous." He put the five on the kitchen table. "Wait for me in the truck, Huddy. I'll be quick."

"Forget it, Spode," Huddy said.

Spode chuckled. "Forget it the man says."

"I'm serious, Spode."

The terrified girl backed away from Spode. "What, you want *more?*" he said. "Five won't get it done? That's a day's pay for your feisty little Pancho, right? Hell, we can work it out, girl. You take personal checks? Maybe you take Visa?"

"That's enough, Spode," Huddy said. "Let's go. We got business elsewhere."

"This is a job benefit, Huddy. A perk."

"Not today it isn't," Huddy said.

I stepped behind Spode and rabbit-punched him as he un-buckled his belt. I put everything I had into the punch. Spode went down to his knees then touched the orange floor with his forehead as if paying homage to Allah. Then his knees gave out and he belly-flopped into the cement. My fist hurt all the way to the back of my neck.

Huddy spun me around. The uppercut to my ribs lifted me off my feet. It felt like a heart attack. Then it felt like nothing.

I woke up in the Hummer. So did Spode. Spode had his gun jammed into the short hairs of my neck again. The barrel was quivering. "I need to *waste* this motherfucker, Huddy," he said, his voice pitched high. "I got a headache that'd make God beg for Tylenol."

"There's some aspirins in the glove compartment," Huddy said. "We'll drop J. P. off someplace."

"They kill people every day here and nobody gives a fly-ing fuck. This sumbitch hit me *twice,* Huddy. My ears are still ringing. You can't let him get away with it. I need to put one in his ear."

"I know you would, Spode. You need to put one in almost anyone's ear. But not this trip. All right, son? We've got other things to attend to."

Spode jammed the barrel of the gun into my ear breaking the skin. "Bang bang, bitch," he said. A thread of blood worked its way out of my ear and down my earlobe.

"You'll have to excuse him, J. P.," Huddy said. "He's overly fond of firearms I'm afraid, and a tad too eager to use them."

Huddy remembered the way back without me having to tell him where to turn, but he didn't know about the bridges.

"You've got to take the Avenida Juárez bridge to get back into El Paso," I said. "Traffic's one-way there, just like it was one-way coming in on the Stanton Bridge. Go past the cathedral on Diez y Seis de Septiembre, then make a left on Avenida Juárez." This time of day traffic there would be the absolute worst.

The afternoon sky was yellow with heat. A strong wind kicked up dust devils in the narrow streets. Tarahumara Indians, women and children in tribal dress, stood begging in groups of three or four on the corners. The drug merchants, backed by local police, had exiled them from their own desperate little farms in the high plains south of Juárez and they came to the city hoping to find a means of survival. The traffickers wanted to grow their product on Tarahumara land, but the Indians, who grew corn and little else, didn't want to. They stood in the way of progress and had to be removed. The drug merchants have the power of eminent domain.

When a traffic jam stopped us short of the bridge, an Indian woman carrying a baby left her spot on the rincón and came to the driver's-side window of the Hummer to beg for money or food.

"I could put a round between her tits and no one would know the difference," Spode said. "And don't try to tell me she wouldn't be better off. Just look at those raggedy ass Indians, Huddy. They are the human version of the common cockroach."

"Spode, you're quite the humanitarian," Huddy said. "I'm going to write to the Secretary General of the United Nations and argue for your Human Rights medal."

"Fuck," Spode said. "We kicked their mongrel asses once from Texas to Mexico City but didn't *finish* the job. That sound familiar to you, Morgan? Remember Korea? The Bay of Pigs? Nam? Remember General Patton being ordered to stop his tanks short of Berlin? How about the first Iraq war? I heard you were there. Soon as we get our dicks up and locked we lose our woodies. It's our national shame. Land of the free and the home of the premature ejaculators. We killed Mexicans by the thousands back then and no one gave a day-old shit, except for a few New England eggheads. But once again we stopped short of taking it all."

"Spode's been to college," Huddy said. "They kicked him out of Arizona State for arguing with his history professors."

"Fucking limpdick pinko clit-lickers," Spode said. "They didn't have a set of stones between them. Zach Taylor would have chained them together and dropped them into the Rio Grande."

"He's referring to the Mexican-American war of 1846, J. P.," Huddy said. "Spode here is a history buff. Whatever you do, don't get him started on the Civil War."

Spode ignored Huddy. "Robert E. Lee was brilliant in the Mexican war. We took half their country," he said. "We could have had it *all,* right down to the Guatemala border, but we signed the damn Hidalgo treaty and only got Arizona, New Mexico, California, Utah, Colorado and Nevada."

"Only?" I said.

Spode jabbed my ear again with his gun. "You think it's a joke? Fourteen thousand American boys died in Mexico. In per capita terms, that'd be over a hundred thousand today. That's a quarter of World War Two numbers. Now the mongrels are coming back in droves to reclaim the territory they lost fair and square. You think the Mexican government doesn't know what's happening? For Chrissakes, that's their *plan*. They aim to take back the western USA by flooding us with wetbacks. California is already more Mexican than white. LA's got its first Mexican mayor in a hundred and thirty years. See how it's coming down? If most of the population is Mexican, then hey, it must *be* Mexico!"

My ear was sore and his diatribe made it ring. "Drop me off here," I said. "I'll walk back. Probably beat you across the bridge, the way traffic is piling up."

"No air conditioner out there, J. P., but suit yourself," Huddy said. "Maybe we'll look you up again if we need a back-street guide to Shit City."

Spode took the gun out of my ear. I got out.

I moved through a crowd of tourists and street vendors toward a man I recognized. I didn't know him personally, but judging from the natty suit he was wearing, his Italian sunglasses, and the way he was scanning the crowd while talking into a radio, I knew he was a plainclothes cop, a judiciale.

"Con permiso, señor," I said.

He looked at me, noted my bloody ear, his face showing a flicker of annoyed interest.

"Esos gringos, en el Hummer?" I said.

The Hummer was moving an inch a minute toward the Santa Fe Bridge. Huddy had his head out the window trying to see what was causing the jam-up.

"Sí?" the judiciale said.

"Tienan pistolas." They're packing guns.

"De veras?"

"Sí, dos pistolas."

"Son sus compadres?" Are they your buddies?

"No, no, señor," I said, raising my hands to show my innocence. "Nomás les vi en un barro." I only saw them in a bar. I lifted my shirt to show him where Huddy and Spode had stuffed their guns. I made my hand into a pistol.

"Qué barro?" he said.

"El Club Chi-Chi."

He looked at me, wondering if I was some kind of nut, then looked at the Hummer, thinking no doubt that it would look mighty fine in his driveway. He lost interest in me. He spoke quietly into his radio and in less than a minute half a dozen men with M-16s materialized out of the crowd and surrounded the Hummer. Huddy and Spode were asked to step out and put their hands on the roof of the truck. They were patted down, their pistols removed. Spode looked over his shoulder at me. I gave him a quick nod and casual salute. After all, he was a *commando*. He shot me the finger just before the judiciales cuffed him.

Mexico, a land of serial revolutions, doesn't allow guns in the hands of civilians. Mexicans are especially sensitive to

Americans coming into their country carrying firearms. This sensitivity goes back more than a century. Spode, the history buff, should have known this. Now they were both going to discover the many charms of the Mexican penal system.

CHAPTER NINETEEN

My answering machine was packed:

"Got to see you ASAP," said Pilar Mellado. "It's crisis time in River City."

"Where the hell are you?" said Luther Penrose. "You won't fucking *believe* what I have to put up with."

"Our interest rates are at an all-time low," said a voice that called itself 'Jimmy Vasquez' of Cibola Savings and Loan.

"Truth is beauty, beauty is truth," said my mother. "That's what we told the kids in high school. Now that makes a lot of sense, doesn't it? Do you understand gravity waves, J. P.?"

"I enjoyed our afternoon together, J. P., but we can do better, don't you think?" said Dani Thrailkill. "I'm off to Phoenix today. Come see me. I'll work your prostate properly, with a spicey gel." She gave me an address in Tempe. I didn't write it down. There were six more messages from people I didn't know offering me things I didn't want.

I studied my face in the bathroom mirror. "You're beautiful," I said. I had a loose tooth and my tongue was cut. My headache started in my brainstem and pulsed its way up to my frontal lobes. I took four Darvocets, washed the blood out of my ear, unplugged the phone, made myself a large Bloody Maria. After that I went to bed with an icepack on my swollen jaw.

Twenty hours of dreamless sleep later, I woke up.

I called Velma. No answer. I called Pilar Mellado. "What have you done with Velma?" I said to her answering machine.

I called Luther. "I might have been wrong," I said.

"You say that with a sense of dismay, as if that's a novelty for you," he said. He was on his high horse. But then he almost always was.

"I've been thinking it over," I said. "Two people on the run can become intimate," I said. "Two against the world, that old romantic theme. You've seen it in a hundred old movies. Think of *The Getaway*. Of course it always ends in one or the other getting left behind or killed."

"Jesus. Life according to Roger Ebert. Thanks so much. Do you have any of my money left? I've decided I want it back after all. I'd also like an itemized account for the rest of it. Keep 10 percent above that for your trouble."

"Aren't we a bit snippy today," I said.

The Valkyries were fussing in the background.

"On the other hand," I said, "there's no evidence of anything romantic going on between Carla and Hector. Not even circumstantial evidence."

I told him about Huddy and Spode and the house in Juárez. I told him that his detective, Ham Scales, gave the bogus address to Huddy Darko, and then suggested Huddy take me along as navigator. "I don't know what Scales is up to, but something's not kosher."

"This Darko and Weems sound like the goons who beat me up," he said.

"They said they weren't."

"And you believed them?"

"They're the kind who take pride in thumping people. They're not shy about admitting it. If they did it, they'd want the credit. Your guys were bounty hunters. My guys were commandos."

"I'm not going to ask you to make sense of that."

"I'm not sure I could, Luther."

"Come over. I've got something else to tell you. I don't like discussing these things on the phone."

Thor or Wotan or whoever set off a trainload of dynamite in the canyons of Valhalla.

"Okay," I said. "Give me a couple hours. I've got a Darvocet hangover."

I hung up. I took a long shower. Ate something I didn't have to chew—a can of slimy overcooked noodles in an over-salted broth, spiked with a splash of Tabasco. Had another Bloody Maria. Called Pilar Mellado again. She picked up.

"What's with Velma?" I said.

"J. P.? Where the hell have you been? I've been trying to get a hold of you for days."

"Something wrong? Is she all right?"

"She's in the hospital. It might be a stroke. She seems okay physically, but her cognitive function is not working very well."

"What hospital?"

"Columbia Medical Center, eighth floor."

"I'll meet you there."

"No you won't. I'm tied up. I've got six other cases to deal with today. But I want to talk to you. You're going to have to do the right thing, and fast."

CHAPTER TWENTY

Monsoon season: wet air from the Mexican Pacific Coast and stationary low pressure cells, along with triple digit temperatures, keep us sweltering from July to September. The Sonoran and Chihuahuan deserts are generally hot and dry, but the monsoon jacks the humidity up to 50, 60 percent and higher. If you have a swamp cooler and not refrigerated air, you discover sweat glands you never knew you had.

I took a long, cool shower, dressed, then drove to the hospital. A thunderstorm was brewing in the malpais country to the west. Streaks of lightning split the blue-black horizon. My shirt was already sticking to my back like Saran wrap.

I found a spot in the parking garage, then walked over the enclosed bridge that led to the main hospital building. I took an elevator to the eighth floor. I asked a hulking male nurse where Velma Morgan was. He took me to a reception desk and checked a clipboard. "Room 834," he said.

She was sitting on the edge of her bed, staring out the window. It struck me how frail she looked. She couldn't have weighed more than ninety pounds, maybe less. She seemed to be evaporating.

"Hi, Mom," I said.

She didn't respond right away. Her attention was fixed on the coming storm. "Hi, honey," she said.

"How you doing?"

"They said it was possibly a stroke. I don't think so. My thinking is crystal clear."

Still watching the storm, she raised her right hand and wiggled her fingers. She did the same with the left. I forced her to look at me by sitting on the wide sill of the window.

"Can you walk?" I said.

"Of course I can walk. I can talk, too. This is me, talking. Can you hear me? Is there anything else about me you think is not working properly? Do you want to hear me sing?" She warbled a few notes of "Sentimental Journey." "There," she said. "Are you convinced?"

"Pilar Mellado wants you to move into the El Descanso nursing home. I think it's a good idea."

"I love lightning," she said, trying to look past me. "It frightened me as a child. That's because I thought it was a random thing, taking lives that didn't deserve to be taken. Poof! Celestial incineration! Heaven bound in a flash! But that's a child's way of thinking. I know now there's nothing random about anything, especially lightning. Lightning is as precise as needlework."

I saw then that her right eyelid was half closed. She caught me looking at it.

"I'm not blind, either," she said. "Not in both eyes at the same time, I can vouch for that."

"Then why are you here?" I said.

"'Do I sit deformed, a naked egg? Did I catch the moon?'"

"*What?*"

"Poetry. The old good stuff, when poets had hearts *and* brains. Stevens, I think. I can't remember it all. Do I have to go to the nursing home because I can't remember it all? Do you remember your father, how she carried him?"

"How *who* carried him?"

"It's a mystery within a mystery within a mystery."

"What is?"

"Don't make me tired, honey."

"I'll talk to Pilar. Maybe we can work something out."

"Work, work, work. I've done enough of that. I've worked all my life. Time to sing, time to fly. 'Crinkled paper makes a brittle sigh.'"

She stood up, lost her balance, sat down again. Her drooped eyelid fluttered. She suddenly looked like a frightened child. I could see the bones in her hand through the papery, liver-spotted skin. She was disappearing piecemeal. I hated to see that. Better to be carried away by random—or needlework—lightning.

A candy striper came in with a lunch tray. "Swiss steak and broccoli and apple sauce!" the candy striper said, enthusiastic with teenage optimism. "And looky here! Boston Cream Pie for dessert! Yummers!"

Velma turned away from the tray, as if insulted. The candy striper fought to hold her smile in place. I told Velma I'd come back tomorrow, kissed her parchment cheek, and left.

I sat in my car with the air conditioning turned up. I called Pilar Mellado on my cell. "She's acting a little goofy," I said.

"Tell me about it," Pilar said. She sounded weary. She always sounded weary.

"Goofy, Pilar, not crazy. No reason she can't go back to her house."

"She didn't tell you?"

"Tell me what?"

"The Virgin of Guadalupe walked into her bedroom last night, just before the stroke. The Virgin was carrying your father's body."

"She didn't mention the Virgin. Looks like she's being cagey. Doesn't that more or less prove she's functional?"

"Less, I'd say. Much less. Here's what you do, J. P., you start making arrangements. Reserve a room at El Descanso, then talk to a real estate agent about putting her house up for sale. The market is up right now. You should get a bundle for it. I'll start the paperwork but you'll need to get a durable power of attorney to make it happen. This needs to get done, J. P. For your sake as well as hers."

I agreed, but knew I would put it off for a few more days. I loved the old girl and wanted no part of betraying her to the benevolent bureaucrats until all options were exhausted.

I drove to Luther's house. There was a black Ford parked in the turnaround behind Luther's vintage machines. It had state government license plates and a short antenna on the rear deck. Luther met me at the door.

"There's a cop here," he whispered. He was barefoot, wearing a loosely belted bathrobe. A tic flickered in the right side of his face. It lifted his lips in an involuntary snarl. He was slick with sweat, pale with fear.

"What's he want, Luther?"

"He wants Hector Martinez. The bastard thinks I know where he is. I told him about you and Ham Scales, how you've been looking for Martinez and Carla. He wanted my computer! I told him I'd never allow the reduction of my intricately crafted prose to a mess of binary symbols. Can you imagine Shakespeare in bits and bytes? He didn't get it. He refused to believe I didn't own a computer. Everyone's got a computer, he said. I showed him my 1926 Underwood. He didn't know what to make of it. He searched behind it, looking for secret wires. He'd already been to the university to confiscate Carla's office computer."

We went inside. I identified myself to a thickset man in a gray business suit. He was wearing snakeskin boots and a white, broad-brimmed Stetson, a replica of the famous "Boss of the Plains" Stetson made in the 19th century. He showed me his ID. Robert T. Eggers, Texas Ranger. The picture on his ID card made his round, cheeky face look parboiled, the small dark eyes hard as drill bits.

"I understand you've been tracking Mrs. Penrose and Hector Martinez," he said.

"I was. I'm not now."

"You located them in Las Vegas?"

"I did."

"And you didn't call the police?" His small eyes fixed on me, the relentless machinery behind them visible.

"Why should I have? They didn't break any laws, as far as I knew."

"Martinez is wanted for murder, Mr. Morgan. I would have thought a professional investigator such as yourself might have, uh, *investigated* the man before spending your client's money."

I looked at Luther. He was nodding vigorously, sucking up shamelessly to the Ranger. "The client," I said, "was only interested in determining if his wife and Martinez were having an affair. I was convinced they weren't and told him so. That was the job I was hired for."

"Well, it's too bad you weren't a tad more thorough," the Ranger said. "Could have saved the state of Texas a whole lot of money and effort. Besides, there's a twenty-five thousand dollar reward for information leading to the apprehension of Martinez. You lost out on a nice little payday, Mr. Morgan. Do you have any idea where they might be now?" I decided not to mention Huddy Darko and Spode Weems, or the little house in south Juárez. "Nope," I said. "Last I saw of them was in a trailer house, between Vegas and Boulder City."

"And do you know what they were doing in that trailer house, Mr. Morgan?"

"None of my business," I said. "I'm sure it was something to do with border issues. Mrs. Penrose is an activist."

The Ranger looked at Luther. "You actually *paid* this man to find your missing wife?"

"I'm asking for my money back," Luther said, swelling now with righteous indignation, the tic in his face flaring wildly.

"Mr. Morgan," the Ranger said. "It might interest you to know that the trailer house is an unlicensed cosmetic surgery clinic. Hector Martinez was there to change his appearance. The woman—Mrs. Penrose—brought him there expressly for that purpose. She paid for the work done on Martinez in cash, something upwards of seven thousand dollars. I'm afraid she's going to be charged with aiding and abetting, and perhaps complicity, once we find them."

"Is he going to be charged, too?" Luther said, pointing to me.

A grin split the Ranger's wide, meaty face. He took off his hat and mopped his brow with a bandana-size handkerchief. His thin hair was soaked in sweat. "Can't arrest a man for playing with a short deck, Mr. Penrose," he said. "If I had my way, I'd charge him with laziness, bad judgement, and a lack of professional standards. You might want to take him to civil court."

The Ranger adjusted his hat, said he might be back with more questions. He got into his black Ford, talked on his radio for a minute, then drove off.

"You going to take me to court, Luther?" I said.

"Don't be an idiot," he said.

"I wonder why Ham Scales passed up the reward money," I said, mostly to myself. "Maybe he didn't do his homework either."

"He must have had his reasons. Twenty-five thousand isn't a lot of money these days, J. P. Maybe Ham was onto something really big."

"Like what? What's Martinez worth to anyone?"

"Make yourself a drink, J. P. You look like you need one."

CHAPTER TWENTY-ONE

"You said you had something else to tell me," I said. Luther was on his hands and knees, extracting his makings from under his recliner. "I shoved my stash way the hell under the chair when that cop pulled up in my driveway. Jesus, I was so scared I almost peed my pants."

"You should cut back on the hemp, Luther. It'll give you emphysema just as fast as cigarettes. Probably faster."

He got into his recliner, rolled a skinny joint. "Don't presume to lecture me, J. P.," he said. "You fucked up royally, according to Robert T. Eggers, Texas Ranger."

I took out my wallet. "Here's the rest of your money, less 10 percent," I said, tossing the wad of bills on his lap. "But I'm not going to pay back my expenses. I did the job you asked me to do."

He waved me off. He didn't care about the money. Like most people who don't need money, day to day accounting bored him. "I heard from Carla," he said. He took a long hit, stared at the ceiling as he held the smoke in his lungs. "She's in Tucson."

"Why didn't you tell this to the cop?" I said.

"Isn't it obvious? I don't want her arrested. I don't want her put in jail for being stupid."

"She's anything but stupid, Luther."

"You're wrong. She's stupid in the way most sentimental idealists are stupid. They make major mistakes because they have contempt for the real world and how the real world works. It's like the ACLU defending the Skokie Nazis' right to assemble. The ideal is their only reality, no blurring the lines allowed. They tilt at windmills. If it comes down to a choice between flesh and blood people and the *cause,* then mere flesh and blood goes in the dumpster. I offer myself as an example of the latter. Cervantes wrote the book on these people five hundred years ago, J. P. You may have heard of it. It's called *Don Quixote.*"

"So you've dropped the notion she's in bed with Martinez."

He took another hit. "She was upset. Something went wrong, but she said she couldn't talk about it. If she's fucking Martinez I'm not going to let it make me crazy. Her safety is all that matters now. I love her, J. P., but if I've lost her I'm not going to make her suffer for it. I still want to protect her."

"Damn decent of you, Luther. But why don't I believe you? What brought about this miraculous change in attitude?"

"I don't care what you believe. You've never recognized my generous side. You don't really know me, J. P. I'm a larger man than you think." He pinched off the lit end of his joint and put the roach into his robe pocket.

"Did she say what she's doing in Tucson? Did she give you an address?" I said.

"No. She said not to worry. Things were getting worked out. I have no idea what those things are. I believe she's in danger, but what can I do about it?"

"Stay stoned?"

"I'd like you to leave now, J. P. Your insults are tiring. I still count you as my friend, but I'm afraid you have a two-dimensional soul, flat and basically uninteresting. You lack the virtue of empathy."

A short stocky woman came into the room. She was wearing one of Luther's pajama tops and nothing else. The pajama top reached her knees. "Come back to bed now, Luther honey," she said. "I'm freaking. This big creepy house of yours gives me the *willies*. I think there's a bat or giant moth in the bathroom. I was on the pot and the thing flew into my hair. Didn't you hear me scream? I damn near knocked myself silly slapping at my head. Why do you leave the damn windows open, anyway? Can't you hear the thunder? It's going to rain any minute."

She wore her makeup in layers and was not as young as I first thought. Her hair was red and seemed to light up the room. She had big glossy hair, 1960s Dallas style, but it was in a state of collapse and hanks of it hung to her waist. Her pajama top was unbuttoned halfway down. Her breasts, like pale gibbous moons, loomed in the opening. "When for God's sakes are you going to be through *talking* to all these damn people?" she said.

"Lelanie Loftsgarten," Luther said. "We met in Barnes and Noble yesterday. Lelanie is an author, too. A poet slash playwright. Lelanie, this is my two-dimensional friend, J. P. Morgan. He lacks the virtue of empathy slash compassion."

"I've *heard* of you," the poet slash playwright said. "You're a banker or something, right? Bankers lack empathy, right? But it's not their fault because that's the way they have to be, or God knows what would happen to the monetary system."

"Thanks for understanding," I said.

"I call her my little Valkyrie," Luther said.

Luther saw me to the door. "You're a goddamned moron," I said.

"Lower your voice," he whispered. "I'm an artist, J. P. I *attract* women. It's compensation for the burden we artists bear. It's also our small reward for the solitary, heroic lifestyle. The concept strains your bourgeois powers of comprehension, I understand that."

"You're a horse's ass," I said.

"The artist has needs the ordinary man, such as yourself, will never fathom."

"You think Carla will write this one off?"

"She doesn't have to know, does she?"

"Goodbye, Luther."

CHAPTER TWENTY-TWO

The thunderstorm blew in on fifty-mile-an-hour gusts and the rain came down with the intensity of a tropical cloudburst. I had to lean into the wind to get to my car. It was definitely Valkyrie weather. Wotan or Thor was mumbling to himself in the black clouds.

A few doors down from Luther's, a sprinkler system was soaking a lawn the size of two tennis courts. Water ran over the sidewalk and down the street. It was an automatic sprinkling system and the robot brain that worked the on-off valves was unaware of the deluge from above.

The plumbing under the sprinklers drew pristine water from the Hueco bolson and recklessly flushed it away. I went to the front door of the house and rang the bell. No one came. The people were gone but their faithful sprinkler system was soaking the already flooded lawn. The system was dumping unreplenishable water from the bolson into the city's storm drains.

Here's the thing: the aquifer goes dry, all we'll have left to drink is HAZMAT tea from the routinely poisoned Rio Grande.

This shortsighted use of the virgin waters of our pristine aquifer is the moral equivalent of selling your children's blood to finance your crack habit.

I am not rational on this subject. That ancient bolson holds agua bendita—holy water. It should be cared for and revered. Lawns, golf courses, and artificial lakes should be illegal here and everywhere else in the American Southwest.

I found the control box next to the front porch, opened the front panel. The controls were set for a one-hour sprinkling every twelve hours. The people who owned this house wanted their lawn to look like a Wisconsin golf course.

People who come to the Southwest to escape the northern winters don't like the barrenness of the desert. So they bring their northern landscaping ideas with them. They just don't get it: water in the Southwest is our most precious resource.

I reset the controls for a monthly watering of two hours. Maybe they wouldn't notice.

"Feeling righteous?" a man standing in the doorway of the house next door said. He had a cell phone in his hand. "I've called the police, señor," he said. His tone was snotty with middle-class invulnerability. He took me for a Mexican—a local, or a mojado in transit.

"Quién es el pendejo aquí?" I yelled. Who's the asshole here? "El hacendado o yo?" The bigshot who owns this place or me?

Thor or Wotan threw a bolt into the Franklin mountains. The flash and thunderclap gave me the advantage: My backup was the old gods themselves. It might even have been a bolt thrown by a home-grown god, like Tlaloc, the Aztec god of rain, not the Aryan foreigners, Thor and Wotan.

Maybe I'm too passionate on the subject of our threatened bolsons. Unbalanced even. The man in the doorway must have thought I was a lunatic—*Crazy Mexican fellow in the neighborhood sabotaging our beloved sprinkling systems that keep our world pleasantly green!*

A second blast of blue light and black thunder underscored my alliance with the irrational. The man darted back to the safety of his house, afraid of me and the god. He slammed the door.

Through the drumming rain, I heard the deadbolt snap in place.

I strolled back to my car, enjoying the storm.

I stomped through a puddle, like Gene Kelly dancing in the rain.

CHAPTER TWENTY-THREE

The phone pulled me out of bed at 7:00 a.m. It was Carla
Penrose. I almost wasn't surprised.

"I may be wrong, but I think you're the only person
out there I can trust right now," she said. "I can't count on
Luther anymore."

"When could anybody?" I said. A dream remnant about a
life misspent was still playing with my head.

"I don't think I can do this alone, J. P."

"Do what alone? What are you doing in Tucson?"

"I'm not in Tucson. I fed that to Luther in case the police
or the Hans Brinker lunatics forced him to give us up. I'm in
Albuquerque. Can you come here, this morning?"

"Hans Brinker? Of silver skates fame?"

"I don't want to stay on the line. I'll explain when you get
here. I'm frightened, J. P. Hector…is *hurting,* badly. Do you
have any painkillers?"

"Darvocet, about a dozen. Some Tylenol 3."

"Bring it all, and don't be followed."

She gave me the name of the hotel where they were staying, the old Hilton La Posada, and hung up.

Carla frightened? She had more grit than Joan of Arc. I've never known anyone less controlled by fear. She could face down a regiment of storm troopers. They might burn her at the stake but she'd never knuckle under to them. Her beliefs were her sword and shield.

I showered, dressed, slipped into my shoulder harness. I loaded the .357 and tucked it under my armpit. I put a pancake holster on my belt for the Browning .25. I've got a permit to carry—good in Texas, not good in New Mexico. I covered my arsenal with a lime-green silk jacket I bought in Juárez ten years ago. A nod to the fashion of the times. I made a pot of strong coffee, then scrambled three eggs with Tabasco, chipotle, and green onions. I split a bagel and put the halves into the toaster oven.

I'm not gun crazy but the fact that Carla Penrose was *frightened* raised some hackles. *The Hans Brinker lunatics,* she'd said. I thought of the document in her files titled, "HBB," and of Huddy Darko's shoulder tattoo. Hans Brinker *what?* Bombers? Blasters? Brownshirts? And why Hans Brinker? You'd have to go five hundred miles north to find a dozen people who owned ice skates.

FOUR HOURS LATER I was in Albuquerque. I got off the I-25 at Central Avenue, and drove to the hotel. Kat and I spent a night at this fine old La Posada—one of Conrad Hilton's first major hotels—the year we were married. We were young and early in the process of discovering each other. We had yet to find the worm in the apple. That would come a couple of years later.

Carla opened the door of her fourth floor room before I knocked. She looked haggard. "What took you so long?" she said.

"My car's got a tremor. It gets the shakes if I push it."

"You didn't tell Luther you were coming here?"

"I wouldn't tell Luther his shorts were on fire."

She looked at me curiously. "I thought he was your friend."

"He is. That doesn't mean he isn't an asshole who deserves what he gets."

Hector Martinez was sitting on the bed, watching a soccer match on TV. He looked like he'd walked into more than one baseball bat. His face was bruised and swollen, the scars from fresh incisions still painfully red.

"Elvis do this to him?" I said.

"Doctor Caravaggio," she said.

"Did you bring the pills?" Hector said.

I gave him a vial of Darvocet. He popped the lid and swallowed two caps without water. It looked as though Doctor Caravaggio had gone overboard with the rhinoplasty. Hector's fine Mayan nose and its wide nostril base had been carved down to a button. Not quite as bad as Michael Jackson's, but bad enough. It could pass for the nose of a nine-year-old Anglo girl.

He'd also been given cheek implants that rounded his face and further emphasized his diminished nose. The round Nordic face and button nose drew attention to Hector's remodeled eyes. Doc Caravaggio had removed the epicanthic folds, giving Hector wide-open, shocked eyes. He now had a permanent "deer in the headlights" look. For good measure, the unlicensed surgeon had plumped Hector's thin lips with collagen injections.

"You want to tell me what's going on with you two?" I said to Carla.

"Do you mean are we lovers? Is that your question?" Defiance animated her face.

"That's not what I meant, but since you brought it up, yes. Are you lovers?"

She sat next to Hector on the bed. She took his hand in hers. "We're close by necessity," she said. "Leave it at that, okay? What's important is the mission we're on. It might cost us our lives."

"What mission?"

"I guess you'll need to know," she said, glancing at Hector. He shrugged indifferently, kept his eyes on the game.

She gave me a thumbnail synopsis. Hector, a graduate student Carla had been advising, was involved in an incident on the border, just west of El Paso. It wasn't clear if it happened in Texas or New Mexico. Hector had been guiding a family into the United States when it happened.

"Wait a minute," I said. "Hector's a *coyote?*"

"Not in the way you ordinarily think of coyotes," she said. She looked at Hector again and I saw how close by necessity they were. Maybe it was platonic love, but platonic love has a way of infecting the flesh. If they weren't sleeping together now, they would be.

"Hector wasn't doing it for money," she said. "He was concerned only with the welfare of the people he was taking across the border. They were good people, on the verge of collapse from heat and dehydration. Hector had set them up with jobs and places to live. That's when the Hans Brinker Brigade came in. The HBB are border vigilantes, but they are not like the typical civilian patrols. Most civilian patrols, like the Minutemen, are non-violent. They see themselves as auxiliaries to the INS. But the Hans Brinker people are a guerrilla army. They want to kill people. Their goal is to create conditions that will touch off a war between Mexico and the U.S. They believe the war of 1846 was never concluded properly. They're vicious, J. P. They use sniper rifles and machine guns to stop trucks packed with illegals. One of them who was patrolling the border by himself stopped Hector's group and ordered them at gunpoint to turn around and go back into Mexico. Hector refused. The man—a kid really and too young to be out there by himself—raised his weapon and Hector went for it. In the struggle the gun, a sub-machine gun, went off. The kid's leg took a bullet and he bled out at the scene. Hector tried to apply a tourniquet above the wound but the injury to the femoral artery was too severe."

"Why do they call themselves the Hans Brinker Brigade?" I said.

"You remember the old children's story, don't you? Where

the Dutch boy, Hans Brinker, notices a leak in a dike and puts his thumb into the hole to stop it from expanding? Hans saves the town by plugging the leak until the men of the town, the 'dikers,' can fix the problem. The Brigade puts itself in that role. They see the border as a low-country dike and themselves as dikers. They intend to stop the leaks and thereby save the country from being flooded with illegals."

"By killing them," I said.

"They think people won't cross if they're in danger of getting shot by snipers. That's the idea anyway. They figure they can get the Mexican army involved by shooting mojados while they're still on the Mexican side of the border. If that happens it might draw the U.S. military into a skirmish with the Mexicans, a prelude to a general war, which is what they want."

"And they're coming after Hector for what—revenge?"

"It turns out the boy who died was the son of the founder of the Brigade, a Phoenix millionaire dermatologist named Stefan Selbiades. It's a very personal thing with them. Selbiades has put a price on Hector's head. Fifty thousand dollars."

"The Texas Rangers think they have jurisdiction. They want Hector for second degree murder," I said. "Texas thinks he's only worth twenty-five thousand—a would-be terrorist." I didn't see any reason to tell her about my run-in with the Hans Brinker twins, Huddy and Spode.

She touched Hector's hand, stroked it. "A man followed us here from Las Vegas," she said. "He was parked outside Dr. Caravaggio's trailer when you were there."

"That would be Bluto. His boss is a creepy peeper named Hamilton Scales. Luther hired him. Bluto works for Scales."

"He followed us," she said. "A big nasty looking man in a cheap suit."

"Bluto. He's here in Albuquerque?"

"I saw him on the plane. He was trying not to look at us but couldn't help himself. He's about as subtle as a fire truck. We lost him by taking a shuttle to Hotel Blue, on Central. We went out the back door, sat for an hour in a dark bar two blocks down the street, then took a cab here. Bluto's not much of a tracker. He's probably still sitting in the Hotel Blue lobby."

I had to ask: "Were you and Hector holed up in Juárez recently?"

"What do you mean by recently?" she said. "I was there about a month ago. Hector hasn't been there for…" She looked at Hector. "What's it been? Two months?" Hector nodded. "Why do you ask?"

"You're not the only one passing misinformation about your whereabouts."

It was clear now that Scales had sent Huddy and Spode on a Juàrez wild goose chase, making sure they took me out of the picture, too. He'd picked the address of the house on Avenida Duranzo out of the phone book. Three birds with one stone.

So the capture of Hector Martinez had become a competition, worth a total of seventy-five thousand. Not a lot these days but enough to rouse the interest of low-end entrepreneurs. Luther's bounty hunters had either lost the scent or were also in the neighborhood waiting for an opportunity.

Hector stood up. He looked like a tired old man. He opened the small fridge and took out a mickey of Jack Daniels. He moved stiffly, as if his entire body had been affected by his facial surgery. He uncapped the little bottle and drank it down, then uncapped another. "I feel like shit," he said.

"I need you to do something else for us, J. P.," Carla said. "I can't do it myself."

"Depends on what you want me to do. I'm not going to assassinate anyone. Last time I checked, that's still against the law."

"I want you to go to the downtown post office and pick up a package. I don't think I should go out, now that I know at least one of the people looking for us is here in town. Then I'd like you to drive us into Mexico. I'll pay you well."

"You want me to aid and abet wanted fugitives."

"I want you to help us further a humanitarian cause, J. P."

"The road to hell is paved with humanitarian causes," I said.

"So is the road to heaven."

"Heaven's a carrot dangling from a stick. Hell is a butcher shop, just around the corner."

"Then you won't do it?"

First Luther, now Carla, asking me for help. Once again I thought of P. T. Barnum and his gleeful announcement that a sucker is born every day.

"I'll do it," I said. "I'd rather do my time at La Tuna than Huntsville. I think the food is better at the federal prison, and the guards more humane."

"Tienes huevos grande, compa," Hector said. You got large balls, buddy.

"Maybe I'm just exceptionally stupid," I said.

CHAPTER TWENTY FOUR

Carla and Hector had registered at the hotel as Mr. and Mrs. Fidencio Ochoa. They paid for their room in cash. The package I was to pick up at general delivery was addressed to—surprise!—*me*. "We couldn't mail it to the hotel," she said. "We didn't know what names we'd be using after Vegas. Sending it to you seemed the most logical choice."

She showed me a stack of picture IDs she and Hector had. They were good quality, made in the USA. Hector's face was his original face. He was still in bandages when he got on the plane at McCarran, so the mismatched features weren't a problem. They'd get new IDs made once his new face healed.

I had to laugh at myself, at my predictability. She knew back at Doc Caravaggio's trailer that I'd come to Albuquerque and run this errand for her. She knew me better than I knew myself. I asked her what was in the package. She became evasive. "I can't tell you in detail, okay J. P.? In part, it's evidence that will clear Hector."

"Like what?"

"Video tape. I was there. I had my little Hitachi camcorder running, but I was about fifty yards away, behind some creosote bushes. I had the telephoto lens out. The picture's jumpy but it shows two men grappling for the gun, then flashes coming from the gun barrel. Anyone can tell it was an accident and who drew the gun in the first place."

I thought about all this as I drove to the Post Office. It had the feel of a badly designed insurance scam—too pat, too much like a written scenario. I didn't push it. The package I picked up was big as a small suitcase and weighed at least thirty pounds. There was a lot more in it than videotape. I tossed it in the back seat of my car.

Then Bluto appeared. Out of nowhere. Good trick for a man the size of a bus. "Hi there," he said. He'd parked his Budget Rental Malibu in front of my Monte Carlo.

He looked uncomfortable in his Walmart suit. His greasy red neck spilled over his shirt collar. He grinned his short-toothed grin and sweat rolled down his cheeks like beads of lard on a fry cook's stove. He took my belt in his fist and jerked upward, taking me off my feet. He held me there, floating in front of him, free of gravity. Bluto could have competed in the Toyota-lifting event in a strong man contest. This was a demonstration, a forecast of what else he could do. I guess I was supposed to be impressed and worried. I was. I still had the bruises from my last dance with super heavyweights.

His grin widened. The last time I got a wedgie I was a light-weight freshman in high school. I remembered the humiliation I felt as my shoes left the ground, followed by the pain of crushed nuts, nearby girls giggling excitedly. The memory came back like a slap. I felt fourteen again.

But I wasn't fourteen, and not as shy as I was back in high school. The crotch of my pants cut into my scrotum and pain combined with the memory of pain. I took the .25 out of my pancake holster and rammed the butt into Bluto's face. His nose exploded like an overripe squash. Blood and snot splashed back to his ears. He let go of my belt and grabbed at his face, howling. I kicked his knee and he went down. Then I kicked his gut. I'd kicked field goals and extra points for the Coronado High Thunderbirds in West El Paso thirty years ago and still had good leg strength. I kicked Bluto's kidney area as if going for a forty-yarder. He rolled away from me, puking. He puked up something green. Enchilada sauce, guacamole, mixed with frijoles. A woman coming out of the post office dropped her mail. Her mouth fell open. Her face pre-faint white. She sat down on the post office steps. "Someone call the police," she said, too softly to be heard by anyone but me and Bluto, and we weren't listening. I would rather have done this to Ham Scales than Bluto, who was just an incompetent hump making hourly wages.

"Make sure you get Scales to pay your doctor bill," I said. "The cheap prick owes you. If I remember correctly there's a walk-in clinic on San Mateo Boulevard. Make sure you get a receipt. Scales won't reimburse you if you don't. And take a cab. I don't think you should drive in your condition."

I left him bleeding and retching on the sidewalk. He'd be pissing blood for a week and wouldn't want to chase Hector and Carla for at least that long.

I drove back to the hotel. I didn't feel good about myself. There was no need to work Bluto over with that much enthusiasm. He'd touched a nerve and old hurts and humiliations came into play. The humiliations of childhood are indelible; they can't be exorcised. If Bluto had just thrown a punch I wouldn't have gone ballistic. Giving me a wedgie, he raised an old demon. I was surprised the old demon was still touchy, and had teeth.

I took a devious route back to La Posada, circling city blocks, making illegal U-turns, turning the wrong way into a one-way street and dodging oncoming traffic for two blocks before I ducked into a side street. I drove through strip mall parking lots and even stopped at a Burger King for a Whopper and fries. If someone was following me, they were too good to make.

A block from the hotel smoke began to stream from the engine compartment of the Monte. I pulled into a parking space and opened the hood with the engine still running. The big V-8 was wreathed in smoke. I could see oil from the valve-covers spraying the engine block. The seals were shot. The engine could catch fire but I'd have to put that worrisome possibility aside until I could install new gaskets. I turned the engine off and walked into the hotel. I took the elevator to the sixth floor.

Carla opened the door. She was in tears, her voice shaky. "What happened to you?" she said. "I thought you ran out on us. Where the *hell* have you been? Hector's been arrested."

A chair was tipped over. The room's lone table leaned against the wall on two legs. A lamp was on the floor, the cloth shade squashed. "Who arrested him?" I said.

"He said he was an FBI Fugitive Recovery Agent. He showed his ID so fast I couldn't be sure."

"Dreadlocks, ear studs, soul patch, twelve-hundred dollar suit?"

"How did you know?"

"He's not FBI. He's a private investigator named Hamilton Scales. He's supposedly working for Luther. I just had a run-in with his employee who'd staked out the P.O. after you lost him. He must have watched you mail the box from Vegas."

She saw Bluto's blood, splattered on my coat. Red on lime-green. "My God," she said. "I'm so sorry, J. P. This is awful."

"It was more awful for the other guy," I said.

I righted the table and set the box on it.

"What does Luther want with Hector?" she said.

"Luther wants you, not Hector. Scales wants Hector. He's after the reward money. How long ago did this happen, Carla?"

"It just happened. Ten or fifteen minutes ago. He had a gun. Hector tried to get the gun away from him. He hit Hector with it. I tried to hit him with the table lamp."

She started crying again. Carla was not a crier, but these tears were for Hector. A lover's tears. I glanced at the bed. The bedspread was off, the sheets tangled. Suggesting recent vigorous activity. The bed had been made when I left for the Post Office. The mussed covers and sheets could have been collateral damage from the ruckus. I looked for tracks anyway, ashamed of myself for looking, but nonetheless curious. It occurred to me that Scales might have caught them in flagrante delicto.

"Did Hector have his clothes on?" I said.

She looked at me, defiant. "He was in his underwear, okay? Why?"

"Scales made him leave that way?"

"He handcuffed Hector, then threw a blanket over his shoulders. I feel so goddamned stupid, J. P. We should have gone to Mexico yesterday."

"There are probably half a dozen professionals looking for you two. What makes you think you could stay in the wind?"

She sat on the bed and held her head in her hands and sobbed. This wasn't like her at all, but it's possible she'd never been in love before. I don't think she ever loved Luther. She admired him, she thought he was brilliant and righteous and unconventional—but it was never ass-over-teakettle lust-driven love.

First love shouldn't happen after you're thirty. But if it does it should be given a name, in the same way the Weather Service recognizes the destructive power of hurricanes by giving them human names. Hurricane Hector had blown Carla's tidy little boat out to sea.

"Maybe we can catch up with them," I said. A 1971 Monte Carlo with a blown valve-cover gasket catching up to a new Porsche wasn't likely. But Scales wouldn't risk getting stopped for speeding. A red Porsche on the interstate would attract the attention of the highway patrol. Every cop with a radar gun between Albuquerque and El Paso would be sampling his speed. He'd have to stay well under the limit, cruising in the slow lane along with the careful grannies in their Sedan DeVilles. That in itself might raise suspicions, but he'd have to chance it.

He'd be heading back to the security of El Paso—no reason to go elsewhere with his prize. In El Paso he could begin negotiations with Stefan Selbiades, which was his purpose from the beginning. He was too greedy to accept the fifty-thousand-dollar finder's fee as final. If Hector had international value, Scales would have offered him on eBay to the highest bidder.

There was a chance we could catch up with him by the time we reached Truth or Consequences, or Las Cruces. If the Monte didn't blow up before then. We had two hundred fifty miles of straight freeway to close the distance between us.

"Let's go," I said.

"I'm sorry I got you into this, J. P.," she said.

"Into what exactly?" I said.

"I'll tell you in the car."

CHAPTER TWENTY-FIVE

"There's money in the box, a lot of it," she said.

We were out on I-25, limping south. I'd filled the crankcase with oil, bought six extra quarts. I also bought a thirty-dollar fire extinguisher.

"How much money?" I said.

"Over a million."

"Dollars?"

"Dollars."

I made the appropriate whistling sound. The next question was so obvious I didn't ask it. But the answer was a surprise.

"Iraq," she said. "It came from Iraq."

I eased back to seventy, five miles under the limit. The old Monte was willing but ailing. A front wheel shimmy made the wheel vibrate in my hands and ribbons of dark smoke streamed past the windshield.

It was a day made for postcard photographers. The Manzano Mountains blazed in the copper sunset. To the south, pink cirrus clouds rose in cotton-candy swirls above a blue mesa. Straight ahead and a thousand feet high a golden eagle floated motionless on updrafts as it searched for prey.

The world is beautiful and the people are sad—a line in a poem I'd read when I was too young to appreciate or believe it.

I waited for Carla to continue. She was frowning, as if deciding what she could tell me, what she could not. A tear escaped her eye. She brushed it away impatiently.

"Hector's youngest brother, Mario, was a soldier in Iraq last year," she said, composing herself. "He was on patrol, in Samara. He and another soldier went into an abandoned house. They found a steel box full of money hidden under a trap door in the kitchen floor."

"I read about that," I said. "But those boys finally turned the money over to their commanding officer. They only kept it long enough to get themselves in hot water."

"That was a different unit. They found *hundreds* of millions. Mario and his friend only found a million and a half."

"How did they get it out of Iraq?"

"The other boy was fluent in Najdi, the local dialect. He'd made friends with an Iraqi businessman. He struck a deal with him. They'd divide the money equally and the Iraqi would mail Mario's and his friend's share to the U.S. They felt they could trust him to do that. He was a decent man."

"Doesn't sound possible," I said.

"Mario didn't think so either. But the Iraqi had a small import/export business. He traveled a lot and often made trips into Syria and Lebanon. Mario said he had a 1980 Yugo with a quarter of a million miles on it. He mailed Mario's share from Aleppo, in Syria, as part of a business shipment. The money came directly to Hector's box at the UTEP Post Office. It was almost too easy."

"So it's Mario's money, not Hector's. Or yours."

"Mario was killed at Al Qaim, in a firefight with the insurgents."

"What happened to the friend?"

"I don't know. Neither does Hector. All we know is that he

was from California somewhere. I suppose he's living the good life with his share."

"It's contraband, you know. You can't keep it."

"Why not? The government would just use it to rebuild Iraq's oil fields and pipelines. That's what the whole damned war was about in the first place—a neo-con ploy to break OPEC's stranglehold on oil quotas. Hector has a much better use for it."

"It's still considered felony theft. The feds will put both of you away for a long time."

"Are you going to turn us in?" she said. "Do you want some of the money to keep our little secret? Name your price, J. P. Fifty thousand? A hundred? *Half?*"

"Knock it off, Carla. I'm thinking about you. And Luther. For Chrissakes, do you have any idea what you've gotten yourself into?"

She leaned against the window and watched the landscape slide by. The low sun caught strands of her short hair, turning them into gold filaments. "Do you believe in miracles, J. P.?"

"I'm from El Paso. We have the corner on miracles."

"Mario put an icon of the Virgin of Guadalupe in the package to guarantee its safe delivery. The Iraqi had to get it through dozens of checkpoints between Samara and the border towns of Al Walid and Al Tanf. He had to drive through the Al Anbar Province badlands, for God's sakes. What are the odds a package with just under a million dollars in it could travel from Samara through the Al Anbar desert to Aleppo, and then to El Paso without being intercepted by some government agency, blasted by a gunship, or jacked by roadside bandits? A million to one? Ten million to one?"

"You're telling me you've become a mystical Catholic? A virgenista? A diehard neo-Commie tree-hugger like you?"

"I was never an atheist, J. P. A lot of Communists back in the red heyday still received the sacraments."

"They needed to," I said. "So what's Hector's plan for the loot?"

"The money is going to Mexico. So are we." She choked a

bit on that "we." She wiped her tears away impatiently. Like any good soldier, she would not allow herself the luxury of a breakdown.

I thought about how she had involved me in their scheme, how I had walked into it like a blind man into quicksand. "You sucked me into the deal, knowing I could be charged as an accessory."

She shrugged. "We needed help. I felt I could count on your sympathy. I know you're not a bigot."

"Thanks for the seal of approval. Maybe it'll be useful to me among the liberals in Leavenworth."

She explained how Hector would build a small tract of safe houses in Juárez for immigrants and buy an existing house in El Paso's Lower Valley to house them once they crossed. It would be a kind of underground railroad for the transients. She called them "transients" not "illegals." Their immediate goal was to give desperate people a little comfort in their search for a decent life. Hector and his friends could weed out the bad apples, like drug mules.

Borders, she said, are political fictions, determined by imperial wars and justified by bogus rationalizations, such as Manifest Destiny. Mexico, with a gun to its head, was divided nearly in half by the treaty of 1848. What was once Mexico became U.S. territory by brute force. Mexican families were cut off from each other by an arbitrary line in the sand. Many of the people who cross over illegally are hoping to stay with relatives until they find work. "Conservatives worry about the so called 'Latinization' of the American West," she said. "But in fact it's only a re-Latinization."

"So what goes around comes around," I said.

"Simplistic, but more or less true."

"The Hans Brinker snipers agree with you."

"On the developing situation, not the solution. They're paranoid killers. We're on the side of the angels."

I almost laughed. Only a kamikaze fanatic could say something like that without irony. Hell, I was on the side of the angels, too—I mean, who with half a heart *wasn't*?—but my goals were not as grand as Carla's. I'd never put my life on the line for a Cause, unless I'd lost my mind. Angels on the side of a Cause had spilled an ocean of blood, too.

Even so, I felt guilty for not feeling guilty about my lack of political purpose. I was capable of that much. People everywhere on the planet had a right to be safe and well-fed and content with their lot—even deliriously happy, why the hell *not?*—but I had no master plan to put that dream into effect. It wasn't going to happen in my lifetime. Some changes in the general population were going to have to happen first. Maybe the genetic engineers could tweak the human temperament until it was peaceful and helpful and generous, instead of restless and destructive and selfish. And maybe pigs would fly and songbirds oink.

I eased the Monte up to seventy-five. Newer cars doing ninety and a hundred flew past. The full moon, big as a dinner plate, filled a wide depression between the peaks of the Manzanos. For no particular reason I thought of Kat, who was not available, and then of Dani Thrailkill, who was. I thought of how I'd like to be in a good woman's bed, feeling a warm body next to mine. Sex, food, and shelter—the simplest imaginable existence. It only takes two people to make a world, a sage once said. More than that, it becomes a confused and unpredictable mess crammed with unresolvable issues. That's all I knew. That's all I would ever know.

"Who knows about the money," I said, "besides you and Hector?"

"The other soldier, the Najdi speaker. But I don't know his name or if he's even alive."

She sank low in her seat, touched her forehead with her fingertips as if she had a migraine. "I didn't want this to become so fucking complicated," she said.

I took that to mean more than the day's events. Something happened she hadn't counted on. Love happened. Falling in love with Hector hadn't been part of the plan. It gave the plan a vulnerability it wouldn't have had if they had remained focused. Soldiers on the side of the angels didn't have the leisure time for a complicating distraction like love.

Carla gave in to her emotions and wept quietly, dozing now and then as sheer fatigue overrode her grief. Then, about ten miles from Truth or Consequences, she sat up as if waking from a bad dream. "Your goddamn car's on *fire!*" she said.

CHAPTER TWENTY-SIX

Blue flames licked through the narrow gap between the hood and the left fender. I slowed to fifty, looking for a place to pull off the road. We made it to the Truth or Consequences exit. I turned into a street lined with flat-roofed modular homes and aging magnolia trees. Retirees from all over the country lived in the cheap prefabs. A lot of them were old enough to know that the town was named after a radio quiz show, popular in the 1940s. The odd name was a mystery to most people now, and the city council had thought of restoring the town's old name, Hot Springs, but never got enough votes to make it happen. No matter what they called it, it would always be Truth or Consequences to me, a town on the south shore of Elephant Butte Reservoir. It wasn't exactly Malibu or Cancun but for the people who lived here it was an econo-paradise, the rocking chair Riviera of southern New Mexico, where the living was easy and affordable.

I popped the hood and got out. A dark snaky flame slithered around the intake manifold and headers. I got the extinguisher out of the back seat and smothered the fire before it could burn through the insulation on the spark plug wires or light up the carburetor. We'd have to stay put for a while to let the engine cool down. I told Carla this.

"Shit, how are we going to catch them now?" Carla said.

"We don't need to catch them."

"What are you talking about? They're probably not more than twenty minutes ahead of us."

"Scales isn't going anywhere. He's going to keep Hector in El Paso until he's able to jack the price up. He can't make it happen overnight. It'll probably take a week. He's not going to settle for the fifty grand Stefan Selbiades ponied up. Money is what this has been about from the get-go. It was never about you. When Scales found out you were traveling with a man with a price on his head you just became the trail marker. If he knew about the half million in that box of yours he would have gone after you with a posse instead of just sending Bluto."

We sat in the car, letting the engine cool. Carla dropped into a deep unreachable sulk. It was infectious. I didn't feel like talking either. If I said anything I'd probably regret it later. There already was enough to regret. My scenario of probable events wasn't convincing, even to me. We sat in the Monte, nurturing our regrets, listening to the cooling engine tick like a clock slowing down.

The ticking stopped a half-hour later. I turned the key in the ignition and the faithful 454 big-block V-8 roared to life. It didn't catch fire again until we were past Las Cruces and almost home. I pulled into the rest stop at the Texas border.

Paint blisters covered the hood like a tropical skin disease. I opened it and once again smothered the engine fire with the extinguishing foam. The spark plug wires didn't look like they'd survive another fire and the batting on the firewall that insulated the cabin from engine noise was scorched, but I was confident the old Chevy would take us the rest of the way home.

I went into the restroom to wash up. It was empty except for one stall which was occupied by a shoeless man. His bare feet were not flat on the floor, as they would be if he were sitting down, but on their sides, one in front of the other. The feet stuck out past the stall door. The man who owned them was lying next to the commode. "You okay, bud?" I said.

He didn't answer. The feet didn't move. I pushed the un-locked door open.

Hamilton Scales didn't look surprised to see me, or especially embarrassed by his condition. He was naked, lying on his side next to the commode, as if he'd decided this was a perfectly reasonable place to take a nap. His head was turned at an impossible angle, almost backwards. His neck had been broken, the top cervical vertebrae, C1, C2, and maybe C3—the vulnerable ones—snapped like dry twigs.

His toes were dirty, the nails long and ragged. It was an odd thing to notice, but it stood out, like a roach in chowder. Scales, who had been so confidently cool, so impeccably and expensively dressed, needed a bath and a nail trim.

Death steals your dignity but replaces it with something more durable: Indifference. Scales' gray filmy eyes looked at me as if I was part of the toilet-stall wall. His bowels had emp-tied themselves on the concrete floor. Scales was indifferent to that, too.

I checked the parking lot for the Porsche. It wasn't there. Hector had taken it, along with Scales' clothes. I went back to the Monte.

"Carla, we've got a new complication," I said. I told her what I'd found. "Looks like Hector killed Scales and took his Porsche."

She sat upright, instantly adrenalized. *"What?* How *could* he have? He was in handcuffs!"

"Maybe Scales took them off so he could use the restroom. Seems unlikely—but possible."

I couldn't believe it either. Hector didn't seem like some-one who could kill with his bare hands. Whoever killed Scales knew something about how to put a killing torque on the cervical vertebrae. But then, I knew nothing about Hector, or what he was capable of. For all I knew he might have been a black-belt Kung Fu master. I asked Carla about this.

"I don't know," she said. "We never talked about such things, but it's possible. I've only known him for a little less than a year."

But oh what a fine short year it must have been, I thought but didn't say.

The news of Hector's escape brightened Carla's mood considerably. "He must have gone to Mexico," she said. "He has family there, in Chihuahua City. He was born in Brownsville, but his parents were from Monterrey. He has dual citizenship. He's safe in Mexico, J. P."

I knew why he was safe and why she was happy: Mexico won't extradite its citizens to the U.S. in capital crime cases. We have the death penalty, Mexico does not.

"It's going to work out for us after all," she said. Her tears this time were tears of joy. "He'll contact me when he gets settled. Then I can bring the money to him."

"Peachy," I said. It didn't matter what I said. Nothing anyone said could bring her down.

I got off the Interstate at the Executive Center off-ramp and drove directly to the Penrose house. "Thank Christ," Luther said when he saw Carla. "You've come home to me at last, my darling! I've been out of my mind with worry!" He grabbed my hand and shook it vigorously, "I owe you J. P. I owe you big time."

"I don't think so, Luther," I said.

He ignored me and took Carla in his arms and tried to smother her with kisses but she pulled away angrily.

"I just stopped by to pick up some things," she said. "I'm leaving you, Luther."

"So it's true," Luther said. "You're fucking the goddamn wetback."

Carla slapped him hard. Luther raised his hand to slap her back, but stopped himself. "Go ahead, hit me," she said. "It'll make it easier for both of us."

I didn't want to hear any more. I went back to the Monte and put out the fire. The hiss of the fire extinguisher blocked all other sounds.

Carla went in the house to pack. Luther stood immobile on the porch. The huge silhouette he made against the interior house light made him look like a cardboard effigy of himself.

I put the fire extinguisher in the trunk and walked back to the house. Luther's face was contorted now, as if he'd had a stroke. "I brought her back to you, Luther," I said. "Sorry it wasn't exactly what you expected."

"*Fuck* her!" he roared into the night. "I gave her everything! I put her through grad school! And now she doesn't want anything to do with me! She was a penniless undergrad when we first met. And *this* is what I get for my trouble?"

"You got no return on your investment, is that it?" I said.

"Fuck you too, buddy boy. I hope she rots in whatever version of hell she and the wetback have cooked up for themselves!"

"Good night, Luther."

He looked at my smoking Monte Carlo. "That's a vintage set of wheels you have there, J. P. But you've neglected it. You're turning it into a pile of dysfunctional junk. You could rehabilitate it for ten grand. But you won't. You won't because you don't appreciate what you have 'til it's gone."

His sudden change of tone was eerie. It was almost a confession of his own failure, but if it made him feel better transferring his mistakes to me, then so be it.

Carla came out with a single suitcase. "J. P., I want you to take me to the San Jacinto Inn on Mesa," she said. "They rent rooms by the week. I'll stay there until I find something more suitable."

Or until the cops pick you up, I thought.

When she cleared the door, Luther said to me, "You told her about Lelanie Loftsgarten, you son of a bitch. Is that why you slapped me, Carla?"

"I didn't tell her a thing," I said, "but you just did, you jack-ass."

He slammed the door on both of us. It sounded like a shot-gun blast. Windows in the neighborhood that had been dark, lit up.

CHAPTER TWENTY-SEVEN

I made myself a half-and-half Bloody Maria in a beer mug and sat out on my small balcony that looked out on the caliche streets of the west end of Juárez. The blinking light on my answering machine nagged at me but I was not ready to hear all the bad news it held. I usually made my half-and-halfs with Cuervo, but I felt I deserved the good stuff tonight, Herradura Gold, made from the glorious agave azul. It had been a long day, full of ugly surprises.

Belief in a theory is grounded in plausibility and buoyed up by intuition. Neither was working for me. Hector was not a killer, not a black-belt Kung Fu whiz, and he wasn't safely in Mexico. He didn't talk Scales into taking off the cuffs and he didn't disarm Scales. He might be wearing Scales' clothes—they were about the same size—but I don't think he was showing them off, along with the Porsche, to friends and relatives in Chihuahua City. It's what Carla wanted to believe, though, and

I wasn't about to suggest the other, darker possibility: someone else killed Scales and had grabbed Hector for their own purposes.

BY THE TIME I finished my third Bloody Maria, I didn't care about the darker possibilities. I watched TV until I fell asleep sitting up.

I slept until ten the next morning. Sometime during the night I'd managed to get undressed and climb into bed, but I had no memory of it. The biggest decision facing me this morning was whether to listen to my phone messages or go out for breakfast at the Hollywood Café.

I opted for breakfast, then remembered the Monte needed some attention. I drove up Mesa to Pep Boys and bought a pair of valve-cover gaskets, a set of spark plug wires, and installed them right there in the parking lot. I carried my own tools— torque wrench, crescent wrench, socket wrench, pliers, and a fancy set of Chinese box wrenches that I couldn't use because they were metric, but they looked pretty in my tool kit. It took about an hour to do the job.

A hunger pang made my stomach growl. I decided to have breakfast at Carrow's, which was only a mile or two north on Mesa from Pep Boys. I drove past the San Jacinto Inn on the way. The San Jacinto had been a fine old motel when Mesa Street was a segment of the old coast-to-coast highway, U.S. 80, long before the Interstate system was built. The new chain-owned motels along the Interstate put the old motel out of business, so the owner turned it into apartments, rented by the week. It was a cheap place to hole up while you scoured the city for more permanent digs.

Carla had taken a second floor room, overlooking the parking lot and the street. I'd carried her stuff, including the box full of money, to her apartment. She registered as "Letty Parsons," a name belonging to a deceased great-aunt.

"I'll put the money into a safe deposit box at my bank tomorrow," she said after I told her that some of the residents in the San Jacinto were parolees, junkies, and general purpose psychopaths.

"Don't trust the door locks," I said. "Prop a chair under the doorknob." I gave her my .25. "It's got a six shot magazine. Anyone breaks in, you've got six hollow points to help him change his mind."

"Thanks, J. P.," she said. "There's no way I can thank you enough. I'm sorry I put you to all this trouble. After Hector contacts me and I join him in Chihuahua City, I'll make it up to you. You've earned at least ten-thousand of our dollars."

"I don't think so," I said.

She gave me a bracing little hug and a dry, sisterly kiss, thinking I was being modest. I wasn't.

Here's how it looked to me:

She wasn't going to Chihuahua City. She was going to jail.

Hector wasn't going Chihuahua City either. He was most likely dead.

And I sure as hell wasn't going to get ten-thousand dollars from anyone jailed or dead.

The whole lunatic scheme was busted, and the fall-out wasn't going to be pretty.

If she was dumb enough to take the Iraqi money to her bank she wouldn't get out the door before she was in handcuffs.

"Stay away from your bank, Carla," I said. "Someone's waiting for you to make that mistake. Rent a locker at the old Union Pacific depot down on San Francisco Street. Your stash should be relatively safe there. Make damn sure you aren't followed."

Whether or not she would take my advice, I had no idea, but I wasn't going to let it interfere with my digestion. My advice would only prolong the inevitable anyway.

I ordered a Denver omelet at Carrow's and took my time eating it.

CHAPTER TWENTY-EIGHT

"Time's up," Pilar Mellado said. "We're taking the necessary and unavoidable steps. Blame yourself, J. P. You might have a week, maybe two, to circumvent the Public Fiduciary's directives. Have a nice day."

The next was a two-day old call from Luther:

"I *can* count on you to be discreet, can't I? There's no need to mention Lelanie to Carla or anyone else, right?" He started to tell me that Lelanie Loftsgarten was a devoted fan of his writing, how she appreciated his intellectual energy, and how *refreshed* and *renewed* he felt after taking her to bed. He started to describe in detail what a great lay she was and how her absolute lack of inhibitions stimulated his creative genius. "The muse is always a woman," he said. "A woman ready, able, and willing to fulfill the artist's needs. That's why so many female artists of any quality are lesbians."

I skipped forward to the next message:

"Your fucking ass is fucking grass you fucking fuckhead." A muscle-throated growler. I half recognized the voice as belonging to Huddy Darko, which surprised me. If Huddy and

Spode were out of jail on the weapons charge, someone must have bought a Juárez magistrate.

Then a voice I fully recognized:

"The bitch is yours, dawg. Take her back to that jerk-off husband of hers, they probably deserve each other. I've got her Mexican fuck-toy. You, uh—what's the word?—oh yeah: *lose*. You want to trace skips for me, the offer is still open. I think you're going to need any work you can get."

In the background I heard the moderate hum of a barely taxed Porsche engine and the Doppler come-and-go whine of highway traffic. Hamilton Scales, cruising ten miles under the speed limit on I-25, calling from his cell phone. Probably his last message to anyone. An image came back to me uninvited—the long skinny body so pale it was almost blue in the rest stop's overhead fluorescents, the dirty feet and ragged toenails, the dreadlocked head turned nearly backwards on the neck. The bland gaze I'd seen before and still see in dreams.

Next:

"This is your mother," Velma said. "I believe you remember me? Perhaps you do not. An annoying woman wants to send me away. She claims I am a prisoner in my own home. Does that make sense to you? Have people lost their minds? Have I missed something?"

I drove to the Upper Valley. Velma was in the kitchen, sipping muscatel. She started talking as soon as she saw me.

"They are going to put my house up for auction. They said I fell and a falling woman is a danger to herself. I did not fall. They found me lying on my back looking up at the image on the living room ceiling. I hadn't noticed the image before. Their spies looked into the house from the patio doors and saw me on the living room floor. They said I *must* have fallen. I did *not*. Go in the living room and look for yourself, then maybe you can stop them from bothering me. I'm an old lady. I can't be bothered by rude people like that. I did not realize we are living in a police state. If I fell why was there a pillow under my head?" She raised her glass of muscatel with both hands and brought it to her lips.

"Mom, it's out of my hands. You go into El Descanso voluntarily or you go by force. I can't stop them."

Her expression changed. Her eyes lost focus.

"And you are?" she said.

"What?"

"Who *are* you, sir?"

"I'm J. P., your son."

"J. P.? What do the initials stand for? John Peter? Josiah Paul? Judas Pipkin? Would you *please* do me the courtesy of identifying yourself before I call my husband?"

I'd been trying to identify myself all my life. I wish I had been named John, Josiah, Paul, even Judas. At least a real name could be a starting place.

"Mom, for Chrissakes. You know my initials don't stand for anything."

"That's preposterous."

"Tell me about it."

Her face was stony, etched now by streaming tears. "I did *not* fall. They claim I fell. But they are wrong. I told them so. There was a pillow under my head. I was lying there to observe her."

I went out into the living room and looked at the ceiling. The old house was in need of some serious maintenance. The monsoon rains had leaked into the attic and the ceiling was stained. If you put your mind to it, and if you wanted very much to believe it, you might see the Mother of Christ looking down at you with unconditional benevolence.

You could put your mind to a lot of things you wanted to believe. It's what we do; it's our great weakness. It makes the world a working asylum. I remembered Luther quoting T.S. Eliot: "The world is a hospital. Half the people are patients, the other half are nurses." I put myself in both categories, some days up, some days down. My lithium-rich bolson kept the mood swings reasonable. But people like Luther's neighbor, who only put their minds to new forms of excess, were pumping our happy water into the Rio Grande where it mixes with toxins and becomes a toxin itself.

"I'll tell Pilar I saw the Virgin, too," I told her. "Maybe she'll put us in adjoining rooms in the nursing home."

"I am not crazy," she said, schoolmarm stern. "I am not senile either. 'The present is too present to imagine.' I believe it goes something like that. "Carpe Diem" by Robert Frost, if I remember the line correctly. Memory! I once could recite the entire 'Evangeline'."

"Pilar hasn't said you were crazy. She just thinks you can't take care of yourself. When was the last time you had food, Mom?"

She looked furtively around the kitchen, like a child trying to invent a perfect lie. The stove was potless, the sink dishless, the counters empty, the cupboards bare. "I think I had something yesterday," she said.

I looked in the fridge. Half a quart of curdled milk, two weeks past its expiration date. One boiled egg. Half a lemon. A black banana. A bread crust smeared with what I hoped was apple butter. A head of lettuce in the vegetable drawer, dark as motor oil.

"You've lost some weight," I said.

"I intended to," she said. "The lighter you are, the closer to the ethereal. You should lose some weight yourself. You've developed a paunch."

She was in her old pink chenille bathrobe. It was open at the neck. I saw the bones between her dry breasts, the ethereal liver-spotted skin. She was dissolving.

"Get dressed, Mom. I'll take you out to lunch."

"Daddy says not eating buys you a ticket out. He's lonely and wants me. But of course there's no guarantee I'll find his dimension when I pass over. Who knows *what* I might find. I might not even find myself there. It's all a miracle and a puzzle. Maybe Daddy will always be lonely. He knows that's a possibility but wants me to stop anyway."

Stop eating. The ticket out. Not something Dad would say, but who was I to argue with a dimension-crossing ghost?

"A nice pork chop sandwich doesn't appeal to you, Mom?" I said, trying to tempt her. "You look awfully hungry."

But she wouldn't be lured away from her fabrications. Which meant she had no choice. She had to go to El Descanso.

I went back into the living room. The Mother of God was still there in the ceiling, regal and forgiving, arms open to receive suffering humanity. You could make yourself believe the watermarks that limned her pale oval face had been applied by an unsteady but devoted hand. If you pushed it, you could almost see the famous infant in her arms.

"Do something," I said. "Give the old girl a break. Please."

CHAPTER TWENTY-NINE

I spent too much of the afternoon in Rosa's Cantina down on Doniphan street, a good place to hide from whatever you need to hide from. I don't know if the bar was named after the Marty Robbins song or if Marty Robbins got the idea for his song from the bar. Or if there was any connection at all between bar and song. Not that it mattered. I liked the bar, I liked the song. It was one of those chicken/egg things that you don't need to think about for more than a minute. Whenever I came here to hide, I filled the jukebox with quarters and played Marty Robbins numbers until the regulars began to look at my neck with knives in their eyes.

I wasn't there to hide, or to drown my troubles. Other than getting my mother to go peaceably to her final earthly crib, I had no troubles at all. I might be accused of aiding and abetting Hector and Carla, but that would be a hard case to make and probably not worth the City Attorney's time. Just doing my job, sir: J. P. Morgan, Claims Investigator and Marriage

Medic, licensed by the state of Texas, and working for the betterment of man and the society in which he carries out his personal mandates regardless how idiotic, misguided, or monstrous.

Carla had troubles and needed a place to hide. Of course, being ennobled by serving a noble cause, she wouldn't think so. Hector had troubles, but there was a chance his troubles were over. By now his corpse was probably feeding the fire ants of the northern Chihuahua or Sonoran desert.

The Iraq money was trouble, but, since I had no designs on it, it wasn't my trouble. It's hard to keep that much money a secret. Money in large quantities sends out signals, like cheese announcing itself to rats. The rats were gathering.

I had a third margarita then drove down Doniphan past the old Asarco smelter and took the off-ramp at the overpass to Sunset Heights and my apartment building.

I had another drink in my kitchen, then called Fernando Peralta, a lawyer I'd played handball with a few times. Fernie worked with Sundown on a few cases and we'd become friendly. I was on a first-name basis with a lot of personal injury lawyers, but I wouldn't trust their advice on how to boil an egg. Fernando Peralta was an estate and property man with an impeccable reputation. We shared a low opinion of the claim chasing crowd.

What I needed from Fernie was a durable power of attorney. I also needed to become sole guardian and conservator of my mother and her estate so I could go ahead and sell her house once she was in El Descanso. Velma wouldn't have a say in the process since I could provide evidence that she was incapacitated due to senile dementia. The Adult Protective Services agent, Pilar Mellado, would carry the ball from there. After a quick competency hearing—a sort of kangaroo court for the doddering—they'd take the old lady out of her house, in restraints if necessary, and deliver her to her caretakers. Life in the new century was going to be one wonder after another.

I made an appointment to see Fernie, then made myself a Bloody Maria in a beer mug and wondered why I was drinking myself into a blackout.

Luther called me in the late afternoon. I dropped the phone twice before getting it to my ear. "The bounty hunters were here again," he said. "They really looked murderous. They want Hector. I told them you knew where he was. I had to, J. P. I couldn't take another beating like that. I'm sorry."

"Thanks for the heads up, Luther."

"They were going to break my legs, for Chrissakes! They had their goddamned can of gas with them. I had to give them something."

"So you gave them me."

"I said I was sorry."

"I'll deal with them, Luther. Don't worry about it."

"I feel like shit, J. P."

"You *could* have run them off with my shotgun," I said.

"I locked it in the trunk of the Packard. I was going to bring it back to you. I couldn't have it in the house another minute. I was itching to *use* it. You understand that, don't you?"

I did. The gun was talking serious bullshit to him, tempting him to eat a load of buckshot. *Nothing to fear, just put me in your mouth and toe the trigger. Ka-boom—instant nirvana, skull full of godly light, and you won't even have a headache.*

I changed the subject. "By the way, Luther. I didn't say anything to Carla about Lelanie. She's not leaving you because of that. I was wrong about her and Hector Martinez. She's in love with him. It didn't start out that way, I'm convinced of that. They were on a mission in Las Vegas, not a honeymoon. After Vegas things got out of control."

"They can both be out of control in hell, for all I care," Luther said. "I'm not going to let it fuck up my life. I've got two hundred and sixty finished pages of *Gotterdammerung Now*, every line a keeper. It's the best thing I've ever done, J. P. It's going to put me on the map. I've contacted an agent..."

I said goodbye before he got up a head of steam on the soon-to-be discovered genius of Luther Penrose. I loaded my .357 Combat Magnum with hollow points, made another Bloody Maria, and waited. I would rather have had my short-barrel Mossberg that was now gathering vintage lint in the trunk of Luther's Packard. Nothing dampens aggressive behavior more effectively than the sight of a chopped semi-automatic 12 gauge.

I left the front door open. I wanted them to walk in. I would be the surprise, waiting in the dark.

I waited until sundown, taking hits of Herradura straight from the bottle, Marty Robbins on my stereo. I felt warm and fuzzy, wishing a woman was coming over rather than a couple of ugly humps. If I closed my eyes, I could see Dani Thrailkill—under me, on top of me, next to me, walking toward me, dancing away, both of us having a great time, sleeping and waking, talking and fucking, talking and not-fucking, having a fine naked lunch, Marty Robbins crooning ballads in the background.

I picked up the phone, dialed Tempe information, but there was no number for her yet. There would be no phone sex tonight, which depressed me a bit. I made another Bloody Maria. The sun had gone down, and it looked like the bounty hunters were not coming over. I sat in my chair in front of the TV, gun in lap, and watched re-runs of Law and Order, Special Victims Unit—raped children, raped grannies, unrepentant disembowelers, fuck slaves imported from Thailand or Swaziland—evening fare for a country on edge and getting edgier. My head got heavy. I let my chin rest on my chest.

Dani said, You're the man I've wanted all along. I said, Would you like to go to Swaziland? She said, Let's. I said, You look like Kat, and then she was Kat, and Kat said, Have you found yourself yet, J. P. I looked into the mirror. There, I said, that's me, Judas Pipkin, Bogus Man unearthed at last, a perfect fossil or vessel. Profound, she said, then walked out the door, suitcase in hand. The slam of the door put me back in the wadi, letting go a three round burst into the conscript. His eyes, up close now, are bright with fear, then recognition. Then—I swear it, I swear it—forgiveness. I don't need your forgiveness. I've been cleared. What I'm doing is justified. But his eyes kept forgiving me anyway.

CHAPTER THIRTY

I didn't hear them come in. For big boys they didn't make the floor squeak much. I got the .357 halfway up but one of them knocked it spinning out of my hand with a baseball bat, the other clipped me with a leather sap. Interesting choice of weapons: ball bat, sap, gasoline, fists, feet.

These goons were country boys in overalls looking to put money down on a doublewide and a duck boat. One of them was big, the other, extra big. Both had blond mullet cuts with short greasy ponytails, earrings like brass gaskets, noses like flat tomatoes. Reminded me of a Wide World of Wresting tag team, Little Big and Extra Big. Their lump-muscled jaws looked like they could chew steak bones into cud. They probably had stout womenfolk with arms like hanging hams and a busload of bristle-headed kids back in Childress or Plainview or Odessa waiting to hear the good news that they'd caught their fugitive and the reward money was in the mail.

They worked me over a bit, enough to make me puke in my own blood on the living room floor. Their punches were short, weighty, methodical, practiced. Kidneys, underbelly, side of the jaw, below the heart. When I got up they put me back down. I tried to roll under the kitchen table where I might be able to regroup, but their steel-toed hobnailed boots found me before I got halfway there. They were as good with their feet as they were with their fists. Small of the back, ribs, side of the head, back of the neck, tailbone.

"You win," I said, but they didn't think they had.

I blacked out. When I came to they went at it again, methodical, slow, steady. Heels, toes, knees, fists. I noticed in a distracted way that I had pissed my pants.

Then they looked at their watches and quit, like they were working for union wages. Little Big went to my sink and poured himself a glass of water. "Damn water always warm out of the tap in El Paso?" he complained. But he drank it down then filled the glass again for his partner. They sat me down and duct-taped my wrists and ankles to the arms and legs of my chair. They carried other weapons, big old single-action Colt .45s. with beautifully scrolled barrels and handsome cherry wood grips. Very western. Extra Big tried to put the barrel of his gun into my nose. It didn't fit but he forced it. The raised front sight broke something. Fresh blood spilled down my lip. He pulled the barrel out and wiped it clean on my shirt. I felt like crying.

Little Big and Extra Big knelt down and put their faces in front of mine. Their combined breath smelled like bacon grease and Cheetos.

"Now," Extra Big said, "you tell us where the Meskin turd-ball is or we might have to hurt you some."

"Jesus, you already have hurt me," I said. I ran my tongue against my front teeth. They moved like they were on stiff hinges.

"Naw," Little Big said. "We ain't hurt you none. We was just introducin' ourselfs. All those pops were mostly pulled. I don't believe we busted a bone. You'd be dead now if we'd a gone at it a hunnert percent, pedal to the metal."

Extra Big unscrewed the cap from his can of gasoline and poured a dollop of it into my lap. "I drop a match, you gonna burn, startin' with your fambly jewels. You can sit there and watch your one-eyed boar get char-broiled, or you can give us the Meskin."

"He's dead," I said.

Little Big and Extra Big looked at each other. *"Dead?"* Extra Big said. "You *seen* him dead? You got proof? Maybe you got a Polaroid pitcher of him bein' dead? We're not about to take the word of a El Paso pimp that the boy we're after's *dead.*"

"Pimp?" I said.

"You don't have to be shy about it," Little Big said. "We know what you do for your grits. But how's a turdball pimp come to know our Meskin's dead?"

I had no idea why they were calling me a pimp but I figured it was smarter to play along. I told them about Scales, how I found him dead and naked, Hector gone. I left out the box full of money, and everything else that would complicate the picture for them. "Other bounty hunters caught up with him," I said.

"What's a pimp trackin' him for in the first place?" Extra Big said.

"Same as you," I said.

"Wait a minute," Little Big said. "You pimp *and* trace skips? You got the time to do both?"

"I lost most of my ladies to the New Orleans syndicate," I said. "The greasers moved in with better money, medical coverage, and 401k pension plans. They lost a bunch a girls after Katrina and needed to re-stock. Pretty much put me out of business."

"Why'd them other bounty hunters kill the boy?" Little Big said. "All's they had to do was turn him over to the Rangers to collect the reward money."

"They weren't in it for the reward," I said. "It was a revenge killing."

I did a song and dance about the Hans Brinker Brigade, its millionaire sponsor and his son, killed by Hector. I didn't mention the reward money the Phoenix millionaire was offering—it would only get them worked up again. I needed them to calm down.

Extra Big wasn't buying. He slapped me hard, tipping me and my chair over. I felt a loose tooth swimming in blood.

"Bull*shit!*" he said. "You think we're fucken stupid? It's *you* what's got the Meskin hid somewheres. You give him up right now or I start lightin' matches."

I heard a heavy faltering footstep on the landing outside my door.

"Here he is now," I said.

CHAPTER THIRTY-ONE

It wasn't Hector of course. It was Luther. He had the Mossberg with him and he looked terrified and crazy. His mouth was moving but he couldn't talk. He could only make strangling sounds, glottal stoppages, as though he was trying to swallow a pound of gravel. Extra Big brought up his Colt but by then Luther had already started blasting.

Extra Big got a shot off but it was a death-reflex trigger-pull and the bullet went into the ceiling making a perfect .45 caliber hole. He'd turned his head away from the blast and the back of his head in the form of red mud plastered itself on the wall. The rest of him sat down, then crumpled. A double geyser of blood from his exposed cervical arteries hosed the room. Luther fired again, this time at his own reflection in the glass doors that opened out on my balcony.

Little Big didn't take the time to raise his gun but dove instead for Luther's legs, thinking that if he got under the shotgun he could grapple it away from him, but his plan was too slow in developing and Luther put two loads of double-oughts into the small of Little Big's back at point blank range, pretty much chopping him in half.

Luther, soaked in blood, the dead arms of Little Big still clutching his thighs, made a high keening wail. He stepped out of Little Big's arms and swung the shotgun around in wobbly arcs, looking for more gunmen in the shadows. He was on a killing rampage and there was one round left in the pipe, which made the situation tricky.

His blood-freckled face was distorted, registering several emotions in quick succession—fear, hate, exultation, remorse, glee. His teeth were chattering and he pointed the shotgun in my general direction. I was still sideways on the floor and taped to the chair. I spit the floating tooth out of my mouth so I could talk clearly. He fired at an apparition over my head. He reached into his pocket and reloaded the Mossberg, then raised it to his shoulder and squinted into the shadows. He fired it again. I felt the compressed wind of the shot blow past my ear like a flight of supersonic hornets.

"Jesus, Luther!" I said. "They're dead! Don't fucking shoot me too!"

He gradually calmed down. He sat on the sofa and laid the shotgun across his lap. His pulse was visible in his fleshy neck.

"You got any beer?" he said.

"Fridge. Help yourself. Put the gun down first."

"God I'm thirsty. I've never been so thirsty. Not even in Riyadh where 125 degrees is normal. I never had to shoot anyone but I was always thirsty."

He put the gun on the floor and staggered to the fridge. He opened a can of Tecate in the kitchen and chugged it down. Then he opened another one and carried it back to the sofa. He looked at me for the first time since crashing the party. "What are you doing down there, J. P.? Get up."

"I can't. I'm tied to this fucking chair. Get a knife from the kitchen. You need to cut me loose."

He went back into the kitchen and returned with a six-inch boning knife. His hand was shaking badly. "Christ, be careful with that, Luther. I keep my knives honed."

"You're a mess, J. P. I told you they were coming. How come you let them get to you?"

I had no answer to that.

Luther freed me from the chair. I hurt too much to stand. I crawled to the sofa and climbed into it.

"You look like shit, J. P.," he said. "Your nose looks bad. I'm going to take you to the Columbia emergency room."

"Not yet. The cops are almost here." I heard sirens in the not too far distance. Everyone in the apartment building and a few people across the street had probably called 911. The Mossberg has a mighty roar. "We'll need to talk to them about this. Whatever you do, Luther, don't lie. Tell it exactly the way it happened."

"Cops? Oh shit, oh shit. You think they'll haul me in? I shot those crackers in self-defense, didn't I? Does that sound like a lie? I mean shit, J. P., they were about to waste you. What was I supposed to do, *reason* with them? Read passages from the Gospels? Do unto others as you would have them do unto you? Kiss your neighbor's ass lest he stick his nine-iron up yours? That big bastard was about to blow holes into me."

"Your timing was pretty amazing, Luther. How did you happen to come by just then? The cops will ask you that."

"I *didn't* come by just then. I've been sitting out front in my car for the last hour or so. I felt bad about sending them here. But I needed to build up my nerve. I almost drove back to Kern."

He was waiting for me to say something appreciative. "You could have come ten minutes earlier, but I'm glad you didn't go home. It took balls, Luther. What you did."

"Yes it did, didn't it?" he mused. "It sure as hell did."

He was still running on uncut adrenaline. His hands shook, and so did his legs. He couldn't keep them still. The heel of his right shoe drummed the floor. His face twisted itself into sudden smirks and smiles and pouts. That would be his medications working. Tardive dyskinesis, motoring the meat. I was surprised that he was able to blow away Little Big and Extra Big while medicated. After Luther's performance—which *did* take balls—I would never be surprised very much by anything again.

He suddenly vomited. When he finished he began to laugh. It started as a childish giggle and degenerated into a madhouse cackle.

"I'm *glad* I did it, J. P.," he said when he was able to control himself again. "These goons hurt the Jesus out of me, and now out of you. Cretins like that have been hurting people all their lives since kindergarten. They *needed* killing. Jesus would have killed them with a fire ax. I feel like killing them again." He picked up the shotgun and held it close to his chest like a child holding a favorite doll.

"Don't, Luther. Killing them again would be hard to explain to the cops."

He gradually came back to planet earth. He got another beer and drank it down in one long pull. He belched. His eyes now looked sleepy and almost sane, the warrior intensity gone.

I said, "Luther, how come you told them I was a pimp?"

"It just popped out. Didn't know what I was saying, I was so damned scared they were going to pour gas on my head."

"I fell into the role pretty easily," I said. "Maybe I was cut out for it."

He looked at me strangely, his tongue protruding and withdrawing beyond his control. He seemed to be tasting the air.

"I'm kidding, Luther," I said.

"It didn't sound like kidding."

"See what I mean?"

Just then Extra Big farted, a terminal release of methane. We both jumped. Luther jerked the shotgun up and blew a hole in the kitchen wall.

CHAPTER THIRTY-TWO

The first wave of cops didn't talk to us. They cuffed us and sat us down in separate squad cars. Other black-and-whites arrived, sirens chirping. The streets were filling up with the curious. A plainclothes cop got into the front seat of my car.

"Things got pretty western in there," he said. "Party take a bad turn?"

I recognized him. He was tall, wiry, had a narrow face, and was prematurely gray. His small ears grew close to his head. He looked built for speed. Raymond Thrailkill.

"Hey Raymond," I said

He looked at me, surprised and annoyed. "I *know* you?" he said.

"J. P. Morgan. I quit the force your rookie year."

It took him a few seconds to recognize me. "Shit, J. P. fucking Morgan. You've munched a few gorditas since then. You used to be Slim Jim Morgan, as I remember. Jesus, you look like you walked into a propeller. We ought to get you to the ER."

"My thoughts exactly."

"But fill me in first, okay? I figure this was a meet of some kind and the bad boys got upset."

"It was and they did."

I gave it all to him—Hector, Scales, Carla, Luther, the bounty hunters, the Hans Brinker Brigade. I left out the stash from Iraq. I didn't want Carla to go to federal prison. The money would get taken care of one way or another.

"Self-defense, then," he said. "The bounty hunters were about to roast your chestnuts when your friend just happened to drop in with the jungle gun. This is how it went?"

"I gave the shotgun to Luther several days ago, after those humps kicked the shit out of him. I'm damn glad I did."

"That short barrel's illegal by four inches," he said. "Class A felony, I believe, under the Texas penal code forty-six oh five."

"I wouldn't be here talking to you, Raymond, without the damn thing."

"The hardware goes to forensics and then the City Attorney will decide what to do about it. Not my call, you understand."

"Sure thing, Ray. Do it right."

He scribbled something in a small notebook. He got out of the car, said something to a uniform, then got back in. "Highway Patrol found the dead nudist in the rest stop yesterday morning," he said, "but couldn't ID him. Prints not in anyone's data base. Thanks for clearing it up."

"I'm a good citizen. I even feel guilty for not voting."

"No one's going to charge you or your friend, unless they find something they're not seeing right now. Looks like self-defense will probably hold up. Those shit-kickers had a rep. They go after skips with rocks and clubs. Fugitive retrieval was just an excuse to bust people up. The money was a perk. No one in Texas law enforcement is going to be unhappy they're gone. Someone from the CA's office will want your statement before the inquest but I wouldn't sweat it. You might have to talk to a grand jury but no way you or your friend will be indicted."

He got out, opened the back door and uncuffed me.

I thought I'd get it out of the way: "I dated your ex, Ray," I said. "She's a fine lady. I'm sorry it went sour between you two."

His eyes got big. There was an adrenaline surge behind them. "What the fuck are you talking about?"

I saw my mistake. Jesus, I'd *believed* her. I guess Dani figured it would be easier for me and maybe more enjoyable for her if I thought she was unattached. I'd violated the single man's prime directive again. This time it wasn't my fault, but the difference was academic.

"She said you were separated, Ray. Hell, it was just a lunch date. I see her at Gold's two, three times a week."

He studied my face with an intensity that could make a corpse sweat. "We *are* separated," he said, "but not because we want to be. Maybe you just heard what you wanted to hear."

"It wasn't like that at all, Ray."

"Innocent, huh?"

"Innocent enough."

He coughed out a small humorless laugh and lit a cigarette. "We're moving to Phoenix," he said. "Dani went there first to get us a place to live. I've been offered a precinct command with the Phoenix PD. They recruited outside the department, which means a lot of prima donnas are going to be royally pissed at me when I get there, but fuck them. Fluency in street Spanish gave me bumping privileges. Every cop in the West will need to have a working knowledge of español before long. The pay is nearly double what I get now. Benefits you would not fucking believe."

He was agitated and talking compulsively, like a man trying to explain why he should be happy when he wasn't. His eyes raked my face, looking for the lie. "Just lunch, huh?" he said.

"At Uncle Bao's—the Mandarin place on North Mesa—after working out. Nothing else, swear to God, vato."

"Knock off the vato shit. We're not goddamned cholos."

"All right, Ray," I said.

"I deal with the baggy pants hair-netted taggers every fucking day, you know?"

"Sure. I'm sorry. I understand, Ray."

His face looked drawn—too much overtime, too much ambition, too much wife. All of it made him seem older than he
was. So worn out and preoccupied he probably had to main-
line Viagra just to raise a floppy. She no doubt milked his prostate just to get his attention.

"She's so damn hot," he said. "Before she got the dispatcher job, she came downtown to Central Command to check
the place out. Every uniform in the shop flexed his pecs and
sucked in his gut. Shit, even the old farts stood around like
movie cops. Al Pacino talking to Russell Crowe talking to Antonio fucking Banderas. She thought that was just cute as hell.
She swings her tight ass and perky little tits through a squad
room, the woodies stand up and salute."

"You're a lucky man, Ray," I said. "But it was just lunch,
nothing more. We talked physical fitness. She's very big on
beta carotene and vitamin D supplements."

I was hurting too bad to give a shit if he believed me or not.
He had good reason not to, but that was his problem, not mine.

"I think I got a couple of cracked ribs, Ray. My nose is fucked
up too. How about taking me to the Columbia ER?"

"Let me get Jungle Jim's story first."

I looked into the other black-and-white. Jungle Jim was being interviewed by another plainclothes cop. *Don't fucking lie,
Luther.* But then, he *was* a fiction writer, wasn't he?

CHAPTER THIRTY-THREE

The apartment manager said the insurance company would cover the clean-up job, but the physical damage to the apartment was major and the repair work would take a few weeks. Luther offered me one of the seven bedrooms in his house.

I had two cracked ribs, a chipped orbital bone, one tooth gone and three others loose, a grade-one concussion, and a swollen but unbroken nose. A buckshot pellet was removed from my left calf. Shotguns are called scatterguns for a reason. The term fits the spray pattern of the chopped twelve gauge semi-automatic shotguns wielded by crazed giants who are somewhat scattered themselves.

The left side of my face was a shade of purple dappled with lighter shades of green. The ER people taped me up, gave me a vial of Lortab and a prescription for more. I tossed both the prescription and the Lortabs, a B-list painkiller, first chance I got. Luther had better stuff in his medicine cabinet.

I took Luther up on his offer. I crawled into a king-size bed covered with afghans and jumbo pillows and slept. Luther woke me up every two hours during the first twelve hours to make sure I hadn't slipped into a coma. Doctor's orders. After that, Luther, to his credit, left me alone. He also kept the Wagner down to a dull roar. Or he played excerpts from Tristan and Isolde, soothing music that rises and falls gradually like ocean swells. Wagner must have been on laudanum when he wrote that tranquil piece.

It was a big, second-floor room, sparsely furnished—bed, dresser, night table—but the walls were packed with art work that found its way into my dreams. Oil paintings of corpulent female nudes having afternoon tea wearing pillbox hats and patent leather high heel shoes; water colors of stark, skeletal men wearing only neckties and golf shoes; woodcuts of expressionless geriatrics using mechanical sex aids on each other; landscapes populated by corpse-eating rodents under cloudless crimson skies. These pieces had to be Luther's. They were lurid and sensational and congratulated their owner on his bold avant-garde tastes. Just the sort of thing Luther would buy to boost his image as a cutting-edge man of letters.

There was some Mexican work, too, religious in content, but Aztec or Toltec or Zapotec in spirit. Gourds sprouting infants and snakes, an Indian Mother of God holding the sun in one hand, the moon in the other, green eel with feathered wings swimming out of her navel. The sun in her right hand, cool as an apple; the moon, a dark ball of coagulated blood, in her left. Taken together, the pictures had the effect of the Hieronymous Bosch triptych, *The Garden of Earthly Delights*—Bosch's nutty rendering of a picnic in hell.

My bruised brain absorbed these images and delivered them to my dreams. The dreams felt like hard work. I woke from them sweating and bone weary, as if I had walked all night in my sleep carrying a hod full of bricks. I ached from the effort.

The dreams made no narrative sense. They were unscrolling spools of images, coming in no particular order. In one dream

I was back in the wadi, thumbing my M-16 to full auto, the shepherd holding a crook morphing into a Hammurabi elite holding an AK.

I smelled the heavy stink of the burning bodies in the Iraqi personnel carrier, human grease crackling. *Light him up, Morgan!* Sergeant Apostoli said. *Light the dumb buttfuck up!*

"You missed your appointment with Fernando Peralta," his disembodied voice said. "He contacted the Nazi woman from Adult Protective on your behalf. He said he's got the ball rolling, whatever that means. He said you'd understand."

It wasn't sergeant Apostoli speaking outside of the dream, it was Luther. He'd bought a pair of wireless intercoms, one for my night table, and one that he carried with him. If I needed anything I was to call him. He called me first.

"Shit," I said. "Is he on the line now?"

"You need to call him back in fifteen minutes. Are you up for it?"

"What time is it?"

"It's almost three. Come have some lunch."

"What day is it?"

"Friday the thirteenth."

"How long have I been sleeping?"

"What is this, Twenty Questions?"

"How long?"

"Long. A couple of days. Maybe three. I've been busy. I'm busy now. Look, I don't like talking on this contraption. Come down, have something to eat."

Voices in the background, picked up by the intercom, sounded like the gabble of arguing chimps. "I'll come down in a minute," I said.

"No need to stress out, bro. Lelanie can bring you a phone."

"I need to get dressed," I said. "I need to walk. What's for lunch?"

"We all had pizza delivered. There's plenty left. The fridge is loaded with cold cuts, too. That's about all I eat now that I've officially re-entered bachelordom."

"We all?"

"Artistas del Paso, bro. I told you I was going to start an art colony."

"Why are you calling me bro, Luther?"

"That's what we are, my man. We bonded in combat. *What?*—you don't feel the ties of brotherhood?"

What I felt were the loosening ties of sanity. I put the intercom down and got dressed. I felt weightless but still toyed with by gravity. I alternately floated and lurched down the long hallway and the staircase that led to the living room.

The strangeness of dreams kept the physical world at arm's length. I knew it was a temporary sensation, but there were no guarantees. A neurologist had talked about broken synapses, warned of *dementia pugilistica*—more knocks on the head could make me permanently punch drunk. I gripped the banister with both hands and took the steps like a toddler, one foot at a time.

Luther was in his recliner, toking on a blunt. Lelanie Loftsgarten was sitting on the floor next to him, a fat green bong between her knees. A dozen or so men and women sat around the room, some smoking, some holding drinks, all of them looking grimly artistic. Manuscript papers were scattered between them. Except for the booze and dope, it looked more like an AA meeting than an art colony.

I went into the kitchen and called Fernie Peralta. We rescheduled our meeting for 10:00 a.m. Monday. He said he'd pacified Pilar Mellado. And the Public Fiduciary had agreed to put the confiscation of Velma's assets on hold.

I found a jar of horseradish mustard and a brick of old cheddar in the fridge, along with a can of Lone Star. I cut the green measles off the cheese and made myself a sturdy sandwich. Gretchen, Luther's thirty-pound cat, jumped into my lap and sniffed the edges of my plate. Her nose bumped a gob of the hot mustard and she jerked her head back and looked at me as if I was an idiot for putting dangerous toxins on perfectly good food.

"Has the big bad pothead been feeding you, kitty?" I said.

Gretchen made a long plaintive yowl. I took a piece of cheese from my sandwich, licked off the horseradish, and Gretchen took it to the floor.

I popped open another Lone Star and headed back to my second floor refuge. I'd thought I'd be able to go out, take a drive to the Upper Valley, get back in touch with my own reality, but I knew now that I was still too unstable to manage it.

I got to my room and shut the door against the drone of the somber artistas. I undressed and fell into bed and back into dream.

He was there, waiting. His filmy dead eyes fixed on me as I let go the second three-round burst. Dead, he raised his arms and pointed to his hemorrhaging ears. The ethylene oxide bomb dropped behind the kill-me berm by an F-15 had blown out his eardrums. He never heard my bad Arabic command to lay down his AK. He heard only the deep eclipsing chime of total deafness.

CHAPTER THIRTY-FOUR

The hot humid night didn't seem as though it was going to end. I slept in sweaty intervals. Each time I woke I thought it was morning at last but only minutes had passed.

I wandered around the house. Luther had never installed air conditioning in the old mansion. The air was dense. Heat lightning lit the windows. My underwear stuck to my skin like second skin.

Luther and Lelanie talked through the night. No matter where I wandered, I heard them. They talked in bed and they talked out of bed. They talked while snacking in the kitchen. They followed each other into the bathroom and continued talking while one or the other peed. They took a bath together and their talking voices were amplified by porcelain and tile.

I heard them and sometimes I saw them. It wasn't pretty. Lelanie and Luther in the dining room, Luther transported, not by Lelanie's energetic fellatio, but by his own voice as he described his visionary ideas.

In the bedroom next to mine, Luther recited passages from *Gotterdammerung Now* as the bedsprings moaned like a rusty teeter totter. When the teeter totter stopped, and after the yelps and grunts died away, Luther quizzed Lelanie, testing her grasp of his innovated methods.

"The new architectonics will knit the real and abstract together like chain mail!" he said.

"Oh *you!*" Lelanie said.

"A bildungsroman carried to the vanishing point of death and transfiguration. Who has accomplished this?"

"My big boy!" Lelanie said.

"Though I dip into the chaos from time to time, I always come back to the surface with the gold!"

"Genius stud-puppy!" Lelanie said.

It struck me that this was the woman Luther should have married: Lelanie, the compliant hedonist. Not Carla, the righteous crusader.

They got up and scampered downstairs toward the kitchen for more snacks. The fridge door opened and closed, opened and closed.

I finally fell asleep for more than a few minutes, but there was no rest in it.

The sun, reliable as ever, came up. It pressed against the windows of my room with the red heat of a forge.

Somewhere a mocking bird ran through its borrowed repertoire, as if every note was original with him.

In the next bedroom, Luther and Lelanie, finally exhausted, snored in two-part harmony.

It was a good day to move out.

CHAPTER THIRTY-FIVE

I took a room at the Las Palmas Inn on east Alameda, an old but decent motel with an L-shaped pool. It was cheap and remote. I left a message on Fernie Peralta's answering machine, telling him where I was. I called Velma and tried to explain to her what was going to happen and why there was no alternative, but she would have no part of it.

"I cannot talk about this," she said.

"What *can* you talk about?"

"Rhubarb pie," she said. Her evasions involved right-angle turns at full throttle. I tagged along.

"Rhubarb pie," I said.

"When you were little you wouldn't eat my rhubarb pie," she said. "You thought rhubarb was a sour word. Pie made from a sour word had to be sour pie. You insisted on this. You were always sensitive to the sound of words, not their meanings. I blame myself. I taught you to be well-spoken and to respect the language. Language is a precious gift. No one seems to realize

that these days. Language has made the human race conscious
of itself. And has therefore given us a conscience. In the beginning there was the Word. The Word told us how to distinguish
one thing from another as well as right from wrong. Rhubarb,
the *word*, brought bile to your mouth."

"But when I finally did eat rhubarb pie, I thought it was the
best pie ever. Especially when you included strawberries and
served it with ice cream on top."

"Strawberries aren't in season," she said.

"There's a season for everything, Mom," I said.

We were suddenly talking in code, but I'm not sure she realized it.

"You can have strawberries every day at El Descanso. Fernie
Peralta is going to call you. He's good people, Mom. It's time
to do this."

"Time is out of joint," she said.

"Just listen to what he has to say, okay?"

She hung up.

I went for a swim. I didn't have trunks but my boxers were
army green and decent enough even when wet. The exercise
was painful, but also mending.

By the next morning I felt reasonably human. I drove out
to UTEP. It was Sunday, and I'd have the campus to myself.
I needed to be in Bhutan for a while, in the rarefied air of the
West Texas Himalayas, to clarify my thinking.

I parked in the south campus parking lot and climbed the
hill to Old Main, the building that was most like a Buddhist
dzong. A soft breeze moved the shrubs in a park-like setting. I
sat on a bench and let the place work its spell on me. I needed
to review the events of the past week from a clear perspective.

Down the hill one of the visiting monks approached Worrell Hall. A gust of wind caught his saffron robe and for a moment I thought he was going to fall. His robe billowed, but instead of falling he seemed to float like a huge butterfly toward
the front doors.

"Lovely little campus, don't you agree, Mr. Morgan?"

The Texas Ranger who had visited Luther was standing behind me. I hadn't heard a leaf or twig crunch under his shoes. For a big man, Robert T. Eggers was light on his feet. He sat next to me, took off his Stetson.

"You waiting for her to show up?" he said.

"Excuse me?"

"I refer to Mrs. Penrose."

"No," I said. "It's Sunday."

"Some of the professors come around on Sunday. You have an idea where she is?"

"Why would I?"

"Is that a 'no'?"

"You could take it that way."

"You're no doubt familiar with the term 'obstruction of justice'? It's an old legal standard and a moderately useful instrument of prosecution."

"You want my opinion? I think Hector Martinez is dead. It's over and done with. There's no need to harass the woman."

"Say he *is* dead. The woman is still going to be charged with aiding and abetting a fugitive. Or maybe you think our laws regarding capital crimes should be applied selectively."

"I can't help you, officer. I think Martinez is feeding the ants somewhere in the desert. You should direct your inquiries to the Hans Brinker Brigade."

"Thanks for your advice. But I think we'll arrest the woman first. We get her, we get Martinez, whole or boned-out by red ants. The so-called Hans Brinker Brigade may be of some interest to students of lunatic behavior, but they are of no interest to us so long as they don't start killing people."

Robert T. Eggers hoisted himself off the bench. "You might want to consider your own situation, Mr. Morgan. Seems like you could bear some of the weight before all this is put to bed." He looked into the bowl of his Stetson for a long moment, then adjusted it on his head. He looked up at the sky. "Going to be a hot one today," he said amiably, then left as quietly as he came.

I walked down the hill to Worrell Hall. The front door was unlocked, but the front office was closed. I went up the stairs to the third floor and made my way down the dark hall to Carla's office. It was locked, but I had my picks with me. Now that I was familiar with the mechanism it took me less than half a minute to move the pins.

The office looked the same. I opened the file drawer and went through the papers I'd already looked at. The file was marked "The Aims and Methods of the HBB" was of more interest to me now than the first time I looked at it. I sat down at her desk and read. I read for half an hour.

CHAPTER THIRTY-SIX

Carla was arrested Monday morning. She met her nine o'clock class, which was either an act of courage or naiveté or both. Probably both. Halfway through her lecture the cops barged in and cuffed her. I don't know what she was thinking. Maybe she thought that she had the moral high ground and couldn't be touched. Her cause was her shield—a delusion the righteous often fall for.

They took her to the detention facility on east Overland, but she wasn't charged with a crime. Instead, the City Attorney got a judge to issue a Material Witness order, which meant they could hold her more or less indefinitely without charging her with a crime.

I called Fernie Peralta and explained the situation to him, leaving out some details he didn't need to know. Fernie wasn't a criminal lawyer but he was a *compa*, a buddy, of the City Attorney. Their wives were good friends too, and they often had dinner at each other's house. Fernie agreed to talk to Carla but warned me there wasn't much anyone could do. A Material Witness order had teeth. He wasn't going to be able to negotiate a Get Out of Jail Free card for her. She'd have a crib in the city lock-up until the Texas Rangers got what they wanted. I asked Fernie to get me on the Approved Visitors list. I needed to talk to her about something I read in her HBB file.

I went to see her on Wednesday morning. She looked happy in her orange jump suit, even thrilled, as if imprisonment proved everything she believed in was true.

"If Hector's alive," I said, "he's probably in Scottsdale, at the Selbiades estate."

We spoke through telephones. A thick wall of Plexiglas separated us.

"No," she said. "He's in Mexico City. He called me."

"He *called* you?"

"On my cell. Monday morning, before I was arrested."

She winked, then mouthed the word *Juárez* plainly enough so that I could read her lips. The phone line we were using was probably being monitored. She was feeding bullshit to the monitor.

Her lips formed the words *Hotel Maria Bonita in Juárez.*

"Mexico City?" I said, going along with the ploy.

"Yes. He's safe in Mexico City."

Get the money, she mouthed. *Bring it to him.*

I shrugged. *Where is it?*

Union Station Depot. Key in my office. Under floor lamp.

I didn't have to form the words. My eyes said it all: *What kind of fucking idiot do you take me for?*

The best kind, her smile said.

She kept smiling. It was the confident smile of someone who knew who she was dealing with. She put her hand on the Plexiglas wall that separated us. "Take what you need," she said, using the telephone again. "You've earned it, J. P. I've seen Luther. He told me what happened to you. I feel responsible. I'm sorry."

I changed the subject. "Selbiades, according to your research paper, is a dermatologist for the rich and the almost-rich. He's a major whacko. There's a small prison on his estate—an underground dungeon, for Chrissakes. He hires illegals to pick his apricots and pears then he has them tortured. He sends them back to Mexico with their whip cuts still bleeding so they can spread the word to other would-be illegals about working conditions in Arizona."

"And he gets away with it," she said, "because he's locked into the political power grid. He's a major contributor to campaign funds, both parties. Millions every year. No one fucks with Dr. Stefan Selbiades—who happens to be an immigrant himself. The irony would be funny if it weren't so goddamn awful."

"Awful people do awful things."

"And good people sometimes stand by and watch."

Which, she didn't have to add, makes them accomplices. The *truly* good fight back. There were no gray areas in her worldview. Come the revolution, I'd be hanged for loitering while the mobs went after each other with sticks and stones.

I changed the subject. "They treating you all right here?" I said.

"I'm an honored guest. They even bring me cookies and dulces. The matrons call me la profesora. They think I'm some kind of celebrity saint. No one treats me like a common criminal."

She seemed vaguely disappointed. What kind of martyr gets cookies and dulces? Where were the whips and chains? The daily body cavity searches, the water torture, the high voltage wires clipped to the genitalia?

"So you don't need me to break you out?" I said. I pressed my hand on the Plexiglas opposite hers.

She smiled. "Hell, I almost feel at home in here. Maybe I was meant for prison. How's Luther doing? I can't imagine him shooting people."

"He might be packing a time bomb that will blow up in his face some day, but as of now he's the man of the hour. Just ask him. The City Attorney's office called the shootings justified. The NRA will probably draft him for their new poster boy."

"Who's this girlfriend of his?"

"Lelanie Loftsgarten. A poet."

"Just what he needs," she said. "I bet she has big tits."

"I haven't noticed."

"Right. Did you notice if she had arms and legs?"

"Let me think. Yes, I believe she did."

"The jolly mating dance goes on."

"No end in sight, it seems."

"I was only twenty-one when I met Luther," she said. "I didn't fall for his good looks—and he had them to spare back then—a young Robert Redford with tics and a lot of attitude. He was an anti-war activist when civil protest had gone out of style. Luther was a hero in my eyes. I thought he was a man who would stand up for a cause. I realized later that he hated the military not on principle but for purely personal reasons. He personalized everything, which led to, or at least aggravated, his mental problems. He didn't give a damn about war or politics. Funny, how you get blindsided when you tie yourself to someone you think you know but don't."

"My motto. I should have it tattooed on my forehead," I said.

"Probably everyone should."

Our conversation seemed over. I moved to hang up the phone, but she stopped me.

"Wait, J. P. I've got another favor to ask of you," she said.

The sucker lights flashed again. I should have walked out. I didn't.

"Don't look so spooked," she said. "It's nothing dramatic. I need some things from the house, that's all. Female things. You don't mind, do you? I don't like the brand of sanitary napkins they give you here. I need panty liners, too."

I thought I heard a burst of laughter from somewhere close by.

Look behind the fat naked ladies, her lips said.

"No problema," I said.

CHAPTER THIRTY-SEVEN

F at naked ladies? Had to be the painting hanging in Luther's guest bedroom. I called him, told him I was coming over.

"I'd rather you wouldn't just now," he said.

"What's the problem?"

"I'm unwell."

"You're sick?"

"Not sick. Unwell. There's a difference."

"What happened, Luther?"

"Nothing happened. Why does something always have to happen? Hasn't enough happened? Maybe something *hasn't* happened. There's a world of possibilities, J. P. Try to imagine it."

"I left something in my room."

"Okay. Come over. But don't expect to stay." I stopped at the university first to retrieve the locker key from Carla's office. I didn't have to pick her office lock this time. The door was ajar.

A janitor was inside, vacuuming her carpet. I waited until he was finished then went in. He didn't like that. He frowned at me. It was his job to clean the office, then leave the door locked when he left. He wasn't authorized to let anyone in.

"Está bien," I assured him. "Soy el esposo de la profesora Penrose."

Whether he bought it or not was hard to tell. The look on his face said, *You don't look like the husband of a professor*, then softened to, *but then what's one of them supposed to look like?* My bruised and swollen face was probably responsible for arousing his suspicion.

"Mi cara fea?" I said—my ugly face? "Un poquito accidente." I rammed my fists together suggesting a collision. He nodded vigorously. He'd been in a car wreck or two.

I laughed—a little fender bender—nothing to us hombres. He could tell it was no poquito fender bender but he appreciated the macho stance. It was understood: Getting a busted face was a small thing for a man to endure. No importa. The matter was settled: I had proven my legitimacy, one man to another. I went into the office, closed the door. The locker key, as she said it would be, was under the floor lamp.

LELANIE ANSWERED THE DOOR at Luther's. "He's unwell," she said. She was wearing a short red kimono, nothing underneath. She had just put it on because she was still fiddling with the sash. Her small feet were bare, the toenails painted glossy black.

"He's sick?"

"No. Unwell. It's not the same thing."

"So I've heard."

"Poor baby looks so lost. I try not to cry when I go into the solarium, but the sight of him makes me weepy."

"What's he doing in the solarium? It's got to be a hundred ten out there today."

"He's meditating."

"Luther doesn't meditate. He medicates."

"That is *not* funny. In fact it's very insensitive. And you claim to be his friend."

I went into the solarium, a room of many glass panes connected to the kitchen. Luther was sitting naked in a canvas chair. Tropical plants with wide obscene flowers grew along the glass walls in deep terra cotta planters. The flowers emitted a prurient scent that ate its way into your brain. A haze of humidity made the foul air spongy. Sweat slid off Luther's broad pink back in rivulets.

"You opening a nudist colony, too?" I said.

Luther scowled at me over his reading glasses. He held a legal pad in his lap and a felt-tipped pen in his hand. The legal pad was covered with scrawls. It looked as if he'd dipped a hundred ants in black ink and let them crawl around on the yellow paper.

"That's unreadable, Luther," I said.

"To you. I wrote this chapter, *Richard Takes Tea With Hitler*, in the German. I've decided the novel of the future should be multi-lingual. Like it or not, we're moving toward one world. A God-awful thought, but inevitable. The isolated self-sufficient nation-state is history. The New World Order is here. The USA is history. It's only a matter of time before people realize it."

"Tea with Hitler? Won't that offend a lot of people?"

"We're far enough away in time to treat the man like an ordinary if somewhat dysfunctional personality."

"*Some*what dysfunctional?"

"Despotism is not a genetic anomaly. Anyone could be Hitler, given the right provocations. Anyone—you, me, Joe Blow. Listen to this."

Luther clutched his chest dramatically. "'Ich habe ein schwaches Herz, mein Führer!' Wagner says. See, Wagner was something of a hypochondriac, as was Hitler. He thought he had heart trouble. These are bunk buddies, commiserating."

"Bunk buddies?"

"I intend to use Sanskrit as well. Hitler was a mystic, you know. The Sanskrit 'su' and 'asti,' suggesting complete resignation to natural impulse, from the prehistoric su-asti-ka or swastika. It's anti-civilization in spirit. There is a su and asti aspect to Wagner's music as well."

"Didn't Wagner die before Hitler was born?"

"I wouldn't expect you to understand."

"What's to understand?"

Luther's face was red as a brick. His curly hair was matted with sweat. He re-lit a blunt and sucked uncarburated smoke into his bottomless lungs. "I'm not going to explain the concept of subjective differentials to you," he wheezed, "or the cohesive interweaving of disparate time fractals. My novel is not time dependent, you see."

"My loss," I said.

"More so than you realize," he said.

"I don't think Wagner would have called Hitler mein Führer."

"The su and asti elements, apparent in the psychology of both men, suggest otherwise."

"You're way over my head, Luther."

"I know," he said.

I went back into the kitchen and took a beer out of his fridge. Lelanie was sitting at the kitchen table, nibbling from a plate of cold cuts and deviled eggs. She didn't look at me as I passed through. I'd ceased to exist in her eyes. I thought I could find a way to live with that.

I went up to my second floor bedroom. I took down the picture of the naked ladies at tea. There was an unsealed manila envelope taped to the brown paper backing. I opened it.

A handwritten note and a collection of photographs fell out of the envelope. The scrawled note said, "Dr. Stefan Selbiades who made his millions in red-rock country real estate is now involved with anti-immigrant extremist groups in Europe. See photos."

I thumbed through the snapshots. Some were of professional quality, others looked like they were taken by amateurs with throw-away cameras. In one high-quality photo there were two men—an elegant, white-haired man shaking hands with a man in a dark double-breasted suit and black fedora who looked like he'd stepped out of 1933. A note on the back of the photo said, "Dr. Selbiades meeting with Fritz Stoudemire, supporter of the Austrian ultra-nationalist, Jorg Haider." Other photos showed Selbiades (the white-haired man) talking to members of Britain's "Combat 18," Belgium's "Flemish Militant Order," and "The National Front of France," all—according to Carla's notes—hard-right anti-immigration groups willing to use violence against foreigners.

"Still gathering information," the note went on, "but in the event that I can no longer conduct my research for whatever reason, please get this material to FBI field office agents Lyle Strimpley and DeWalt Frederickson. Selbiades has modeled his Hans Brinker Brigade along the lines of the more violent of these European ultra-nationalistic organizations.

"Selbiades' long-term aim is to get the US Government involved militarily. He'd like nothing better than to see half a million US troops guarding the border from San Ysidro to Brownsville. If that happens, a small incident could spark a major war. Selbiades of course intends to provide as many incidents as it takes.

"Follow the money. I'm sure he makes substantial contributions to some or all of the European groups. An international conspiracy of this scope should interest the FBI as well as the State Department."

I re-taped the envelope to the backing of the naked ladies, and hung the painting back on the wall.

I went back downstairs. Luther had come out of the solarium. He had his legal pad with him and was now wearing flowered Bermuda shorts and running shoes.

"Listen to this, J. P.," he said. "I'll translate as I read from the German. 'Adolf and Richard, comfortably seated before the roaring fireplace in Hitler's Berchtesgaden retreat, spoke in low, yet excited, tones. "I need something," Adolf said. "A little…ah…pick-me-up, if you understand me, Richard." Just then, as if on cue, Dr. Theodore Morell entered the room, cautious as shadows, and, after asking Wagner and Hitler to drop their pants, injected the buttocks of both men with the cleverly misnamed Vitamultin—a powerful methamphetamine—then gave them a vitamin cocktail to drink.'"

"I don't mean to be a nag, Luther," I said, "but I still don't see how you can put Hitler and Wagner in the same room together, or the same book for that matter."

"I know this is a stretch for you, J.P, but try to understand. Literature is not literature if it is not free to present ideas without regard to conventional narrative constraint, or any other type of restraint. I am attempting to transcend and transform the expected. Hitler, for example, will ask Wagner to compose a new anthem for the Third Reich—not to replace Deutschland Uber Alles, but to augment and enhance it with symphonic effects. Wagner will agree to this."

"I get it now," I said. "Hitler's channeling Wagner."

"No he isn't." He turned a page and began to read again: "Adolf gave some oval pills to Richard. 'These are called Pervitin,' the Führer said. 'They will stimulate your creative longings. I planned the invasion of Russia after taking several of these.' Hitler picked up a bayonet and regarded it fondly. 'What is in these pills?' Wagner asked. 'Ask not, my dear Richard, what is in the pills,' Hitler said, making playful stabs at Wagner's stomach with the bayonet. 'Know only that it sets the mind on fire! You will fall in love with my little oval pills!'"

Luther waited for me to acknowledge his genius.

"Terrific," I said. "Wagner a meth head. Makes sense." I changed the subject. "Want to go for a ride? If you're finished meditating, I mean."

"Yes. I'm unwell. But I think it's because I've been housebound since the...episode. Who are we going to kill today?"

"No one, I hope."

Lelanie, who'd been hanging back, stepped close to Luther. "Don't go with him, Luther baby. He's insensitive to your condition."

"I know that, sweetheart," Luther said. "That's why I value his friendship."

Lelanie stamped her small foot angrily. "That makes no sense at all, sugar cakes!" she said.

Luther slipped his hand under her kimono and kissed her. "You go upstairs and crawl into bed. Before you know it, sugar cakes will be back."

"Sugar cakes," I said when we were in my car.

"Oral fixation," Luther said. "She thinks of me in terms of food. She's a latent cannibal, J. P."

"She's probably got a lot of su and asti," I said.

"Endless hunger," Luther said, grinning lewdly.

CHAPTER THIRTY-EIGHT

I didn't stop at the Union Depot. No way was I going to carry a box with half a million dollars in it across the border. If Hector was actually in Juárez we could make a safer arrangement to transfer the money.

I headed for the Bridge of the Americas that crosses over the Rio Grande into the eastside of Juárez. The Maria Bonita hotel was on Avenida San Lorenzo. I found it after making half a dozen wrong turns; at one point I was heading *back* to the border.

"You want to let me know where we're going?" Luther said.

"There's a chance Hector Martinez is here."

"Do I get to twist his head off and shove it up his ass?"

"He didn't take Carla from you, Luther. Carla took *him*."

"Takes two to tango, J. P. But never mind who took who. I've got my pride to consider. The man is bedding my wife. How do you think that makes me look?"

"It's an image thing with you?"

"It's always an image thing. Unfortunately we live in a fish-bowl of images. There's no escaping it. Potential humiliation lies around every corner. The cuckold, my friend, is society's clownfish."

"So Lelanie's purpose in life is to re-build your image?"

"She also writes her little poems and plays a mean game of Scrabble, if you don't mind creative spelling."

"You're a beautiful human being, Luther."

I reached into the glove compartment and took out the .357. Luther looked at me as if I'd lost my mind. "You get caught with that, they'll put you in Cereso and throw away the keys."

"I don't intend to wave it around."

"What *do* you intend?"

"When I figure it out you'll be first to know."

We went into the hotel. The desk clerk looked a little confused when we asked for Hector's room number.

"You are friends of Señor Martinez?" He said *friends* as if he found the word entertaining.

"We have business with him," I said.

"Verdad?"

"Something wrong?"

He looked down at his guestbook. "No señor," he said. "Está bien. Señor Martinez is in room 22B, second floor."

But something *was* wrong. I stepped away from the desk, and took Luther aside. "Go up and see who's in the room. If it isn't Hector, just say you've got the wrong door. Then come get me."

Luther came down after a minute or two. "Goons," he said. "Skinhead types. Muscle shirts and death-head tattoos. Made me wish I had my shotgun."

"My shotgun, you mean."

"That gun is part of me. I'll need an exorcist to get rid of it."

"It belongs to the crime lab now."

"You know the people up in that room, J. P.?"

"Huddy Darko and Spode Weems. Hans Brinker Brigade commandos. They work for Stefan Selbiades, Scottsdale dermatologist and certified nut case. He's also a real estate billionaire who wants to touch off a shooting war with Mexico. Probably wants to expand his real estate interests to northern Sonora and maybe east to Chihuahua. The annexation of Baja is also in their game plan."

"Whoa. What the hell are you talking about? You're going to have to fill in the blanks, J. P."

I did. I even told him about the money and where it came from.

Then I told him to drive my car downtown to the Mercado and pick up some things. Running errands was an affront to his dignity but there was enough intrigue in the air to kick-start his adrenaline, and that was enough to override his pride.

While he ran the errand, I sat in a bar across the street from the hotel. I ordered a Pacifico Light, but didn't drink it. I kept my eye on the front doors of the hotel. I guessed that Huddy had registered as Martinez. Which must have made the desk clerk do a double-take. Huddy looked about as Latino as a polar bear.

About an hour later Luther pulled up to the curb in a cloud of dust, brakes screeching. He got out carrying a paper shopping bag. I joined him at the front of the hotel.

"I don't want to go past the desk," I said. "There's probably a back way we can use, by the pool."

The pool was empty. A few American couples sat at tables, under Cinzano umbrellas, sipping margaritas. The back door of the hotel was not locked. We went in, climbed the back stairway to the second floor, found room 22B. The door opened before my second knock.

"Thought you'd never get here," Huddy Darko said. "We expected the beaner's squeeze, then found out she was in jail. We figured she'd get a friend to bring the cash. Nice to see you again, J. P. You got it with you?"

We went in. Spode Weems was lounging on the sofa in his shorts, watching an Argentine telenovela. He was cleaning his fingernails with a Buck knife.

"Who's your friend?" Huddy said.

"He's my bodyguard."

Huddy found this amusing. "Not much of one, judging by the condition of your face."

"How did you get Hector to set up Carla?" I said.

Huddy's grin widened. "Now that's the first time I've heard you say something truly dumb, J. P.," he said. "You can get anyone to do most anything you want, you push the right buttons. You didn't know that? In the Cisco Kid's case it was pruning shears on the scrot. The Latino male, along with most other males, has a strong aversion to getting his balls clipped. We also used some of that liquid nitrogen the doc freezes warts with. It comes out of an aerosol can at two-hundred-something below zero. You don't understand pain until you've had liquid nitrogen sprayed up your nose. It wasn't easy for the beaner, but in the end he delivered. Told us all about his brother in Iraq and the money he smuggled out. The doc's got another surprise for the poor bastard."

"I thought you just wanted Martinez. What's the money got to do with it?"

"Nothing much. But since there's a lot of it, we thought it'd be a shame to let it fall into the hands of the bureaucrats. We—Spode and me—already collected the reward from Dr. Selbiades for bringing in the beaner, but then the doc had to pay off a Mexican judge to get us out of that shit-hole slam. He wants to recoup some of the payoff. That was clever of you, J. P. I got a real burr up my ass about it. Cost us some standing among the brother commandos."

"I bet I know who this fat fuck is," Spode said, pointing his knife at Luther. "He's the candy ass who lets the beaner hose his old lady. Am I right, Fat Fuck? He probably wishes we took the beaner's jewels off. That'd level the playing field for Fat Fuck. Jesus, look at Fat Fuck twitch. What's with that, Fat Fuck? You got yourself a nervous tic? That come from thinking about the beaner stuffing his chorizo up your old lady's taco?"

Spode chuckled, appreciating his metaphors.

Luther managed to stay out of it, though I could see his pulse working in his neck and I could hear him breathing.

"Nice job you boys did on Hamilton Scales," I said.

"You *saw* that, did you?" Huddy said. "The asshole had it coming. He sent the three of us on that wild goose chase. We lost some valuable time. It was a pleasure to do him. He had an easy neck. Snapped like a dry stick. Necks are a specialty of mine. I'll probably do another before the day is over. Now, J. P. Did you bring the money or did you make the second biggest mistake of your life?"

"No money," I said. I didn't ask him what he thought my biggest mistake was. Probably getting born.

"Had some suspicions? Can't blame you for that. We'll just have to go get it. You don't have any idea of refusing us, do you? If anyone has a claim on that stash of Iraqi dollars, it's me and Spode. You can see that, can't you?"

"Right now the money's up for grabs," I said.

"Sure, but we're going to grab it first." Huddy took a folding knife out of his pants pocket. It had a wide five-inch blade. "We weren't about to bring guns into Mexico again, but I think knives are a bit scarier. Cut and slash, stab and twist. Ever see intestine come out of a deep belly-cut? Looks like a gray balloon. Ooh-whee, I'd rather get shot."

"I'll try to accommodate you, Huddy," I said. I pulled the .357 from the pancake holster at the back of my belt. Huddy studied the gun, more disappointed in himself than surprised. Spode, who had been watching the sexy telenovela, looked like he'd been caught playing with himself in the girls' locker room.

I cocked the gun. "On the floor, face down," I said.

Huddy backed up a step, shaking his head. "Uh-uh, I can't let it go down this way."

"Tie him up, Luther," I said.

Luther dug a roll of duct tape out of the bag he was holding. He took a step toward Huddy.

"I'll cut you a new shitter you come near me, fat boy," Huddy said.

Luther looked at me. "He's not cooperating, J. P."

I pointed the gun at Huddy's head. "Take your pick," I said. "Duct tape or wadcutter. The gun's still loaded for target practice. Wadcutters make a clean entry hole. Can't say that for the backdoor wound."

Huddy grinned, like he held a trump card. "You won't do it," he said. "You're not the type, J. P."

"I agree. Thanks for realizing it."

This puzzled him. Then he brightened, as if I had exposed a weakness he could exploit. "You've never shot anyone, have you?"

I didn't answer him.

"I didn't think so," he said. "It's not easy, like in a Clint movie."

"That's a fact," I said.

He looked puzzled again. He frowned like a behavioral psychologist closing in on the truth. "It takes a special kind of cold to shoot an unarmed man, J. P. I just don't think you belong to that breed. You're a nice guy."

"You're not unarmed," I pointed out.

He dropped the knife. "Now I am," he said.

He took a step toward me, then another. "We can work this out," he said. "Fifty-fifty split. Hell, let's make it sixty-forty in your favor." He smiled generously. He reached out to shake my hand.

"Allah akbah," I said.

"*What?*"

The first wadcutter went through his hand and into his chest. He stumbled backward. He looked at his hand, as if surprised that it had failed to catch the bullet. Then he looked at the spreading red stain on his shirt. He stooped to pick up his knife with his good hand. I shot him again. A head shot this time, just above his right eye. He was dead before he hit the floor, the wadcutter turning his brain into flapjack batter. His boots knocked together a few times then stopped.

Maybe this was what he thought would be my biggest mistake. Maybe he was clairvoyant. The thought shouldn't have bothered me but it did. Blame my mental state.

"Son of a bitch!" Spode said. "This *sucks!*"

"It gets worse," I said.

CHAPTER THIRTY-NINE

"What do you mean it gets worse?" Spode said. He'd lost his hard-case voice. He sounded like a kid in the woodshed, pants dropped for a hide-tanning.

"I guess I mean this, Spode," I said. I clubbed the side of his head with the butt of the heavy Combat Magnum, thinking of the kid in Juárez he'd clubbed with his gun. He dropped like a sack of meal. I took the bottle of tequila out of Luther's shopping bag.

I'd over-prepared, ready for whatever situation presented itself. There was a lot of other stuff in the bag that I wouldn't need: clothesline rope, a length of chain, two padlocks. I didn't think I'd have to shoot anyone.

I uncapped the tequila, took a hit, passed it to Luther who gulped it down like lemonade. Then I whacked Spode again with the tequila bottle hard enough to give him a brain-squeezing hematoma. I needed to make sure he stayed out for a while. I wiped the bottle clean of prints with my handkerchief.

I adjusted Spode so that his outstretched arm was in line with Huddy's head, then put the neck of the tequila bottle in Huddy's hand. I wiped my prints off the .357 and gave it to Spode. With his finger on the trigger and my finger on his, I fired another shot into Huddy. Now Spode would have gunshot residue on his skin. That's about all it would take to convince the cops that he was the shooter.

It occurred to me that I was probably overdoing it. I didn't know how serious the Mexican cops practiced forensics but I suspected they wouldn't spend much effort on this scene. It should be clear to them: The big tattooed gringos had a little disensión—a disagreement, claro? The drawn knives would feed this notion. Mira: one gave the other some chingazos to the cabeza with the tequila bottle; the other managed to squeeze off a couple of killshots before he collapsed. Bueno, and good riddance to these fucking gringos maricónes.

When I was satisfied the orientation of Huddy to Spode was right, I picked up the phone book and called the cops. Not just the cops—*all* the cops. I called every police organization in the city, starting with the nearest precinct, the Locales, on Avenida Abraham Lincoln. I called the Judiciales, and the Municipales. I even called the Policía Federal de Caminos—the highway patrol. I told them all the same thing: "Homicidio! En el hotel Maria Bonita! Andale!"

Spode had at least a grade three concussion, and maybe a cracked skull. When he woke up in a day or two he'd be in a Juárez hospital, cuffed to the bed frame. The concussion practically guaranteed he wouldn't remember the events of the last few minutes. The cops might even convince him that he'd shot his partner after a spat. Whether he remembered what happened or not, Spode was going away for a long long time—for a second illegal weapons charge if nothing else.

I asked Luther for his makings. He looked put out but I knew he was holding. He couldn't leave the house without emergency weed. He gave what he had to me. I rolled a pair of slim joints and dropped them on the night table. It wasn't

enough to make the cops think Huddy and Spode were involved with the traffickers, but it would help tilt the scales
against them. *These gringos came here looking for puta y mota,
but things went loco. Often happens with these culos from el
norte. They turned on each other como hungry dogs. El mundo
is a better place without them, sí? Not even their mamacitas will
miss pendejos such as these—verdad?*

I checked the scene one more time, wiped my prints from
everything I'd touched. "Okay, let's get out of here," I said.

"Wait a minute," Luther said. He sat on the bed and picked
up one of the joints I'd rolled. He lit it and pulled smoke into
his lungs with such hunger you could see the joint visibly
shorten.

"You can't wait until we get across the border?" I said.

"My fucking nerves are shot, for Chrissakes. I need a few
tokes."

He made the paper crackle a few more times, then pinched
off the lit end and put the roach next to the other joint. "Besides," he said. "It looks more authentic this way. Why would
they roll two numbers and then ignore them?"

We went out the back door. The gunshots hadn't brought
out the curious. It wasn't a good idea to be too curious about
gunshots in Juárez. There was a serious turf war going on between drug cartels and gunfire was not unusual. Stray bullets
often killed people who were too close to the combatants.

When we got to the car I handed Luther the keys. "You
drive. I'm a little shaky," I said.

Luther idled the car away from the curb and drove down
the avenida. He did a good job of imitating a sane tourist. Cop
cars flew by us on the other side of the road, sirens yelping.

"Why did you have me buy all that junk?" Luther said, after
we were on Avenida Abraham Lincoln, on our way out.

"That's the only question you want to ask me?"

"For openers."

"I don't know, Luther. I guess I just wanted to be prepared
for whatever. I haven't been lately. I didn't plan on shooting
Huddy."

We crossed the bridge back into Texas. We got on the interstate and headed toward downtown El Paso. Luther took the slow lane. We idled along at fifty miles an hour.

"I think you made a big mistake, J. P."

"And what would that be?"

"The gun you left behind. It's registered to you. They'll be able to trace it."

"It isn't registered to me," I said. "I bought that old magnum at a swap meet in Lordsburg twenty years ago. I paid for it with cash. Sixty bucks, I think. It's probably not registered to anyone."

I felt cold, even though it was over a hundred degrees. My legs were shaking with unused adrenaline. My hurt jaw hurt more from being clenched. My teeth hurt. My eyeballs hurt. My mind, what passes for it, hurt.

"You okay, J. P.?" Luther said.

"I haven't been okay since 1991," I said.

"We need to get drunk, buddy," he said.

"Seems reasonable to me."

CHAPTER FORTY

Luther drove with a dyskinetic foot on the accelerator. He'd let the speed drop down into the forties, then stomp it up to seventy. After a minute or two at seventy the Monte would gradually lose speed again, sometimes down to thirty-five. He was driving people around him nuts. Horns sounded, middle fingers waved, threats we couldn't hear were screamed. I could tell Luther's brain was racing as he went over the events in the Maria Bonita.

I could also tell he was about to hold forth.

"I don't want to hear about it, Luther."

"I haven't said a goddamn word!"

"You're chortling. You think what I did was a good thing."

"It *was!* What? You've got second thoughts? You should have let them cut us up?"

"I did what I had to."

"That's right! You did! So feel *good* about it. That guy needed killing about as bad as anyone ever did. Just like the crackers in your apartment."

"So we've bonded again? Is that it? Who should we kill next, bro?"

"Your sarcasm is bringing me down, J. P."

"Sorry, Luther. It's all on my head this time. Not yours."

"What, you're getting religious? You're a choir boy now?"

"Far from it, I'm afraid."

"Let me re-state my point, old friend. People die. That's in the job description. It's sad when good people die, not sad when shitheads die. The fewer shitheads in the gene pool, the better off the planet will be. Stay with that thought, J. P. It's the only one you need."

"Okay, but quit the fucking chortling."

"Chortling is a perk. You smoke the bad guys, you get to giggle and snort a little."

"Could we stop talking about it now, Luther?"

"How about them Cowboys," he said.

LUTHER EXITED THE INTERSTATE at Sunland Park. He took the North Mesa exit and drove to Fausto's, a disreputable little cave in the walls of the city.

I did straight shots of tequila, three of them, then switched to Bloody Marias. After the third Bloody Maria I stopped shaking. My breathing relaxed. I was able to take full easy breaths without hyperventilating.

Luther calmed down too. He calmed down too much. The bottom fell out of his adrenaline-fueled high. He looked hunted. He kept glancing toward a dark corner of the bar. He'd glance at it, then turn quickly away, then sneak another apprehensive look.

He looked at me, eyes wide and yellow-tinged with fear. His lower lip quivered, his tic newly energized. "We'd better go home," he said, his voice almost childlike. We could have been twelve-year-old kids again, baitfishing with flashlights for catfish in the Rio Grande, hours past our curfews.

"What's wrong, Luther?" I said.

"I'm hallucinating. I should probably go home and take

some medicine. The big man you shot is sitting at a table over there by himself. He's staring at us."

I looked in the direction of Luther's timid nod. Huddy Darko raised his bottle of beer in salute. I saw the perfect red dimple in his forehead where the blunt-nose wadcutter entered, mushroomed, then blew his brains through the back of his head. I saw dark blood pooling on the floor. I saw his feet moving, as if he still had the idea he could run at me and knock me down.

I thought of my Iraqi conscript, half the size of the approaching apparition. *His turn now*, I thought. *I'm ready. I apologize for taking your life, sir. I offer mine in redress.* I fought back a ball of puke. Sanity swam downstream. I tried to reel it in.

He was Huddy's twin in biker leathers. Big, bald, bad. No blood on him. Just jailhouse tattoos on his massive arms. Blue and scarlet. Skulls, barbed wire, and cryptic symbols. A strawberry birthmark on his forehead mimicked the bullet hole. He got up from his table and came over.

"You two undertakers need something to pull yourselves up?" he said. "You look like you could use a kickstart."

"We okay sir," Luther said. He'd planted his elbows on the bar and hid his face between his forearms.

"I've got some excellent crystal out in my saddle bag," the big man said. "I want you to know that my lab is safe and non-toxic. My lab conforms to the government's pharmaceutical standards. Hell, my kids play grab-ass in there and they're star pupils at Cabeza de Vaca Middle School!"

Luther looked like he was imploding. His neck disappeared, his chin drooped to his chest. "No sir, or maybe a baggie of ganja if you have a variety, that would be good sir." Luther said this from inside his protective arms, his shaky voice muffled, almost inaudible.

"Jesus, Luther, it's not Huddy," I said.

The biker stepped back and took a good look at us. "Let's see if I'm reading this situation in the proper light—crazy fat man and his depressed male nurse? Correct me if I'm wrong here. The fat man's on leave from psychiatric lock-up but he got out of hand, and now you've got some tall explaining to do to the keepers?"

"You're only half-wrong," I said. "But no, we don't want any crank or weed. Thanks for the offer."

"Take my word for it, you undertakers need something. Never seen anybody so fucking down as you two. I pulled a dime in Pelican Bay on a bad murder-two rap but never lost a night's sleep even though my cellmate was a flatland loony from East Montana. I never knew where the crazy hayseed was coming from day to day. I read *The Power of Positive Thinking.* Kept me upbeat in the number one hard-time house in the USA. Now listen up you two gravediggers, I got a Ziploc bag of schedule-two thrusters I could let you have for a bill. Guaranteed to turn a narcoleptic into a midnight tap-dancer, I shit you not."

"No no," Luther whined. "Thrusters take down your manhood, sir. Wormwood, sir. Mires the bull in quicksand. My lady, she won't tolerate a floppy. She requires wood. Most ladies do."

The biker tried to look at Luther, but Luther was still hiding his face. "I see you degents are drinking tequila," the biker said. "Now *that* shit will take you down under the floorboards. It'll corrode your liver. You'll look at life with a jaundiced view."

"Appreciate the advice," I said.

"Undertakers don't take advice. They got to figure it out the hard way."

"I changed my mind," I said. "I'll take the thrusters."

The biker went outside, came back with a baggie of small white pills. I gave him a twenty. He kept his hand out. I gave him another twenty. He kept his hand out. I took my money back. He said, "All right, it's your lucky day. You can have them for forty."

I gave him the money, he gave me the pills. "Thanks," I said.

"You'd better get your compadre back into lock-up," he said. The fat man's not happy on the loose. He needs his cage."

I thanked the biker for his advice. He went back to his table where he became the ghost of Huddy Darko again. I swallowed two thrusters with the dregs of my Bloody Maria.

"Let's get out of here, Luther," I said, half-dragging him off his stool.

We went out into the blazing afternoon. A temperature sign on a bank across the street said 112°. I could have sautéed onions on the hood of the Monte. I opened the door and oven-hot air billowed out. I took the wheel this time since Luther was not back to normal.

There was no normal for Luther. There were just deviations from a hypothetical position on a hypothetical line. True for all of us of course, but not something I needed to dwell on just then.

Luther fell into a lockjawed silence. He looked in the back seat from time to time. Whatever he saw back there didn't panic him, but his contained fear was so palpable it made my skin crawl.

I drove too fast. I needed to run away from Luther's hallucination before it became mine. I ran away from it all the way to his house. I turned the corner to his street too fast—the thrusters had kicked in—and Luther's door swung open. He'd been leaning on the handle and the force of the sharp turn sprung it loose. He tumbled out of the car and into the street. I hit the brakes and got out. He wasn't hurt beyond a few scrapes. "Sorry, Luther," I said.

"They did it," he said, indicating the phantoms that had followed us out of Fausto's. "They put their boots to me." He said it with such conviction that I found myself looking into backseat while he picked himself up off the pavement.

He got back in and we idled up the street to Luther's mansion. I parked, set the brake.

"We're home, Luther," I said. "We're safe now."

"Home. Safe now," Luther echoed mechanically.

I had a hard time believing it myself. I checked the backseat again, looking for the ghosts of beatings past.

CHAPTER FORTY-ONE

L uther went straight to the bathroom to get his meds. I heard him talking—pleading—with whatever phantom had followed him in there. From the pitch and intensity of his voice it sounded as if he were trying to convince the phantom to go back to the shadow world that spawned it. The phantom wasn't listening. Luther wept and begged. The ordeal went on and on.

I sat on the sofa next to Gretchen. She'd been lying on her side, dozing. She raised her head to see who'd had the gall to disturb her nap. Seeing it was me, she rolled over on her back exposing her downy belly. She had a big, well-fed belly that required petting. I stroked her for a few languid minutes. Her purrs rumbled like an idling semi.

The purr of a big cat is tranquilizing. I rested my hand on her belly but she wasn't having any of that. She reached for me, claws extended, as if to say, Keep petting or I'm going to hurt you. Very human. Her back legs kicked my forearm. Nothing serious. No blood drawn, no harm intended. She was just feeling lovingly assertive after a long boring day.

Luther finally came out of the bathroom. "I'm going to bed," he said. "I've taken my pills. I'll probably sleep until tomorrow afternoon. Try not to let any assassins in the house, will you?"

He was back to his old self. Which wasn't great but preferable to the self he'd been exhibiting the last few hours.

"No more specters?" I said.

"Thanks to the pharmaceutical ghost busters," he said. He shuffled off to his bedroom, leaving me with Gretchen.

I went into the kitchen and made myself a sandwich of cold cuts and sliced cheese. Gretchen followed me. I gave her pieces of pastrami, smoked salmon, and deviled egg. She was an old cat, accustomed to eating human food. It was too late to put her on a sensible diet. She was close to thirty pounds and apparently enjoyed being a big tail-less butterball with kitchen privileges.

There was a note taped to the side of the fridge:

> Luther hon, I've gone shopping. Someone from New York called. Jonathan Traybull or Craybull of Yelburton, Inc. He wants you to call him back. I think it's good news about *Gotterdammerung*. The number is on the pad next to the phone. Love you, you grand old monster.
>
> –Lelanie.

I gave Gretchen another wad of pastrami, then left. I drove back to my motel room where I took a long cool shower, then went to bed. When the thrusters wore off I slept and didn't wake up until ten the next morning. I made coffee in the small pot the motel provided, then called Fernie Peralta. He wasn't in his office. I called his cell. He picked up on the first ring.

"Where've you been, J. P.?" he said. "The competency hearing for your mom takes place in twenty minutes in district court."

"This is a formality, right?"

"More or less, but the old girl's got some fight in her. It may not be the slam dunk you and Pilar Mellado think."

"She sees virgins, Fernie. She talks to my dad. She doesn't eat."

"Everyone sees virgins around here. If that's the criterion for putting people away, they'll have to stack cages in the Sun Bowl."

"Who's the judge?"

"Henry Carstairs. He's adjudicated a lot of dementia cases. He generally favors the elderly. If they can sign a check and find the toilet he turns them loose. He's an old cowboy. He doesn't like government sticking its nose into the lives of the citizens. He's big on independence."

"Where do I go?"

Fernie gave me the directions.

The hearing was in progress, in a small room in the county courthouse, when I arrived. Velma was sitting next to Pilar Mellado. She looked tiny and frail, but not frightened. Three people, two men and a woman, sat in the same row as Pilar and Velma, but separated by a dozen seats. Fernie was at Judge Carstairs' bench, talking to him in confidential tones. Carstairs, a heavily jowled man, looked more like a football coach than a judge. He was dressed casually in a bright yellow shirt with pearl snap buttons and bolo tie. He had a wide, generous mouth and a bent, warhorse nose webbed with broken capillaries. Fernie, a short, dapper man, came back to take a seat behind Pilar Mellado. I joined him.

"Who are the suits?" I whispered, indicating the two men and the woman.

"They're the DMU—the Decision Making Unit—of Adult Protective Services. They've just presented their findings to Carstairs."

Fernie opened his briefcase, pulled out some papers. "Your mom wouldn't sign the papers giving you guardianship. Or power of attorney, for that matter. It's up to the judge now. She's a sweet old lady, J. P. I'm sorry both you have to go through this."

Judge Carstairs looked up from the Decision Making Unit's report. He took off his reading glasses and laid them on the papers before him.

"Mrs. Morgan," he said. "Can you give me any reason at all why you've stopped eating?"

Velma stood up. She was wearing one of the dresses she used to teach in and high-top tennis shoes. Her white hair was combed back neatly and held in place by amber barrettes decorated with plastic daisies. They were the kind of barrettes little girls wore fifty years ago. "What I eat," she said, "how much I eat, and when I eat, these are private matters, sir. They are no one's business but mine."

"That's true, ma'am. On the other hand if we allow you starve yourself to death the county will look pretty foolish, not to say culpable. Don't you agree?"

"I'm trying to lose some weight," she said. "Is that a crime now?" Lying wasn't her strong suit. It made her look shifty rather than noble. She looked down at her tennis shoes.

The judge paged through the papers before him. "I understand that your late husband has instructed you not to eat. Can you confirm this?"

"What my late husband says to me or what I say to him is also a private matter," she said, retaking the moral, if unstable, high ground.

"I see. Do you converse often with your late husband?"

"Not often. Only when he has something on his mind. He's very lonely in the dimension he finds himself in."

"Forgive me, Mrs. Morgan, but your husband is deceased," the judge said gently. "You understand that, don't you?"

"What is death but a transfer?" she said. "'I and this mystery, here we stand.'"

"Interesting, Mrs. Morgan, but not helpful to your case."

"'Death is the mother of beauty; hence from her alone shall come fulfillment to our dreams and our desires.'"

"Talking nonsense, Mrs. Morgan, is not the way to go," the judge said.

"'We live in an old chaos of the sun,'" she countered. She looked genuinely daffy now, her daffy smile triumphant, her old daffy eyes alive with meaning.

The judge collected his papers. Fernie leaned toward me. "Slam dunk after all," he said.

The judge cleared his throat. "I'm genuinely sorry, Mrs. Morgan. But I have no choice but to find in favor of Adult Protective Services. There is no absolute test for competence, but it is my opinion that you are not capable of caring for yourself. I hereby assign guardianship to your son, Mr. J. P. Morgan, who will…"

"'Get with child a mandrake root!'" Velma shouted. "'Chief Iffucan! Fat! Fat! *Fat!* I am *personal*. Your world is *you! I* am my world!'"

"Did the lady just call me impotent and *fat?*" the judge said.

I stood up. "She's not insulting you, Judge. It's poetry. My mother taught high school English for thirty years."

"And I'm sure she was a fine teacher. But this is not a school house." The judge tapped his gavel and stood up. "We're done here, folks. I've got another hearing in ten minutes. Why don't you all go have some lunch now."

"Look!" Velma shouted. She pointed at the wall behind the judge's bench. We all looked. Even Judge Carstairs turned to look.

"The Virgin!" she said. "She's *here!*"

The wall was yellow with age. Small cracks in the paint defined a figure. I hadn't noticed it until now. It looked like a veiled woman with outspread arms. There was no face behind the veil, but if you stared at it long enough you saw benevolent eyes below a generous brow. The forgiving arms of the veiled woman seemed to reach out to all of us.

"An old cracked wall that needs paint," Judge Carstairs said, breaking the spell. And then that's all it was, an old cracked wall. If you looked hard enough, if you squinted, you might see whales, mountains, the outline of Peru. Or the Virgin, depending on your interests and needs.

The judge left the room. Pilar Mellado, an angular, harassed-looking woman with stiff black hair she kept brushing back out of her face, came over to me. "I'll take her to El Descanso now, J. P. With your permission of course. Your mom's house is essentially yours now to sell. I'd get right on it. You're going to need to start paying her rent soon."

Pilar took Velma by the hand and led her away. The old woman looked confused. I caught up to them. "Mom, this is the only way," I said.

She glared at me as if I was a rude stranger intruding on a family matter.

"I don't know you, sir," she said.

CHAPTER FORTY-TWO

Hot wind grained with sand stung my eyes. Fernie Peralta caught up with me in the parking lot. "You okay?" he said. "I just had the clerk notarize the power of attorney and the guardianship papers." He opened his briefcase and handed them to me. "You've got complete control now of your mother's estate."

I fumbled with my car keys. Dropped them. A dust devil corkscrewed through the parking lot, raising a mini-tornado of sand and detritus.

"Got some grit in my eyes," I said, picking up my keys.

"You've been through a lot lately," Fernie said. "Let me buy you a drink."

"Jesus, I hope I'll swallow the rat poison before I start telling my kids I don't know them."

"You don't have any kids," Fernie pointed out.

"You know what I mean."

We went to Padrino's, a downtown bar. Fernie ordered a dry martini. I had a beer and a pickled egg.

"How's your friend doing?" Fernie said.

"What friend would that be?"

"The guy who shot the Neanderthals who attacked you. Isn't he old Judge Penrose's son?"

"The same. He's crazy as ever."

"Everybody should have a friend that crazy."

I was tempted to tell Fernie about Huddy and Spode. The impulse to confess—to someone—was strong, but I decided I'd better keep it to myself. I didn't think Fernie would be under any legal compulsion to contact the Mexican police, but I wasn't sure.

"Who is this Hector Martinez?" Fernie asked.

"You've heard of him?"

"His name came up in the inquest. Seems the bounty hunters along with the state police were after him."

Fernie, being an estate attorney, wasn't up to date on wanted felons. I told him about Carla and Hector. How I'd been tracking them, along with Hamilton Scales. I told him how Scales had his neck broken by Huddy Darko of the Hans Brinker Brigade, and that Hector had been tortured and was probably also dead by now. I didn't mention the Iraq money.

"I've heard of Scales," Fernie said. "His reputation has a stink on it. What's the Hans Brinker Brigade?"

I told him what I knew. He shook his head, not in disbelief but in recognition of the rising madness that afflicted the border.

Fernie was a güero, a pale-skinned Mexican with little or no Indian blood. Some locals with a hard-on for Mexicans that were too white dismissed him as a pocho, meaning he had embraced Anglo culture and values and therefore rejected his own heritage. He'd been a regional golden gloves welterweight champ, did a tour in Iraq with the 82nd Airborne during Desert Storm, had a law degree from USC, spoke three languages fluently and two others competently. Given all that, he never forgot where he came from. He was a Lower Valley kid, an all-league wide receiver for the Isleta High School Indians, and a champion of Mexican-American causes.

Busy as he was, he found the time to do pro bono work for several poor families in east El Paso county who had been screwed by unscrupulous real estate developers. The developers convinced these people, many of whom lost their minimum wage jobs to Mexico when NAFTA went into effect, that they could become part of the "ownership society" by using what little savings they had to buy cheap half-acre plots in the desert. The improperly platted tracts had no water mains, no electricity, no sewer lines, no paved roads. The hard-working poor built their sub-standard houses on these worthless tracts of land, forming colonias almost as desperate as those across the border in the slums of Juárez. They trucked in their water and cooked on kerosene stoves. Some of the houses were built over hazardous waste dumps. Fernie went to bat for them, and secured some impressive judgements against the developers—when they could be tracked down—to make him a hero for the underdog. "The only thing those scumbags developed was their lust for a quick buck," Fernie once said to me after a handball session at the Y. "They fuck the poor because the poor are easiest to fuck—the history of the world in a nutshell."

Fernie ordered another round. After a quiet few minutes he said, "I'm sorry about your mom, J. P.," he said. "I think Judge Carstairs would have found in her favor if she had promised to start eating again. She's a feisty old lady, and not all that whacky. There are whackier people running for public office."

"Thanks for your help, Fernie," I said.

"I didn't do much. You've got the hard part, compa."

I said, "What do you mean?" but I knew what he meant.

"You don't want her to die thinking you betrayed her. But that might be a hard case to make."

We finished our drinks. Fernie paid the tab. We got up to leave.

"Oh, by the way," Fernie said. "That outfit from California Sundown hired? The honeymoon's over. Huge cost overruns and mediocre results in the field. They liked to rent expensive B cars while on the job—Boxters, Beemers, even a Bentley. Sundown won't admit it, but they'd like to have you back, J. P."

"Thanks, but they're going to have to kiss my rosy red ass first."

"All you'd have to do is drop your pants and bend over."

We shook hands and went our separate ways.

My separate way took me to the Union Depot. I found the locker, opened it, and took out the box. The Iraq money was wrapped in plastic bags, the bags sealed with strapping tape. I didn't bother to count it. I was more interested in the videos Carla had mentioned. There were six 8 mm cassettes in the box, all with the same label: Accidental Shooting. Six numbered copies. I took one of them, then put the box back. On my way back to my motel room, I stopped at a Radio Shack and bought an adapter that would let me play the 8mm tape on a standard VCR.

It occurred to me that what I was about to do was not in my self-interest. It also occurred to me that I didn't have a clear idea anymore of what *was* in my self-interest or even what "self-interest" meant. Maybe the self had its own agenda and I was its vehicle. A familiar but disturbing thought better left alone.

I drove to my motel, wired with emotions I couldn't account for.

CHAPTER FORTY-THREE

I stopped at the First Strike gunshop on the east side of town and bought a box of 230-grain, half-jacket hollow points for my 1911 Army Colt. The Colt was the last gun I had available. I'd never fired it, thinking of it as an antique. For all I knew, its workings were rusty and jammed with sand. I stripped it down, cleaned it, oiled it, dry-fired it. It weighed a ton but it could stop a truck.

Phoenix was a short day's drive from El Paso. I didn't like the town. Or rather, what the town had become. The developers and planners over the last twenty years had turned it into a green paradise, commandeering vast amounts of Colorado River water to do it. Golf courses, artificial lakes, spongy green lawns and fruit-bearing orchards everywhere. If you didn't know any better you might think you were in the tropics where the annual rain fall was measured in feet, not a stingy six or seven inches. Precious water was being used as a cosmetic and not protected as a necessity. California, Nevada,

Utah, New Mexico, as well as Arizona, all had their collective snouts in the trough, sucking up the only thing that made life in the desert possible. By the time the river reached the border, the Mexicans could measure their share of it in teaspoons. A prolonged Rocky Mountain drought, where the waters of the Colorado originated, would make the great cities of the Southwest vanish like mirages.

I got to the city by late afternoon. It was one-hundred-sixteen degrees according to the electronic clock on a strip mall bank. I checked into an older motel in Chandler, just south of Tempe, which was just south of Scottsdale. Scottsdale motels were pricey and no one was paying me for this trip.

Stefan Selbiades, MD, was listed in the Yellow Pages of the greater Phoenix directory. I called his office. I told the receptionist that I had an irregular mole on my leg that had changed shape practically overnight, and that I was terribly worried about it. I actually said "terribly," in an upper-crust Hyde Park-on-the-Hudson accent. I thought that would impress her. Westerners, by tradition, and in spite of their creative blustering, were intimidated by eastern sophistication and eastern money. I sounded like FDR talking to Fala, his Scotty.

She wanted to give me an appointment for the following week but I insisted on seeing the doctor in the morning.

"I'm flying to Singapore tomorrow afternoon on business that will keep me there a month," I said. "You must get me in. This thing on my leg is scaring the dickens out of me! I've heard Doctor Selbiades is the best. I need peace of mind! They'll probably give me acupuncture or craniosacral massage in Singapore! Has anyone ever been cured of a melanoma by acupuncture or craniosacral massage? I daresay not."

I daresay not? She hesitated. Then caved.

"I can squeeze you in between the ten o'clock and eleven, sir," she said. "Be here at ten-thirty. The doctor will give you a cursory examination. If it actually *is* a melanoma, you might have to cancel your trip to Singapore."

"My life is more important to me than anything I might accomplish in Singapore," I said gravely.

"Of *course* it is," she said, echoing my gravity. "Life is a gift. It's too bad that the only time we seem to realize this is when our mortality comes knocking."

"How true," I said. "How very true."

She was a scolding moralist who needed to have her superior ass kissed on a daily basis. I obliged.

I had a light dinner at a restaurant across the street from the motel. The restaurant had a bar attached. It was a dark, generously air-conditioned bar. The drinks were generous, too. The Bloody Maria I ordered came in a tumbler big enough for goldfish. I had two of these, then went back to my not generously air-conditioned motel room. I stripped and sat in the wisps of cool air from the rattling vent.

It occurred to me that Dani Thrailkill had probably found an apartment in the area by now and that it might be close by. Maybe within walking distance. I tried not to think about it. I remembered our afternoon together. I tried not to think about that either. But triple-X images of that afternoon flashed through my recklessly disobedient brain.

I dialed Information and the electronic voice of Information gave up the Thrailkill's new phone number. I wrote it down. I sat staring at the numbers, remembering her words, *Come see me, J. P., we'll have a great time.*

But I didn't come here to see her. Did I?

I tore up the number, which was listed in Raymond's name. I watched TV for a while. Then went to the front office to ask the clerk if he had a VCR I could borrow. The clerk was a pimply kid of twenty or so. He gave me salacious leer.

"Rented some porn?" he said.

"Snuff flicks," I said. I gave him my best Psychopath Comes to Phoenix look. He held his dirty little grin in place by will power alone. I went back to my room.

I hooked up the VCR. The tape hadn't been edited. The first images were quick and random: Hector driving Carla's Corolla, shot from the passenger's seat. Carla walking toward the camera out in the desert somewhere. A telephoto shot of a circling hawk or eagle or vulture. A close-up of a desert tortoise.

Then scenery flashing by as the car sped down a two lane desert highway followed by a minute of empty blue screen. The screen came back to life suddenly, and I watched Hector approaching an armed man in combat camouflage. There were several people behind Hector, obvious illegals—women with babies, a couple of old men, half a dozen young men, two grannies in shawls. The man in camo raised his automatic weapon. It looked like a Mac10 or an UZI, hard to tell what it was, even with the telephoto lens extended. Hector approached the man, gesturing wildly, shouting. The man backed away from Hector, stumbling, his weapon held at an awkward angle. I could hear Hector and the armed man shouting at each other. The man with the machine gun fired a burst into the air. I could hear Carla's foreground voice saying *Oh Jesus, Hector be careful,* but too softly for Hector to hear. Hector gripped the barrel of the gun, pushed it down and away. The rapid pops as it fired half a dozen rounds on full auto made both men jump back in surprise, but only one man fell, screaming and grabbing at his leg. Hector took the gun and tossed it aside, then knelt beside the wounded man. The camera wobbled and I was looking at sky, at earth, at creosote bushes, then at Hector, up close now, as he took off his belt and cinched it around the upper thigh of the wounded man to stanch the arterial flood. *Carla,* he yelled, *see if you can raise a 911 dispatcher on your cell. Tell them where we are and that we need an ambulance. I've got to take these people out of here. They need water.*

The tape ran for less than five minutes. It seemed even shorter. I watched it ten times.

Sleep was not an option. I sweltered in the sagging mattress, the twisted sheets damp with sweat. When I managed to doze off for a few minutes, Dani was under the sheets with me, ripping my reluctance to shreds. She stopped what she was doing and looked at my leg. *Melanoma,* she said. *There, on your thigh. You said you were clean! Why did you lie?* Then Raymond, hollow-eyed and in uniform, entered the dream. I told him to get out, he didn't have probable cause. *Melanoma is probable cause,* he said. He was carrying an AK and an opened folding knife. *Here, I'll cut it out of your leg. Protect and serve, that's what I do, vato.*

I woke from these sweaty melanoma movies with the vague impression that I was closing in on the thing I was chasing, then realizing that the thing I was chasing was chasing *me,* and had been all along. The feeling didn't go away until I'd had three cups of motel room coffee and a cool shower.

I wondered if this trip to Phoenix was conclusive evidence that I had lost my mind.

I decided there was a good chance it was.

CHAPTER FORTY-FOUR

Stefan Selbiades' dermatology clinic stood alone at one end of an L-shaped strip mall, separate from the seamless storefronts that huddled together under a single awning. The clinic, obviously here before the mall was built, was a one-story stucco with an art-deco look—a relic from another time, back when Phoenix was an un-airconditioned bus stop between El Paso and LA.

The building had rounded corners with decorative glass-brick inlays. Its streamlined modernity defied the Indian motifs the other businesses employed to attract tourists. A mixed bag of images taken from cultures separated in space and time and world-view decorated the storefronts and stood in stark contrast to the white glare of the skin clinic. Thunderbirds, Kokopelli the flute player, images of plains Indians in feathered head-dress, replicas of the Aztec Stone of the Fifth Sun, along with Dia de Los Muertos skulls and skeletons, had been applied randomly to the storefronts. Taken together, they formed a pastel frieze that turned serious Native American art into gibberish.

I arrived right on the dot at 10:30 and the receptionist, "Candy" according to the nameplate on her desk, ushered me to an examination room after I'd filled out the usual forms. Candy looked about as sweet as battery acid.

The people in the waiting room felt they were being by-passed. Their annoyed grumblings made this clear. Most of them were elderly and, because this was Scottsdale, *rich*. Arizona, like Florida, has a large population of the ailing old who've taken their money south to escape the bone-aggravating chill of the north country.

Arizona sun is cruel to old skin, keeping the dermatologists busy. Most of the people in the waiting room had desert skin—crusty keratoses on their arms and necks that looked like rust deposits, carcinomas big as nickels on their cheeks and noses and chins. Hairy wens, stubby warts, and sebaceous cysts were also there, competing for space in the facial topography. A pampered few who had relatively clear complexions were probably there to get their semi-annual Botox shots and their shrinking lips plumped up with collagen.

Dermatologists are not among the elite in medical circles but the work is relatively easy and it pays well. The scorn of brain and heart surgeons does not depress them very much. Their malpractice insurance is miniscule compared to what these riskier specialists have to pay.

Doctor Selbiades' clinic had a number of examination rooms and the good doc moved briskly from one to the other, racking up Medicare dollars faster than the government could print them. I didn't have to wait long for him.

He looked better than his photos. For one thing he wasn't as old as I'd thought. The photos Carla had in her file made him seem in his sixties, maybe even seventy. He was closer to fifty and lean as a long distance runner.

"Drop your pants, Mr. Morgan," he said. "Let's have a look at that mole."

"I don't have a mole," I said. "I came here to collect Hector Martinez, or what's left of him."

He didn't react. "I'm supposed to know what you're talking about?" he said. He had a slight accent, maybe east European, but his diction was flawless.

"Huddy Darko said Martinez was here. Told me all about your little shop of horrors. I don't think Huddy was lying."

This got a reaction. His eyes widened a bit and he turned his head slightly as if trying to slip a punch.

"If you'd like to call the police, go ahead. I think they'd find your dungeon interesting," I said.

"Huddy Darko," he said, as if trying to place him. "You know Huddy, do you?"

"I killed him," I said. "Spread his brains around a Juárez hotel room. In self-defense, of course."

He relaxed a bit, the corners of his thin mouth lifting in a philosophical smile. "Someone was going to kill him sooner or later. Mr. Darko lacked diplomatic skills."

This amused us both. I laughed a bit. I'd taken a couple of thrusters before coming here, to rev up for a busy day, and they started to kick in. I was amped up enough to feel giddy about the coming events, whatever they were going to be.

"I am very well-connected, Mr. Morgan," he said. "I have highly placed friends on the police force as well as in local government. You can't threaten me with my friends."

"And yet you haven't picked up the phone."

He brightened, struck by a realization. "That *woman* sent you," he said. "That preposterous El Paso woman. The crusading professor. Champion of the mongrel races. Am I correct?"

"Carla Penrose is in jail, being held as a material witness. The cops want Hector. I can save you, Carla, and the police a lot of trouble if you'll just turn him over to me."

He sat on the stool next to his examination table. He adjusted his slacks so that they maintained their perfect crease. He was wearing highly polished penny loafers with tassels. He said, "I'm afraid I'm not reasonable on this subject, Mr. Morgan. Martinez killed my son."

"It was an accidental shooting," I said. I took the tape out of my shirt pocket. "This proves it."

He took the tape, slipped it into his jacket. "What can this possibly prove to me? The facts cannot be changed. My beautiful son is dead. We called him Willy."

"Your beautiful son was on patrol for the Hans Brinker Brigade, your brainchild. Sending a boy out there with an automatic weapon and a lot of dangerous ideas in his head was irresponsible. You want to blame someone for his death, start with yourself."

I'd hit a nerve. He flinched. "You have no right to speak to me this way," he said. "And you don't have the first notion about my ideas."

"You've got snipers out there thinking they're saving the country. More people on both sides of the border are going to wind up dead thanks to your ideas."

"War is a constant, and it is inevitable. We are made for serial warfare. My men are merely in the vanguard of the next conflagration."

"How old was Willy, sixteen?"

"He was nineteen, and dedicated to the preservation of this nation and its values. We are under siege, Mr. Morgan. Perhaps you don't believe that. Our borders have to mean something. We either have a country we can call our own, or we do not. I suppose you think I'm a xenophobic racist."

"For openers."

"Let me be clear about something. Anyone with a modicum of sense is a xenophobic racist when it comes down to a safe place to raise a family and work for decent wages. Or don't you think so? It probably hasn't occurred to you that Mexico is one of the most racist and xenophobic countries on the planet. The ruling class—men of pure Spanish heritage—have been abusing the Indian populations of Mexico for five hundred years. Now they are sending their little brown men north—thousands every week—to purge themselves of their ignorant Indio brethren. Our aim is to stop the flood. If it means eventual war with Mexico, fine. Bring it on."

"I didn't come here for the lecture, doc. Take me to Hector Martinez or I'm going to start knocking the bullshit out of you right here."

"I have appointments…"

"Cancel them. No one's going to die from squamous warts. Tell your receptionist you're not feeling up to par."

"I think you're bluffing, Mr. Morgan," he said, his voice shaky.

I gave him a backhand slap hard enough to knock him off his stool. One of his loafers came off and skidded across the room. Selbiades landed hard, on his tailbone. He yelped in pain. "My coccyx," he said. "I've bruised it!"

I stuck the .45 in his ear. "Your tailbone isn't the only thing I'll bruise, doc. I'm just about pissed off enough to put a dum-dum into your cortex."

He was more inclined to believe me now. He got to his feet, found his loafer, and we left the examination room. Selbiades stopped at Candy's desk and told her he wouldn't be back until tomorrow morning. Whiplash from the slap I'd given him had mussed his hair. A shock of it broke loose of its careful grooming. It looked like he had a rooster's comb.

Candy started to say something to him, then decided against it. She looked at me, concerned and puzzled.

"The doc isn't feeling well," I said. "Probably something he ate. I'll come back tomorrow morning, if you can fit me in." It was a lame bit of play-acting.

"I thought you were going to Singapore this afternoon," she said, skeptical and maybe a little alarmed.

"Singapore will have to wait, Candy."

CHAPTER FORTY-FIVE

"What is the body's largest organ?" Selbiades said.

"The liver?"

"Try again."

"The spleen."

"No."

"The brain."

"You're guessing aimlessly. No, it's the *skin,* Mr. Morgan. The skin is the border between you and all that is not-you. It is the body's first line of defense against the anti-self. It aptly illustrates the importance and legitimacy of *borders.* You see?"

I drove north on Scottsdale Road, out into desert real estate where million dollar mansions notched the horizon like sandcastles at the beach.

"The health of the skin determines, in large part, the health of the body," Selbiades said. "Dermatology is cutting edge medicine, yet we are perceived by the public as upper echelon cosmeticians. *Nothing* could be further from the truth."

He didn't expect me to respond, and I didn't. He was full of himself, a natural pundit who felt obligated to enlighten the uninformed. I kept the .45 in my lap. I didn't think I needed to wave it around. Selbiades wasn't the type to make a ruckus. In fact, he seemed eerily tranquil.

"You have good skin," he said. "No blemishes, fine pores, excellent stratified epithelial tissue. May I touch you?"

"May you *what?*"

"Don't worry, I just like to feel the texture and resilience of healthy epidermis."

I put my hand on the gun. "No touching."

"Yes, of course. I understand. It's just that *skin* is my turf, so to speak." His long, manicured fingers reached for my face, but stopped inches away. I saw a slight tremor move them.

"Generally speaking, the body is the doctor's realm," he continued. "A hegemony established over the bloody millennia. We claim it, and with good reason. Call it arrogance, but really, the body is our hard-earned territory. We don't take the personality that occupies the flesh with any seriousness. It's an ephemeral thing at best. The desires and doubts of the hamster who turns the wheel are of no interest to us. All bodies are more or less the same, but the personality within is a hodgepodge of impulses, longings, and half-baked and often contradictory beliefs. A nasty tangle of competing wishes and emotions."

"Even yours?" I said.

"No. In my case, and perhaps in yours, disciplined thought based in knowledge is the great corrective."

"I doubt it."

"Ah, then you've given these notions some thought?"

"Not much. But one snow job is about as good or bad as another."

"Do you actually believe that?"

"Sometimes."

"Relativism," he scoffed. "The bane of our era. It's infected society at every level. In a relativistic world there is no clarity, and there can be no heroes—just plodding time-servers and their bored masters. I sometimes wonder if the country is worth saving."

The lectures ended when we arrived at the iron gates of the Selbiades estate. He had to get out of the car to open the gates by hand since the electronic key was in the glove compartment of his Alfa Romeo which was parked behind his clinic. His tailbone was giving him trouble. He walked stiffly, as if someone had rammed a brick up his ass.

I drove for another half mile before we reached the house, a three-story gray stone Victorian complete with turrets, weather vanes, and gingerbread trimming, all of it surrounded by a plush lawn big enough to accommodate a nine-hole golf course. If the word "quaint" had meaning, then here it was, all fleshed out. The Selbiades mansion rose like a resurrected idea from another time against the stark desert backdrop. A heavily irrigated strip-orchard bordered the lawn—beautiful green trees that sent a haze of mist into the parched air. A fairy tale rainbow bloomed above the leaves.

I held the gun on him as we climbed the steps to the veranda. Tall double doors with carved columns on each side formed the impressive if overstated entryway. Entering the house was like stepping through a time portal. Velvet drapes hung against tall windows stopping the desert sun from pouring its blinding light into the carpeted front room. The slow ticking of a grandfather clock added to the effect of time travel.

The furniture was dark, the chairs and sofas deep with overstuffed cushions. The walls held paintings of ancient military campaigns. In one painting wild-eyed fusiliers laid siege to a cadre of wounded men bravely defending a forgotten barricade. The painting hung above the mantle of a fireplace big enough to roast a four-hundred pound Iowa hog.

"Do you like my clock?" Selbiades said. "It's a Jacob Strausser. Made in Nuremberg three hundred years ago."

"It's ten minutes slow," I said.

"It comes from an era when men did not organize their lives by the minute hand."

A woman came into the room. She was gray as Selbiades

but not as slim. Where he had hollows, she had smooth white hillocks of flesh. She was smiling in a way that made you think it was the only expression she could allow herself. Her opaque blue eyes seemed disconnected from anything resembling a thought process.

"Would you like tea?" she said. "We have black and green. We have orange pekoe. We have gunpowder, and we also have white."

"Not just yet, my dear," Selbiades said. "The gentleman and I have some business to discuss."

The smiling woman cocked her head slightly to one side, imitating cerebral activity. "Oh? Is the gentleman a doctor colleague?"

"No. He's a prospector," Selbiades said.

The woman accepted this explanation and went back to wherever she came from. I said, "You think I came here for money?"

"Money is usually at the root of most foolish enterprises."

"I want Hector Martinez," I said. "Turn him over to me and I'll be out of your hair."

"You've put yourself through all this trouble just to please the insane El Paso woman?"

"That must be it," I said.

"You're not *sure*? You don't have the passion of the *cause*, whatever that might be?"

"No. I'm just pissed off at people like you. I do my best work when I'm pissed off. Being pissed off gives me a sense of identity. I'm pissed, therefore I am."

"Ah, very good. A somewhat different take on Descartes. You would be a fine commando, sir. What would I have to do to recruit you to our Brigade? We need angry young men who are educated and *capable*. Too many of our recruits are *just* angry and have very little else to recommend them. If I could only make you see the world from my viewpoint. Our borders are ulcerated, Mr. Morgan, you can't deny it. They desperately need healing. Help me heal them. Help me close the ulcers that allow filth to enter the body. I'll give you the rank of Squadron

Leader, sir. It pays fifty thousand a year, with benefits and vacation time."

"Pension plan?"

"You mock me. But consider this: you are a drifter, sir, a loner and a trifler. You have no reliable base—either in a belief system or in economic security. This will come to haunt you in your later years. A man has to stand for something lest he crawl to his grave in tatters. You face an ignominious future, Mr. Morgan. I'm offering you a life belt. Stand up for *something*, man. Stand up with us. The continuity and integrity of our very culture is at stake."

"Pass," I said. "Hector Martinez, doc. Turn him over now."

He shrugged. His expression soured. "Follow me then. I'm finished with him."

He led me down a carpeted hallway to the kitchen. His smiling wife was sitting at a small table reading a romance novel called *The Scarlet Ravagers*. The cover art was teasingly lurid: a muscle-bound pirate carrying a woman aboard his ship. It seemed the woman was in the throes of orgasm, as if the idea of abduction and rape, which had an important role in her erotic daydreams, was now being fulfilled. Mrs. Selbiades looked up, the fixed smile in place. "I have water in the kettle," she said. "Listen for the whistle." She went back to her adventure with the pirates.

Selbiades opened the door of a pantry and went inside. There was another door at the back of the pantry. I had to duck to get through it. This second door opened on a wood staircase that went down to a cellar. Selbiades turned on a light. I followed him down the stairs into a brilliantly lit room.

"Your famous dungeon?" I said.

"That's a very crude term. I prefer to think of it as a triage area."

The room was done in square white tiles, floor and walls. The floor had a drain in it as if the room needed to be hosed out occasionally.

There was an operating table in the middle of the room. Surgical quality lights hung above the table. Glass-door cabinets full of neatly arranged surgical instruments lined one wall.

A naked woman stood against the back wall opposite the staircase. Her wrists were tied to D-rings that had been imbedded in the wall. Her ankles were chained together. Her head hung down, as if she'd been drugged. Selbiades went to her. "How are you today, my dear?" he said. He stroked her face. The woman didn't react to his touch.

Her pubic hair had been shaved and the pubic mound looked wounded. Her breasts were also bruised. Selbiades continued to examine her. He touched her breasts with his long trembling fingers, and then he knelt down and examined her pubic region.

"Excellent, my dear," he said. "We're coming along just fine. A few more days and you should be completely healed. What a delight you shall be then!"

He lifted her chin with a knuckle but she kept her head down. He persisted, and finally was able to force her head up so that I could see her face. He pushed her hair away from her forehead.

"Lovely, don't you agree, Mr. Morgan?"

The plastic surgery—the work of Doomed Elvis in Nevada—had pretty much healed and the swelling had gone down. Hector's face had a narrow, button-nosed look that matched his new body.

"The bone structure of the face is quite appealing," Selbiades said. "I find the overall effect intensely erotic."

"Jesus Christ," I said.

"I'd planned to give her to one of my commandos," Selbiades said. "But now she's yours, Mr. Morgan. You asked and now you shall receive. You have a fine brown virgin on your hands. When you take her, she will bleed. Look how she trembles in anticipation! What more could a man desire? She's all yours for better or worse. Go ahead, kiss the bride. It may take her a while to rid herself of the idea that she once was a man, but if you keep up the hormone injections the macho pose will become history."

"Why didn't you just kill him?" I said.

"I'll tell you exactly why I didn't just kill him. My son Willy was worth a hundred of his kind. Do you actually think his *death* could be enough to compensate me? No, I required extreme *suffering*, and what could be more painful to a Mexican macho than to turn him into a woman? And believe me, he is *all* woman now. I used the penile inversion technique perfected at the Clinique du Parc in Casablanca, along with daily hormone injections. Her breasts unfortunately are mere implants, but the nipples are quite sensitive. All else is real. His scrotum became labia, his penis became vagina. I even gave her a hymen made from a piece of tendon taken from her jaw. She's a fully functional virgin, able to experience and appreciate intense orgasm. Isn't modern surgical technique truly miraculous?"

"Turn him loose," I said.

"Yes, of course. She's all yours, Mr. Morgan. I just hope you two will take advantage of what I've accomplished here. I recommend the honeymoon suite at the Sedona Hilton. Take her there, have a grand time. Make her cry with pleasure. But be gentle with her, she's still recovering from the surgeries."

He untied Hector's wrists and removed the chains from his ankles. Hector crumpled to the floor. He stayed down a full minute, then gradually got back to his feet.

He had no expression on his face, but his black eyes were pits of hate.

I took out my handkerchief and wiped down the .45. I held the gun in the handkerchief and handed it to Hector. Hector chambered a round.

"What do you think you're *doing?*" Selbiades said.

"The only reasonable thing I can think of," I said.

Hector shot Selbiades low, below the navel. The skin doctor screamed. He rolled around on the tile floor, smearing it with blood. Hector shot him again, this time in the groin. The third shot went into Selbiades' right eye. It must have hit the orbital bone and got deflected because instead of exiting at the back of his head it came out his left ear. Half the contents of his skull came with it. Hector shot Selbiades again, opening a gutter in his chest with a tight three-shot volley.

He looked at me briefly, then turned away. "Thanks for your trouble, compa," he said, his voice hoarse but still masculine. "I appreciate it. Tell Carlita I loved her."

Hector put the gun to his own head and fired the seventh shot.

Upstairs, the teakettle screamed.

CHAPTER FORTY-SIX

I went back upstairs to the kitchen. The teakettle was still whistling the shift change at General Motors and Mrs. Selbiades was still reading *The Scarlet Ravagers*. I sat down opposite her. She didn't seem to notice.

"I'm afraid I've got some very bad news, ma'am," I said. She didn't look up. Her eyes were locked on her miscreant sailors and their booty. Her refuge.

I tried another tack. "Who's winning?" I said.

"Pardon me?" she said, finally acknowledging another presence in the room.

"The bad guys or the buxom beauties?"

She looked at me, puzzled. Apparently she hadn't heard the shots—or she'd heard so much coming from Selbiades' little shop of horrors by now that she'd learned to not hear it, in the way people living next to busy airports screen out jet noise. Maybe the screaming kettle had something to do with it. Whatever it was, she'd clearly carved out a separate reality for herself and was determined to stay in it.

"It's never about who wins," she said. "It's about finding the good in people you never expected could *ever* be good. In the end, everyone wins because love triumphs over all."

"Evil doesn't have a chance then," I said.

"It isn't real, you see. Evil is people simply not understanding each other." She'd made herself believe this; it excused a lot in her bizarre life.

"Thank God for romance novels," I said.

"Oh, I *do*. At evening prayers. Stefan and I kneel together in our nightclothes before turning back the covers. His prayers are more practical than mine, I suppose. He speaks to God in familiar terms, something I could never do. But Stefan lives in a much larger world than I. Would you like tea now?"

"Noisy little kettle you have there, ma'am."

"I always have my tea when Stefan goes into the basement with those poor people he tries so hard to help. Now then, young man—orange pekoe? Earl Grey? I have a very nice Javanese. Maybe you prefer a medicinal tea, such as chamomile."

My hands were shaking a bit. Medicinal tequila would have been nice but I didn't think she had any. "I'll take a raincheck ma'am," I said. She kept looking at me, waiting for something. It was an odd bit of human connection. I felt obligated to acknowledge it. I said, "I'm sorry about your son, Mrs. Selbiades."

"Willy? Oh, he's fine," she said. "There's nothing to be sorry about. He's taking a semester at sea. He's high in the rigging of a three-masted bark called La Paloma Blanca, off the north coast of New Zealand. I can almost see his beautiful gray eyes scanning the horizon for landfall. When he returns I will be gone, but return he shall."

"Like MacArthur to the Philippines," I said.

"Like Rhett Butler to Tara," she said.

She went back to her book. Romance novels and other fantasies had gotten her through her grief. More grief was on the way, but she'd weather that too, satisfied that it was all due to a misunderstanding and everything would work out for the best and things that were would once again be things that are. A cozy delusion.

"You'd better not go into the basement, ma'am," I said. "There's been an accident."

She looked bewildered. "Accident?"

"Your husband. I'm afraid he's been shot by one of those poor people he tries so hard to help."

"What could you possibly be talking about?" she said. Defiance was not her strong suit. Her mouth twitched at the corners, she blinked back tears. She fingered the pages of her novel as if she might ignore me and go back to her ravaging pirates. But then she put the book down.

"Show me," she said.

"I don't think that's a good idea, ma'am. The police will take care of it."

"Police? I don't want the police. The police never come here. What would I tell the neighbors? We are respectable people."

She got up and went to the pantry door. She hesitated, then opened it and went inside. I followed her down the creaky stairs.

"It's bad, ma'am. I don't think you should go in there," I said.

She didn't seem to hear me. She stepped down the stairs carefully, one deliberate step at a time.

"I've never been in here," she said. "Not since Stefan had his young men remodel it for his charity work."

She walked over to Selbiades and looked down at him with detached interest, as if she'd found an exotic new flower in her garden. She didn't look at Hector at all. She lost her smile suddenly and said, her voice lower by an octave, "I *told* you! I *told* you, Stefan!" But this low galvanized voice was as unsustainable as the realization that produced it. She coughed, exorcising it. She started to faint, caught my arm. Her eyelids fluttered and her eyes rolled back but after a few seconds she collected herself. She became calm and eerily cordial again. "I'm sorry," she said. "But it all seems…too *much.*" Her lips twitched, her

plump cheeks quivered, as she tried to re-establish that constant smile.

"Far too much," I agreed.

"It's so…unreal," she said.

"So over the top," I said, weary of madness—hers and the
world's.

"I mean, of *course*, it *is* real, but somehow…"

"Unreal," I said, finishing the thought—which was not a
thought but the failure of thought.

"Things are never what they seem," she said.

"Truer words were never spoken," I said.

"I suppose you think I'm in shock."

"That's a real possibility, ma'am."

She grinned coyly at me, like a sixth-grade flirt in the lunch-
room. "Well I'm *not!* I am quite composed," she said. She put
a finger to her lips, sealing them—as if we were now bound to
silence by secret pact.

We went back upstairs. She sat down at her kitchen table
and picked up her book. She didn't start reading right away but
stared off into the melancholy distance.

"Something like this was bound to happen," she said. "It's
not totally unexpected. The people who need help the most are
often not very grateful."

"Happens all too often," I said. She looked at me without
recognition, as if I were a stranger who had suddenly materialized in her kitchen.

"Young man," she said. "Would you mind going out into
the orchard and telling Stefan to *please* come into the house
now? I've told him a hundred times if I've told him once that
he shouldn't go out in the sun without his cap. You'd think a
dermatologist would know better."

She went back to her book. The furrows in her brow
smoothed. Her dementia protected itself from the larger madness she had to live with by inventing a more comfortable reality. A perfectly reasonable response. Insanity is the mind
looking for high ground and finding it. The rest of us wade
through the muck.

I found the library, just off the front room, picked up the phone and dialed 911. I reported the murder/suicide anonymously and hung up. I wanted a Crime Scene Unit here before a commando showed up and got it into his head to clean up the mess and bury the bodies out in the desert.

I returned to the kitchen and found a note pad. I wrote: "This was a man named Hector Martinez, wanted in Arizona, New Mexico, and Texas. He was sexually mutilated by Dr. Stefan Selbiades in revenge for the shooting of Selbiades' son. The video tape proves the shooting was accidental and that Martinez in fact tried to save the man's life." The scrawled words looked like they'd been written by someone with late-stage Parkinson's disease.

I went back to the dungeon and left the note next to Hector. I took the videotape out of Selbiades' coat pocket and put it on top of the note. I didn't sign the note. If the cops wanted to talk to me about it, fine. I could do that. There was nothing in it I couldn't stand by. I stopped a moment to regard the two bodies.

They seemed very real.

I'm religious on rare occasions. This was one of them.

"Qué le vaya bien, compa," I said to Hector. Good journey, buddy.

I recommended Selbiades to the deepest circle of hell: "May horny devils ride your skinny ass until your bones turn into snakes," I said to Selbiades. I could have done better than that but I wanted to get the hell out of there.

I drove back to Tempe on Scottsdale Road. Two Hummers with camouflage paint jobs came toward me. When they passed by I saw they were filled with big men sitting shoulder to shoulder, wearing camouflage fatigues: HBB commandos, coming to report to their commandant after their morning patrol. They all looked like replicants of Huddy and Spode—stern and regimented and eager to inflict pain. We traded scowling glances. I stepped on the gas and the old Monte roared. Two cop cars—the response to my 911 call—came burning up the highway. They'd get to the Selbiades house before the commandos figured out what to do with the bodies.

I picked up my stuff from the motel in Chandler, then got on I-10 and headed east. This wasn't going to have a neat ending, but after all the facts came out Hector would be cleared and Selbiades would be exposed for the ghoul he was. With its financial head cut off the Hans Brinker Brigade would become a footnote in someone's dissertation on the varieties of American paranoia.

I would have a lot of explaining to do, and maybe I wouldn't be able to cover my involvement with complete honesty, but I wasn't too worried. The antique .45 couldn't be traced to me, and I didn't think anything the addled Mrs. Selbiades said to the cops would be taken seriously. The screams of tortured migrants could not be completely drowned out by the whistling tea kettle, and that must have driven her slowly around the bend. My story: I came looking for Hector, found him and Selbiades dead in the dungeon.

The hardest thing ahead of me was telling Carla what had happened. I did not look forward to that. Somewhere east of Tucson I stopped for gas at a truck stop. The elevation here was over four thousand feet and the air was much cooler. A breeze rippled through my shirt as I pumped gas into the Monte's tank. It felt like reprieve.

A redtail hawk circled above the truck stop looking for easy prey. It knew that mice and other small rodents were attracted to the dumpsters and the edible garbage people tossed out of their car windows. Food chain dramatics—they never end.

By nightfall I was in Las Cruces. An hour later I was back in my motel room, ready to fall into bed and sleep for a couple of days.

CHAPTER FORTY-SEVEN

B y the evening of the next day, the weather had changed. A front blew in all the way from the Canadian steppes, bringing with it a silver overcast and a dry wind. I took a one-minute shower in the holy waters of the Hueco bolson, drank a pot of coffee made with that lithium-rich water, read the freebee newspaper provided by the motel without actually reading it, and watched CNN to see if the United Arab Emirates had invaded Sweden while I was gone. The world I'd left behind was intact, warts and all. For which I said a prayer of thanksgiving to whatever gods supervised Chaos.

I needed now to reconnect to the ordinary madness of everyday life. The deeper madness of the extraordinary had drawn down my reserves. The waking nightmares, as well as the sleeping ones, needed to be lost in the traffic snarls of the commonplace.

I called a real estate agent I knew up on Thunderbird Drive and set up an appointment for the following day. I called El Descanso and asked for my mother's room. The switchboard operator put me through. I let it ring ten times before hanging up. The nursing home was close to the real estate office. I'd stop by to see her after putting her house on the market.

I called Fernie Peralta at home for no reason other than to hear the voice of the sanest person I knew. He wasn't in, and that was fortunate. In my present mood I'd probably tell him everything that had happened in Scottsdale, and that would have put him in a compromising legal position as an officer of the court. If anyone put me in Scottsdale at the time of Selbiades' murder and Hector's suicide, and if I was then asked to give a deposition, or if I was called to testify before a grand jury, then I'd tell my story. Otherwise, the nasty business died with me.

"FOUND YOU AT LAST, you slippery bastard," Luther said. "What are you doing in this shithole? Your apartment is all fixed up, nice and clean with fresh paint and new shag carpeting. Looks like 1950 all over again. They even gave you a fancy chrome dinette set."

It was noon. I'd slept another twelve hours, this time without being stalked in my dreams by commandos or scalpel-wielding skin doctors. Luther, who looked like he gained another fifty pounds, filled the door to my room. Apparently I hadn't locked it, or the flimsy lock hadn't held against his weight.

"What do you want, Luther?" I said.

"Get dressed, we're going to celebrate," he said.

Lelanie pushed him out of the way and came in. I pulled the bed sheet around me but not before she got a full view of J. P. Morgan in the buff. She pretended to be unimpressed.

"Celebrate what?" I said.

"Tell him, Lelanie," Luther said.

She smiled at me, holding back.

"Tell me what?" I said.

"Luther sold *Gotterdammerung!*" she said after the suspenseful lull.

"Turn around, Lelanie," Luther said, "so the man can get out of that sheet and into some clothes. We've got some partying to do."

"Congratulations, Luther. Who's the buyer?"

"I'll tell you about it later. Get dressed, we're going to the Paso del Norte for drinks. Hop to it, boy!"

We went to the classy old hotel in Luther's classy old Packard. The Paso del Norte had one of the prettiest bars on the planet. A domed skylight that looked like a giant Tiffany lampshade hovered over the circular mahogany bar, dappling it with pastel patches of light. There were about a dozen men in thousand-dollar suits and eighty-dollar haircuts sitting in groups of three and four, getting their afternoon martinis, whipping out their cellphones from time to time. I had a beer and ordered a pastrami sandwich from the restaurant. The sandwich would be my first food in two days.

Luther was being coy, but I wasn't going to ask him again who bought his book.

"*Tell* him, hon," Lelanie said. "Tell him who your publisher is."

"Yelburton House," he said, "an imprint of Zellman and Rutledge. They published that bestseller a few years ago about the Romanian child prostitute Czar."

"Big advance?" I said.

"You know money isn't important to me, J. P.," Luther said.

"No advance," I said.

"Twelve hundred and fifty dollars after Luther signs the contract," Lelanie said. "Another twelve-fifty on publication."

"In that case I'll have another beer," I said.

"Go ahead, make light of it, J. P.," Luther said. "I don't care about the money. This could be my breakthrough."

"I'm sorry, Luther. I don't mean to rain on your parade. Congratulations. I mean it."

"Of course they want him to make some changes first," Lelanie said. Luther shot her a deadly look.

"*Before* they send you a contract?" I said.

He looked at me, aggrieved. He knocked back a shot of

George Dickel sour mash, his fourth. Chugged some beer. "It's a business, not a charity. That's what they *do*," he said. "They want a product they feel they can sell. So they have suggestions."

"Like what?"

"They want him to get rid of that old dippy guy, Vahg-ner," Lelanie said. "They don't like all that nineteenth century hanky panky sturm and gangbang stuff. You know, bustles and petticoats and endlessly boring talk in stuffy drawing rooms? Passion in the perfumed moonlight with violins a-trilling? They thought all that junk was too cornball for today's audience. They want it to be about Hitler's meth jones, period. They want Hitler stoned to the eyeballs as his army marches into the Russian meatgrinder."

Luther gave her a withering look.

"Oh honey!" she said. "I'm just telling J. P. what they said. When all is said and done, it's going to be a much better novel!"

"I've started the rewrite," Luther said, sheepishly. "I'm envigorating my metaphors. I see them as timely grenades that stun the reader out of his apathy."

Dark storm clouds like hungry wolves growled over Bavaria.

Something like that would soon find its way out of Luther's 1926 Underwood. But what the hell, he'd gotten some recognition from a New York publisher and who was I to poke fun.

"You can do it, Luther," I said.

"They liked my swastika research," he said. "They didn't know the swastika was the first abstract symbol invented by mankind. Or that every primitive culture on earth used some form of it in their arts. Aboriginal mound pottery found along the Mississippi was covered with swastikas. Ancient Hindu coins also. The cross with all its dreary history is a form of it."

"How does meth figure into all this?" I said.

"That's the part I'll have to work out. I see meth as the premier wartime drug. When the country goes to war the people turn to meth. We see it functioning that way today. Nazi troops ate it like candy. Our GIs liked their Benzedrine inhalers. Rosy the Riveter had her over-the-counter pep pills, Bennies and

Dexies. Maybe it breaks up enough brain cells to uncover buried archetypal figures. After he drops a few hundred milligrams of Pervitin, I'll have the Führer hallucinate a burning swastika that follows him around like his faithful dog, Krank. Who knows? Yelburton's giving me a year to work it out."

Flares of black lightning from cerebral clouds of methamphetamine amped up the Fuhrer's brain as his Wehrmacht steamrolled Poland.

"What do you think, J. P.," Luther said. "Should I look for another publisher who'll go along with the Wagner stuff, or should I just kiss the Pope's ring and be done with it."

"Kiss the ring, the foot, the ass, kiss whatever section of anatomy needs to be kissed to get the book into print. But be a proper whore—make them pay you something up front."

"I bow to the superior wisdom of a man who hasn't read a book since 1990," Luther said, sliding off his stool.

Lelanie grabbed his arm and held him upright. The stocky little woman was strong as a dock worker. "Gee, sugar cakes, you're *so* drunk," she said. "Let's get you home to bed."

"She's hungry," Luther said to me, grinning salaciously.

"You old potty-mouth!" Lelanie said, delighted.

"There's no quit in this girl," Luther announced to the entire bar. "She hums like a hive, if you get my drift." The haircuts leaned away from their cellphones and turned to have a closer look. "Uh-uh fellas, hands off," Luther warned. She's all mine."

"Stop that, you big poop!" Lelanie said. "You're embarrassing me!"

On that note we left the Paso del Norte.

WE DROVE AROUND TOWN in the yellow Packard, the three of us in the front seat passing a pint bottle of schnapps back and forth like teenagers on a spree.

That pretty much finished the day. Luther dropped me off at the motel. I shook his hand, congratulated him again, kissed Lelanie's cheek, and went inside.

I called the real estate agent I'd stood up, apologized, and made another appointment for the following day. I packed up, checked out of the motel, then drove to Sunset Heights and my refurbished apartment.

Home.

CHAPTER FORTY-EIGHT

The real estate agent had seen Velma's house and the considerable acreage that went with it. His appraiser set the value of the place at two-hundred sixty thousand. The agent said that, in today's hot market, I could probably ask two-eighty. Possibly three.

El Descanso charged five thousand a month to house and feed and care for Velma. Two-sixty would last about four years at that rate. After that, the Poor House. I shook hands with the agent, agreeing to his 6 percent cut, then left his office feeling a little sick.

El Descanso was about two miles from the real estate office. Its grounds were extravagant, complete with tiled fountains, modern statuary, and an unlikely copse of aspens, Austrian pines, and Russian olive trees. The landscaper, like so many of them, had ignored the fact that we live in the northern Chihuahua desert. Inside it was like any other mid-scale nursing home.

I found Velma's room on the second floor of the three-story building. Her cubicle was only slightly larger than her kitchen pantry at home. It was nice enough: a hospital-quality bed, a big window with a view of the blue tile roof of a high school, a TV with remote, two chairs and a small sofa. There was a painting on the wall next to her bed, a landscape titled "Eternal Serenity." The colors were cheerful, the sunlight generous, but the artist had managed to make the natural world look like a painted corpse.

She was sitting in one of the chairs watching a soap opera on the small screen TV. She didn't look at me. Her eyes were fixed on the intricate goings on at General Hospital.

"Nice cozy room you've got here," I said, trying to be upbeat. "They treating you all right?"

She didn't answer. Then I noticed the tube. It descended narrow as a garden snake from a bag on a steel pole. It traveled over her shoulder and across her chest. It made a sharp turn, climbed her chin, and entered her nose. A band of clear tape on her upper lip held the tube in place. I got up and went into the hallway. I found a nurse.

"What's the nose tube for?" I said.

After a moment she looked up from her clipboard. "Excuse me?" she said. She was young and pretty and crisply professional. She was so tight with professionalism she almost squeaked.

"There's a plastic tube in my mother's nose," I said.

"Your mother is...?"

"Velma Morgan, room 213."

The nurse looked at her clipboard. "Morgan, Velma," she said. "Yes. Admitted August ninth."

"What about the tube?" I said. "Why does she have a goddamned tube in her nose?"

"It's just a feeding tube, sir. It goes from the nasal passage down into the esophagus. She refused to eat. This is the only way she can receive nourishment. It's only minimally discomforting. Her throat might be a little sore, but it's nothing I'd worry about."

"I *want* you to worry about it," I said.

"Sir, the stroke partially disabled your mother," the nurse said. "Her left side is more or less immobile. There's a slight chance she will recover some function with therapy. The neurologist thinks her cognitive ability has been affected. She tried to pull the tube out several times with her good hand. That's why we're using the restraint."

"The *what?*"

We went into the room. Sometimes you don't see what you can't bear to see. I saw it now: the sagging left side of her face, the vague eyes, the clear plastic tube that siphoned nutrients from the hanging bag and delivered them up her nose and down her throat and into her stomach. Her wrist was strapped to the arm of her chair, immobilizing her trouble-making hand.

"This isn't what I expected," I said. "For Christ's sakes, she didn't come here to be force-fed. When did she have the stroke? Why wasn't I notified?"

"We tried to reach you, Mr. Morgan," she said. "Evidently you were out of town."

"I carry a cell phone."

"I don't believe we had the number."

I sat down next to Velma, my eyes stinging. She still wouldn't look at me. "I don't know why I agreed to this, Mom," I said. I was talking to myself.

"The final stage of life is often not what we'd imagined it to be," the nurse said.

I lost it. "What did you just say to me?"

"The final stage of life…"

"I heard you the first time. Where did you get that, out of a fucking handbook of useful clichés?"

She stepped back, almost stumbling. "We can't tolerate that kind of language here, sir," she said.

"A torture chamber requires a more polite language? Is that what you're saying?"

She stammered a bit before her professionalism reasserted itself. "Try to understand the situation, sir," she said. "What would you have us do? Let her die of self-inflicted starvation? She became more difficult to deal with after the stroke. Very uncooperative. The staff can only be expected to do so much."

"I guess five grand a month doesn't buy a hell of a lot in the way of TLC," I said. I eased the feeding tube out of Velma's nose as gently as I could. I peeled the Velcro strap from her wrist.

"You leave her the fuck alone, now," I said. "If she doesn't want to eat, that's up to her. I'm going to sit here with her. If anyone tries to put a goddamn feeding tube up her nose, they'll have to get past me."

Everything that was wrong with the world seemed to come down to this—a little old lady with a tube up her nose and her arm strapped down so she couldn't pull the goddamned thing out.

I had no plan. What was I going to do? Sit there until she died of starvation, the way she wanted to? Would I be charged with murder?

The nurse left the room. She came back a minute later with two male nurses. The larger of the two said, "You'll have to leave the building, sir. *Now.*"

He was a muscle guy with a pretty face. It was too pretty to take chances with. He had a nice straight nose, good cheekbones, a fine jaw, Hollywood teeth. He needed to keep all of it in mint condition. I stood up. My scarred and busted up face made him take a quick step to one side, out of the way of a possible right cross. He almost knocked over the other male nurse.

"We're leaving," I said.

"What did I tell you, James?" Velma said to my dead father, hovering somewhere above, or slipping out of a wall. "I told you the boy would come to his senses." Her speech was slurred, but clear enough. Her left eye closed and opened in a slow confidential wink.

I picked her up and carried her down the white antiseptic hallway and out of El Descanso. I put her in the Monte and drove her home.

CHAPTER FORTY-NINE

A week later Carla was released from the detention center. She wasn't exactly off the hook. Theoretically, there was an aiding-and-abetting charge pending, and a possible obstruction-of-justice charge as well. But the City Attorney and the Texas attorney general's office were no longer actively pursuing the case since it was now clear that Hector Martinez didn't murder anyone and was, in fact, the victim of a sadistic lunatic. The charges against Carla were moot and in all likelihood would be dropped. She went back to her teaching job, although tenure now was not going to be automatic. In fact, it was unlikely. Carla had been at the epicenter of too many extracurricular activities of the disruptive kind. College administrators don't want loose cannons on board. They want compliant, team players. The lessons of the 1960s and '70s had not yet faded from campus memory.

Selbiades' wife gave some indication to the Phoenix police that there had been a stranger in her house the day of the murder/suicide, but her description was variable and vague and interlarded with wandering flights of fantasy. Sometimes the stranger was a pirate with an eye-patch, other times he was a Mexican gardener who her husband was going to help. In any event, what happened in the dungeon was pretty much open and shut.

The cops decided the Colt .45 belonged to Selbiades. Selbiades was a gun collector and he favored the weapons of the Pancho Villa era. General Pershing, whose men chased the Mexican revolutionary into the Sonoran desert, carried a 1911 Colt .45. The police thought that Selbiades' gun might have been the one worn by Pershing himself. Hector had somehow managed to take the pistol away from Selbiades then killed him with it before he took his own life.

The unanswered questions stayed unanswered. Selbiades' highly placed friends did not want the embarrassing weight of their association with him to fall on their shoulders. They convinced themselves, and others who might have needed to be convinced, that there was no point in raking through the ashes of what was being called the "unfortunate event." The Hans Brinker Brigade? No one had ever heard of them.

I HAD LUNCH WITH Carla at the Hollywood café on the day she was released. She looked ten years older. The news of what happened to Hector had a searing effect on her spirit. There was a gray streak in her hair that wasn't there before. Her eyes were fierce and stricken at the same time. Meeting her gaze head-on took an effort of will. I broke it off, fumbled in my pocket for the key to the Union Station locker where the half million presumably still sat.

"What will you do with the money now?" I said.

"It's Hector's money. I'll do what he'd planned to do."

"Watch out for the Feds. You make deposits over ten grand, the red flags will go up."

"I'll work it out. I can pay cash increments for the work that needs to be done in Juárez. I'll buy a house in El Paso in my

name. Maybe I'll even live there a year before I turn it into a
safe house for migrant workers. I'll be known as the coyote
with a heart." That she was able to laugh at herself surprised
me a little.

Then her eyes went misty and distant. I knew she was imag-
ining life with Hector in that safe house, salvaging the lives of
desperate people, salvaging their own lives in the process.

She swallowed hard. "Did Hector say anything before…"

"He said, 'Tell Carlita I love her.'"

She blew her nose on a paper napkin, shook her head impatiently. She wasn't going to let her emotions blind her to the
work ahead. "I turned my research on Selbiades over to the
FBI," she said. "They acted as if I'd given them the war and
pestilence predictions of Nostradamus. They were not interested in what they called 'periodic anomalies.' Shit, the future
of this country is going to be shaped by periodic anomalies."

"The butterfly effect."

"Except these butterflies are in our backyards and their effect is immediate."

"Chaos rules," I said.

"It wants to. But we create resilient islands of sanity and
kindness in spite of it. That's our damn *job*. It's the *only* damn
job."

We let it go at that. When a conversation becomes an exchange of metaphors, you know it's time to take a walk. I liked
Carla Penrose, but she almost got me killed. Her charisma was
dangerous. I'd joined her cause and had become its foot soldier
without fully realizing that I'd enlisted. Her mojo, wherever it
came from and however it was applied, was too strong for me
to buck. I didn't want to be dragged into that riptide again. I
needed to maintain my apolitical stance.

When we got up to leave the Hollywood, I said goodbye, not
hasta la vista. Goodbye is forever. She kissed me but her lips
were cool. So were mine.

CHAPTER FIFTY

Velma regained feeling on her left side a few days after I'd brought her home. She was able to move around the house with the aid of an aluminum walker. I drove her to a physical therapist three times a week. I moved in with her and planned to stay until I could find a permanent 24/7 caretaker. Adult Protective reluctantly agreed to this, warning me that there would be frequent surprise inspections.

She was so happy at being sprung from El Descanso she agreed to eat. She credited her recovery to the Virgin on her living room ceiling, to Dad's cross-dimensional influence, and to her own stubbornness.

The day Pilar Mellado came by I fixed Velma a lunch of broiled catfish, basmati rice, and greens. "I want you to eat in front of Pilar. You give her the slightest reason to doubt the new arrangement, and off you go, back to El Descanso."

"I'm not afraid of her," she said, sticking her chin out.

"Now see? That's exactly the attitude I want you to lose. You want to fight City Hall? They'll win every time."

"Brave new world come true," she said.

"It isn't that brave or that new," I said.

"In my day, we took care of ourselves."

"In your day they put grandma in the attic so they didn't have to listen to her make funny noises."

She wasn't really interested in arguing. She'd gotten her way, at least for a while. If she could stay in her home another year, or even another month or two, she had her victory.

"When Pilar comes," I said, "don't talk about virgins, other dimensions, or visits from Dad, okay?"

"You want me to tell lies?"

"Just don't volunteer your views."

"What if she asks me about particulars?"

"*Then* you can lie."

A WEEK LATER I WAS following a woman who claimed she found an eyeball in her guacamole at Casita Linda, a Tex-Mex fast food chain headquartered in San Antonio. Sundown Fidelity was the prime insurer for the local franchise. I was working for them again, on a contingency basis this time. They were apologetic, admitted it was a mistake to let me go, praised my past performance. I accepted both apology and praise and agreed to look into the case. Besides, I needed money because I'd hired Olga Calderón, an illegal alien, to look after my mother full time. Fernie Peralta was working on getting Olga temporary Resident Alien papers, although most workers from across the river are undocumented. Everyone knows this, including the Citizenship and Immigration people, and not a lot is done about it. It's an El Paso thing, and not a big deal. It works. The rest of the country, if it could put its insanity aside for a minute, could learn a lot from El Paso.

The eyeball belonged to a dead cat. I found the cat in an empty lot next to the woman's house the day after she filed her suit. The cat was in a shallow grave covered with rocks and marked with a crucifix made of Popsicle sticks. I didn't need ground-penetrating radar to find it. The grave was covered with excited red ants—enthusiastic flesh-eaters. One of the cat's eyes had been gouged out, post-mortem I hoped, with a teaspoon. The spoon was buried with the cat. Slam dunk.

The woman, who claimed to be having traumatic stress episodes because of the incident, was suing Casita Linda for two million five. She was charged with extortion, fraud, false witness, and whatever other felony seemed fitting. Luckily for the restaurant the eyeball-in-the-guacamole story never made it into the local papers. The story, which would have hurt the restaurant even though it was false, was nipped in the bud. Sundown sent me a nice fat check for the job, and the manager of Casita Linda gave me a handful of half-price dinner coupons.

OLGA CALDERÓN, BEAUTIFUL AND stately, had emerged from the river like a gift. I'd had dinner at La Hacienda, a bar and restaurant on the north bank of the Rio Grande. The building is part of the first U.S. army fort in West Texas, built in the 1850s. The barroom is decorated with military relics—old muskets and carbines hang on the walls, along with long and short bayonets, sabers, and regimental flags. The bartenders and waiters look as old as the building. The drinks they serve are generous and the dinners are wonderful, if swallowing fireballs is your thing.

I took my after-dinner Bloody Maria out to the patio. There was a raucous wedding party occupying most of the tables. I walked around the wedding party and down to the bank of the river below the patio. A thick stand of desert willows and salt cedars muted the romantic mariachi guitars and the raised voices of the partygoers.

The orchid-like flowers of the desert willows danced in the slight breeze coming off the water. The blooms were like a thousand tiny tongueless bells.

I sat down on the dry hardpan bank. I thought, *This is my place on the planet. This is all I know. Love is connection, and this healing place is what I am connected to. It's what allows me to survive.* My wounds had healed, at least the visible ones. The hidden ones were slower to mend.

My sense of connection to the place had to do with the flow of time. In the big important cities of the north, time can't stop. There are no suspended moments that allow connection to take root. Time in the north is relentless. It moves in one direction with the determination of a mechanized army. Here, it nods off. It slows, it reverses flow, it confuses itself. Mañana, ayer, hoy? Tomorrow, yesterday, today? Who cares? Ahora, the moment, is all. With a little tequila in your veins you can sense time's reluctance to follow an undeviating straight line, and how we are perfectly and magically trapped in each infinite moment. You could build a cathedral in honor of that notion.

THE RIVER MOVED PATIENTLY toward the Gulf of Mexico, its water burnished by the late afternoon sun. All along its great length, from here to Brownsville, men and women on both banks struggled to find a decent life. The economic forces of the world seemed determined to keep the people on this border desperately poor, and their environment laced with toxins.

And yet, good things happen.

I saw a head floating in midstream. It was a fine head that could have been taken from an Aztec frieze. Long black hair floated around it like a cast off shroud. The head moved slowly toward me, its lips moving.

Ayúdame, it said. Help me.

The head had a neck, and the neck had shoulders, and the shoulders had arms. It became a torso moving across the flow of the river.

Her face was untroubled, even though she was submitting herself to the river's secret currents in which many waders before her had lost their footing, got pulled under, and drowned.

Her face was lovely in its serenity and indifference to danger. And the zinc gray water around her turned *blue,* as if she, by her presence, had de-toxified it.

Ayúdame, she said.

I went down to the water's edge. Water streamed off her white dress and beaded her long black hair. In a display of cutting-edge intelligence, I said: Usted es una ilegal?—You're an illegal?

In my defense, I was dumb with food and tequila.

Todos somos ilegales, she said.

I was familiar with the phrase. *We are all illegals.* It was scrawled on the concrete bank of the Rio Grande on the Mexican side, across the Santa Fe Bridge. It was there to remind the gringos that they were occupiers, that the lands north of the river had been taken from Mexico by force or arms and dollars. But it had another meaning, as well. The land on both sides of the river belonged to God: We are all squatters without sanction.

Ayúdame, she said.

I waded out to her. I gave her my hand. She put all her weight on it and I went headlong into the river and started to float downstream. I couldn't regain my footing and a deep current pulled me under. I came up spitting, hoping I hadn't swallowed a lethal dose of toxins. My head was above water, but the current still muscled me downstream.

Olga, her powerful thighs churning under her thin dress, came after me. She grabbed my shirt, then my belt, and pulled me to my feet. Together we struggled toward the bank.

"Gracias," I said, as we waded, arm in arm, out of the river and up the dry bank.

"No problema," she said.

This formal exchange after our slapstick moment in the river made us both laugh. Olga had, for a big woman, a shy, tinkling laugh. Her speaking voice, though, was low and resonant. *Musical,* I thought, anticipating already how Velma would like to hear it.

Olga had a sealed plastic bag with her. She signaled for me to turn around. I finally understood her and let her take her wet dress off in private. She put on her dry dress, another white cotton shift, the one she kept in the sealed bag. She had no shoes, wet or dry, and her feet remained bare.

"Necesito empleo," she said.

She was young and strong and almost six feet tall. Mestizo, but more Indio than Spanish, she had strong cheekbones and wide flat lips and deep-set eyes. Eyes that did not shy away from mine, or, I imagined, anyone else's.

The river had delivered her to me, and she delivered me from the river, this powerful brown goddess who needed work.

"I am Olga Maria Calderón," she said. She leaned to one side and twisted water out of her black hair. "I can wash the clothes. I can do the iron."

"That's great, Olga," I said.

"I can cook the food. I can drive the carro." She mimed gear-shifting, steering, and honking. She looked out the side windows for cross traffic.

"Better and better," I said.

"También, I can speak the inglés," she said.

We shook hands, sober as diplomats making binding promises.

"This is our lucky day, Olga Maria," I said.

We went into the patio where the wedding party still roared. We sat at a small iron table on the edge of the festivities. The mariachis noticed us and strolled our way. Olga combed her hair with her fingers, drying it out by feeding air into the thick tresses.

I saw her lips moving. A prayer? She was looking at me, but her eyes were flat with indifference. If it was a prayer of thanks it didn't include me as the object of her gratitude. I was just the unwitting instrument of cosmic intervention. I could live with that. Almost imperceptibly she said, "Región de los sueños." She was looking at the wedding party, the relative wealth it celebrated, and the broader view of El Paso, and beyond El Paso, America: Dreamland.

"Olga Maria Calderón," I said.

Her musical name on my lips startled her. "Sí, señor?" she said.

"I've got work for you."

CPSIA information can be obtained at www.ICGtesting.com
Printed in the USA
LVOW11s1938161115

462793LV00006B/715/P